Raven

A Cinzento Academy novel

Sue Loh

Cover art by Alano Edzerza

www.edzerzagallery.com

http://EvilPlanToSaveThe.World

@suedeyloh

To the people who supported the creation of this book via Kickstarter: My heartfelt thanks for your trust and support, and here's hoping we achieve our common goals.

To my children and their peers: May you wander your own paths without the misdirection of labels.

With love and gratitude, Sue Loh

Mark —
thanks for helping me
to save the world!
— Sue Loh

The amazing thing about software – it's as powerful as your imagination. If you are a kid with big ideas and a clever mind, there's nothing more empowering. – Reed R. Robison

To Brielle and Kayla, I hope this book helps to inspire you to persevere through any obstacles you encounter. Love Mario & Andrea

Corinne and Devin, never let fear of the unknown get in the way of what is right, and you light the way to our future.

Day One

Noob

"Hey, it's Friday all day, baby!"

Scrappy's voice carried across the half-empty dining hall and echoed off the quartz floors and the floor-to-absurdly-high-ceiling windows. Fireball shook her head, picked up her breakfast tray, and headed for the table at which Scrappy sat with the other three members of their team. She was smiling, though. It was hard not to smile at Scrappy's cranked-up squee level.

In this case, his excitement was warranted. If plain vanilla Fridays were great, this one was made of peanut butter ice cream with Reese's Pieces on top. Benjamin, one of Cinzento Academy's most recent graduates, was having a buy-out party and housewarming tonight at his brand-new, off-campus apartment. Everyone on a working team was invited, as well as select members of the Academy staff – meaning Mom, Carver, and Benjamin's favorite profs. It was a highly anticipated event.

Benjamin's graduation was a Big Deal, in part because he had opted to buy out his tuition *and* continue to work for Cinzento. Fireball was hoping to do that herself someday, though she was only sixteen – years away from hosting her own BOP. Benjamin was the first person she'd known as a student who'd decided to stay with the company, and she was a bit agog at the idea of seeing his new digs: an entire one-bedroom apartment of his very own.

Fireball slid into a seat at the table and swept her dark gaze over the other members of her team. "So-o-o. What's on the agenda for today?"

"You tell us, O Fearless Leader," said Scrappy, smothering his pancakes with genuine maple syrup all the way from eastern Canada. "And bear in mind that I'm hoping you say, 'loafing and squeeing over Benjamin's BOP.' Please say that." He put a fist under his sharp chin and batted his eyelashes at her.

"I think what's on the agenda is performing a maintenance cycle on the Raspberry account and an alpha test of that new Alligator patch."

That was Cricket, whom Fireball was convinced could hold more information in her dainty head than most computers could cram into several exabytes of storage. The Raspberry account had nothing to do with fruit, nor was the Alligator patch related to aquatic reptiles. For reasons that even Fireball was not clear about, the students at Cinzento's live-in academy (aka, Mom's Home for Wayward but Brainy Boys and Girls) liked to give things playful pet names – the academy itself, the various work products, their clients, and even themselves. Raspberry was Rasmussen-Berringer – a legal firm whose client files Teams Raven and Peregrine had digitized and migrated to a new, secure network, which other teams at Cinzento oversaw. Alligator was a security patch intended to take a massive bite out of any malware that poked even one dainty toe into a Cinzento-protected system and backtrack to the source instigator.

Get it? Alligator? Eats *all* malware and sources it to its inst*igator?* Har-har. That had been one of Scrappy's. His finest, he would have said. Fireball thought it passably clever.

"We ought to be able to finish up those two by lunch and have the whole afternoon for antsy-pating Benjamin's BOP," she said.

"Well, except that we've got group study this morning," objected Books. "You guys can daydream your way through that if you want, but I'd advise against it. You know what happens if you don't keep your grades up."

He punctuated the warning with a stern look at Scrappy, who was simultaneously grinning and cramming pancakes into his mouth. Scrappy was the only member of Team Raven who knew firsthand what happened when you let your grades drop. He'd been suspended from writing test suites until he brought his logic grade back up to a respectable B. Books's dire expression didn't seem to faze the other youth one bit. He merely grinned more broadly, showing everyone at the table his mouthful of masticated pancakes.

"Yuck," said Books's sister, Whiz, looking away.

Books just rolled his dark brown eyes and went back to sipping his coffee. At eighteen, Books was the token "adult" on the team – or at least he seemed content with that role. Fireball admired that. In fact, there wasn't much about Books she didn't admire. He was smart, serious, reliable, and really, really nice to look at. She let her gaze linger on that über fine face, now wearing an expression of intense study as he pored over something on his Pad.

"Earth to Fireball."

Fireball peeled her gaze from Books's face to see Whiz looking at her quizzically.

"What?"

"I asked if you'd scoped a bus that'll get us to Ben's tonight."

"Uh, not yet. I figured I'd do it today sometime."

"I'd get on that if I were you," said a voice above Fireball's head at approximately the same time a bowl of melon balls appeared on the table in front of her. It was proffered by a strong, brown hand with no-nonsense, unvarnished fingernails.

"Aw, Mom!" groaned Fireball. "I didn't ask for fruit."

"No, indeed. I see that your breakfast is composed entirely of carbs and sugar. You didn't ask for fruit, kiddo, but you will eat fruit."

Fireball rolled her head back and looked up at the woman every student at Cinzento Academy called "Mom." She stood, arms crossed, head atilt, eyeing Fireball obliquely through the tail of her hazel eyes.

"I'm not *five*," Fireball said perversely. "Five-year-olds need to be told what to eat. I'm more mature–"

Mom rolled her eyes. "Oh, *mature.* Says she whose brain won't be fully connected for another six or seven years."

They had a similar dialogue virtually every morning, and every morning it ended with Fireball eating fruit. Sometime in the misty past, someone had referred to Mom as She Who Must Be Obeyed, and the idea – if not the nickname – had stuck.

3

Occasionally, one of the kids would refer to Mom as Shewhombo, but that was not clever by half, Fireball opined. Mom was just Mom. They knew her by no other name, though Books claimed he had heard Carver refer to her once as "Mar," which could be short for Mary or Marlene or Margaret or a bunch of other M names. Sometimes, when bored, the kids would conjecture about what Mar was short for. It would never occur to them to just ask. Such things were Simply Not Done. Besides, it would kibosh the fun of speculation.

Mom was one part lunch lady and one part drill sergeant... if the drill sergeant had an infectious laugh and a dry sense of humor, never punched out, and demonstrably loved her recruits. The other two parts were counselor and parent. Fireball felt she could tell Mom just about anything and the woman would understand. She had it on good authority that the other kids felt the same way. Mom was probably in her fifties, but the kids didn't think of her as an adult, so much as an older kid whose experience in the world demanded respect. Mom was the fixer of boo-boos, the shoulder you cried on when you felt alone in the world, and the bringer of unwanted fruit.

At least, Fireball thought, it was melon balls this morning and not stewed prunes.

"I'll check bus schedules right after breakfast," Fireball said now. "How many of these–"

In answer, Mom reached a long arm between Fireball and Cricket, who sat to her left, scooped up a serving spoon full of melon balls, and plopped them onto Fireball's breakfast plate in the lee of her half-stack of pancakes.

"That many," she said. "Anyone else here who didn't put fruit on their plate, ditto. See you at the BOP tonight, if not sooner." She turned and started back toward the kitchen, then paused and turned around. "Oh, by the way, I hear there's a new student coming in today. A boy. Your age." She turned and strode off toward the kitchen, light from the tall windows bouncing vividly off her close-cropped presently green hair.

"Why'd she tell us 'bout the new kid?" Whiz asked. "Low probability he's in our team or even in our form."

This was true, Fireball mused, as she chewed her melon balls (not half bad, really). Team Raven was something special at Cinzento – students of the Academy, yes, but so much more. They were one of a handful of topflight student tech teams with a particular and focused set of computer skills, more qualified to handle the prime client cyber security accounts than many of the adult full-time workers. The chances of the new kid being in their class or on their working team were pretty slim. Even if he had the computer chops, they'd most likely not be geared toward the deep level security required for inclusion on Team Raven.

Everybody's smart phone went off just as the PA system went live; a cheerful female voice said, "Time to prep for first session, students. You have fifteen minutes until your first session."

The room was suddenly filled with the sound of chairs scraping on the quartz tile of the floor. The newbies and elementary-level kids. They always bolted at the first bell. Team Raven – with over a decade of experience between them – finished their breakfasts at leisure, poured to-go coffee into their thermal mugs, and left for their first session.

~~~

During group study, Team Raven pored over materials on *Pedagogy: Teaching Technical Skills for Retention* and drilled each other on real-world application. All part of the job description for the team; they had not only to defang viruses, defend, declutter, and defragment client systems, but to teach the clients' tech teams how to keep those systems defended, decluttered, and defragmented. This was not always easy, for it was sometimes hard to get an adult who considered himself knowledgeable about such things to take instruction on a new security system from a teenager – especially a teenaged girl like Fireball with hair that faded from auburn to fiery orange and who wore a raven totem around her neck on a leather thong. Or one like Cricket who looked like she'd walked straight out of some Japanese goth manga.

There were times when Fireball seriously considered that she might be wiser to adopt Whiz's practical, efficiency-minded take on dress and hair. Whiz wore her über-kinky hair cut close to her head, and dressed in jeans and pullover or button-up shirts of decidedly nondecorative design. She always looked crisp and professional and was quicker in and out of a bathroom than even the two male members of the team. Fireball imagined being practical for all of two seconds before discarding the idea as ridiculous and inhibiting.

She was pondering a mnemonic to help a client remember to Save Early, Save Often and Always Back Up First (*Sesoabuf? Bufseso?*) when Carver entered the room with the new kid in tow.

"Heads up," murmured Scrappy, his gaze flicking to the door. "Newbie at twelve o'clock."

Five heads swiveled to assess the situation. At the other table in the room – Team Nightingale, whose specialty was connectivity – conversation stopped, and everyone there turned to look as well.

Carver stopped just inside the door, frowned, and pointed at the Nightingale team table. "Nightingales, back to work. You're spooking your new classmate."

He then continued on his way to the Raven table, giving everyone a good look at the new kid. He was Hispanic, average height, with thick, wavy black hair that barely touched his shoulders, making it quite a bit shorter than Carver's. Kinda cute. His eyes were large, dark, and wary, his expression somewhere between neutral and grim.

Fireball couldn't blame him. She remembered what it had been like to be the new kid. She'd been ten and dumped at the school by Child Protective Services when her mother got busted for stealing to support her drug habit. She'd been a tough little nut on the outside, scared spitless on the inside. This kid just looked... numb. Or apathetic, maybe. She wondered what his story was. Everyone here had a story.

"Hey, Ravens," Carver said, coming to halt at their table. "This is Angel, your new recruit. He's a natural troubleshooter, and I think his particular skill set will fit very nicely with yours. Angel, this is Team Raven. Fireball, here, is the team lead. She specializes in system integration. Books, there, is our networking and communications guru and research department;

his sister Whiz is our interface designer and experience modeler; Cricket is a fiend when it comes to security and hacking, and Scrappy focuses on software/hardware integration and performance issues."

Each team member murmured a greeting as Carver introduced them; Cricket smiled shyly when he called her a fiend and seemed to grow a little in size. As for the new guy, Fireball doubted he even heard who Scrappy was or what he did on the team. His eyes had stopped on Cricket and stuck to her as if glued.

Fireball shook her head. Bad sign – going all crushy on a teammate, first day. Well, he might have to learn the hard way that it did not pay to develop a Thing for someone who'd get to see you at your worst on a daily basis. Fireball knew that one firsthand and in spades. She was in awe of Books, while he had no one on his radar but Cricket, who was oblivious of his attention and probably would be just as oblivious of the new guy's.

Carver was looking right at Fireball now, so she listened up. "Fireball, since you're team lead, I'd appreciate it if you would mentor Angel, or assign him a mentor to help him adapt his skill set to Cinzento's needs. See me after lunch and I'll fill in some more details. That okay with you, Angel?"

The kid pulled his eyes from Cricket's face, gave the others a skittering glance, then nodded. Fireball thought he also mumbled, "Yes, sir," but she couldn't be sure.

It was hard for her to think of Carver as a "sir," notwithstanding he was twelve years her senior and headmaster of the Academy. Or maybe he was the dean. He'd been one of CZA's first grads – an orphan of Squamish origins who'd had his entire extended and nuclear family wiped out in a single horrific boating accident in Puget Sound. He took a special interest in orphans, which made Fireball wonder if the new kid was also one. Sensitivity protocols (and just plain niceness) kept her from asking. She'd get the full skinny on this guy from Carver later, if necessary.

Carver sketched a salute at the team, patted the new kid on the shoulder, and left the room, giving Team Nightingale another warning look.

"So, Noob," said Scrappy, "have a seat."

The kid was watching Carver's receding back, his brows drawn together in a worried frown.

"Hey!" said Scrappy again. "I'm talkin' to you, New Guy!"

The kid jumped and turned around, blinking as if the sound of Scrappy's voice had blinded him. "I'm... what?"

Scrappy grinned broadly. "What you are, Noob, is the fledging member of this team. That means you do whatever I say."

"No, it doesn't," said Fireball, pulling out the empty chair on her right. "It means you do whatever *I* say, within reason. Have a seat. Tell us a bit about yourself, Angel."

"Noob!" objected Scrappy. "I called it. No one here goes by their birth name. Heck, some of us don't even *remember* our birth names."

"You may ignore *Darrell*, for the moment," Fireball told the new kid. "What's your story? You don't have to tell us the whole thing – if it's too awful, I mean – but the basics."

Something shuttered behind the kid's eyes. "I'm, uh, seventeen. I was going to a charter school in Tacoma, but my mom and dad were killed in a fire where they worked about seven months ago." His voice came out in a practiced monotone, steady, controlled, fake as fake. "I went to live with my aunt and uncle, but that didn't work out." A pause and a grimace. "They sent me here because I want to do programming."

"You any good?" asked Scrappy.

The dark eyes flicked up to Scrappy's narrow face. A tiny spark of fire lit them for a moment. "Yeah. Yeah, I *am* good."

"We'll see."

"Cut the macho BS," said Whiz, rolling her expressive eyes. She was the youngest member of the team at fifteen, but she looked older; she was taller than everyone on Raven but her brother. Her head was older, too. "Last thing we need is some doofus competition. Welcome aboard, Noob. Sure you'll fit right in."

Fireball wasn't sure, though she wondered if Whiz's positive attitude would make her the best option for the kid's mentor. For sure there'd be Kudos in it for her, and Kudos could help down the line with a Buy-Out. But the kid's skill set put him in Scrappy's bailiwick, and any raw recruit drew test duty. You learned how code worked by learning how to make it fail.

"I'm going to assign you to Scrappy to learn the ropes," she told him, "since you'll be using your troubleshooting skills first. So, I second what Whiz just said – be BS-free and you should fit in just fine. Now, let's see if what we're studying at the mo' makes any sense to you." She slid her Pad toward him so he could see the text of the lesson. "You know what pedagogy is, recruit?"

"Uh... no."

"Gonna be a long morning," said Scrappy wryly.

Fireball nudged him under the table with the toe of her boot, but inwardly, she had to agree.

Big Trouble at FuBarCorp

It *was* a long morning, as it happened, though not for any reason Fireball could have anticipated. Before lunch – literally *right* before lunch, when the kids were mere feet from the dining hall doors and could smell the goodness wafting out of the kitchen – Carver reappeared to inform them that they had a new and very urgent project.

"I need you in your lab right now to go over the situation."

"But," said Scrappy, "*lunch.*"

The others made famished noises.

"I'm with the kiddos on this one," said Mom. She stood in the double-wide dining hall doorway, hands on hips, giving Carver the hairy eyeball. "They need to eat, Carve, especially if you're going to be drilling them on some super-important project. Last thing the Company needs is pilot error caused by low blood sugar."

"Mom," Carver said, meeting her eyes, "there's really no time for a leisurely lunch. We have a situation on our hands."

"Yeah? Mr. Grayson know?"

"He's the one who sent me down here."

She shrugged. "Okay, fine–"

The kids groaned, including the newbie.

Mom was still talking. "– but they are not to miss meals. So I'll be bringing sandwiches up so they can eat while you yak at 'em."

"Yes, ma'am. Of course you will." Carver jerked his head toward the elevator core down the hall. "Let's go, guys. They'll be vacuuming crumbs out of their keyboards for days," he added, but Mom had already charged back into the dining hall.

~~~

"First," said Carver, "we have a new client, Foster Bowman Myrle."

The team, seated in their workstation chairs, had swiveled to face their headmaster as he paced the length of the generous open area between Raven Lab's computer stations. His arms were folded over his chest, and his face was composed and sober.

"The megabank?" said Books. "Wow. That's a coup for the Company, isn't it?"

Carver nodded. "Yes. Mr. Grayson has wanted to land that account for years. So this is a pretty big deal."

"What's so urgent, Boss?" asked Fireball. She leaned back in her chair, instinctively avoiding a collision between her head and the rings of Saturn in the solar system mobile that hung above her workstation. The breeze of her movement sent the planets into a slow dance around the sun.

"FBM has had – and is still having – a sudden rash of network problems; CPUs overheating, systems going offline, subroutines stalling, data flow being interrupted. If that weren't enough, their chief tech officer has resigned, and the CEO – Conrad Myrle – has hired us to troubleshoot their corporate systems and fix them."

"Starting point?" asked Whiz.

"None that their people have been able to identify, though there is a chronological log of the failures that they've tentatively identified as part of the overall issue. If you open the FBM log overview document on your Pads, you'll see two spreadsheets. One is the chronological order in which the bugs were encountered; the other is the order in which they actually occurred – date and time-stamped."

The kids all picked up their work Pads and opened the document in question. No clues leapt out at Fireball, but she heard Cricket make that little trilling sound that had inspired her handle. That meant the other girl had seen something significant in the sequence of hiccups.

Sandwiches arrived at that point, including one for Carver, and the team devoured them while they went over Foster

11

Bowman Myrle's current system specs: network storage capacity, throughput, nodes, et cetera. Internet connectivity was also a source of interest since it was possible – even probable – that whatever was wrong at FBM had snuck in through that access.

Noob had been issued an Academy Pad on which to do his classes and manage his workflow. Fireball shot discreet glances at him to see if he was paying attention to Carver and absorbing the information. Absorbed was pretty much the message his face told. He was clearly taking in the contents of the spreadsheets and, if his sudden complete stillness meant anything, he was thinking about it, too. Fireball wanted to ask what he thought, but he probably wouldn't even be working on this stuff with them.

When Carver was finished with his presentation about Foster Bowman Myrle, he left them with this: "Mr. Grayson wanted me to be sure to tell you that Conrad Myrle is heavily invested in the success of this assignment. There is, he tells me, a lot of money and prestige riding on pleasing this client. And your involvement in this is not to leave this group of people. As far as anyone outside Team Raven knows, this is just another maintenance contract."

"Why?" asked Books. "That's highly irregular."

Carver made a wry face, then said, "Yeah, it is. But that's all straight from Grayson's office."

"What about the Old Man?" asked Fireball. "What does *he* say about this gig?"

The face, again. "The Old Man found out about this project about the same time you did. He is probably not that happy that he wasn't involved in the negotiation."

"Oooh," said Scrappy. "Is Zander in trouble?"

"No. And please don't get in the habit of calling him that. It's better if you remember that he's Mr. Grayson to you. Okay?"

~~~

Team Raven started assessing the situation immediately – or at least most of them did. Scrappy was stuck giving the new guy his first assignment, which was to run test scripts on the data collection model for the Raspberry account. Scrappy was hopeful that it would take the newbie all day to do it, leaving him free to do *real* work with the rest of the team.

First step was introducing Noob to his test boxes, which sat in an unused bay next to Scrappy's. There were several of these in their roomy but cozy computer lab to allow for the growth of the team. Unlike the "lived-in" workstations, they lacked any personal touches, like Fireball's miniature planetarium or the library shelving that surrounded Books's machines or Cricket's Halloween and Day of the Dead–themed stuff. Everyone had their own style. In Scrappy's bay, every surface was covered with science fiction–related memorabilia (Fireball insisted on calling them toys): A TARDIS and a Dalek from *Dr. Who*, a *Millennium Falcon* from *Star Wars*, a handful of *Star Trek* action figures, a little stuffed ET, and an Iron Man, because he was the only legit SF character on the *Avengers* team. The rest were all fantasy, and Scrappy didn't do fantasy, though he had to admit a grudging admiration for Loki.

The new kid's test box was a standard unit identical to the ones used at Rasmussen-Berringer that would be running the system programs. Its sidekick was a hot rod – a no-holds-barred beast of a machine maxed out in every way that the tester could use to debug the system code before rerunning the test script. When Scrappy sat Noob down at the dual workstation and showed him the ropes, the other kid was transfixed and transformed. His eyes lit up, his mouth made an almost-smile, and he listened attentively to everything Scrappy told him and repeated it back with greater detail, clearly showing that he understood what he was being asked to do.

"Man," he said as he opened the first test module to go over it with Scrappy, "this is one hot box. I mean, the sheer horse power is amazing. Is all of Cinzento's equipment this state of the art?"

"Every last bit," Scrappy said with more than a little pride. "Well, except for the stuff – like this test machine here – that has to be a perfect example of what the client's going to be running our software on. That's sometimes total garbage. But we have to deal, y'know?"

Noob gave him a look. "Do you ever just tell the client that their equipment is so subpar they have to replace it?"

"Yeah. Sometimes it comes to that. Or we tell 'em that we can't give 'em what they want because of the state of their systems. They always argue – 'cause these corporate types don't know tech from their... well, from beans. Sometimes they just buy new equipment and sometimes they go to someone else who they're *sure* will be able to give them what they want in spite of how antiquated or inconsistent their equipment is. Every once in a while, they come back with their corporate tails tucked between their legs and ask us to design a system they *can* use on their Neanderthal computers or they ask what equipment they *should* have. Then we do a needs analysis – Fireball usually spearheads that – and hand it over to one of our system packaging teams to find the client what they need at the best price." He grinned. "We are loved and reviled for our prowess in the field."

Noob seemed impressed. "How do you have time for studies?"

"Morning for study, afternoons for application... usually, that is. This is sort of an emergency." He paused and chewed his lip. "Wow. We're supposed to be going to a BOP tonight. I hope this doesn't kibosh that."

"A bop? That like a dance?"

"No. A party. Specifically, a Buy-Out Party. Our buddy Benjamin graduated from CZA last year. He's earned enough to buy out his tuition. He's gonna be working for the company – but with a straight-up, he-gets-to-keep-it-all salary. A *big* salary. Good code monkeys are in short supply these days, and demand is sky high."

"Oh, right. Carver said something about that to me when he was explaining why the Academy was created in the first place. I... wasn't paying a lot of attention to the history lesson, sorry." Noob shrugged. "I figured I'm here and I've got nowhere else to be, so I'll learn the ropes as I go."

"Oooh, Mr. Gloomy. Snap out of it, dude. You're never gonna get any Kudos for that attitude. This is a plum gig, this is. You should be friggin' happy you ended up here."

"Happy," Noob repeated. "Sure. Except for the losing my parents part."

Ouch. Hit that tripwire dead on. Scrappy put a hand on Noob's shoulder. "Dude. I don't even remember my parents. I'm half-convinced I didn't have any – that I was hatched or left on Cinzento's doorstep by a stork."

"Yeah, well, that's where we're different. I *do* remember my parents. And it hurts."

Faced with Noob's discomfiting desolation, Scrappy made the universal hands-off gesture. "O – okay. Got it. No family talk. You good with this test suite? You've done testing before?"

Noob sat up straighter and seemed to square his shoulders. "Yes and yes. I know the drill. I used to do module testing for my... for my mom and dad. To practice what I was learning at school." His eyes drifted to the code he'd been scrolling through on his coding machine. He frowned. "Um, what's this little loop here?"

Scrappy leaned over his shoulder to look. "Standard stuff. It's a timing loop mostly. To make sure the program hasn't hung."

"Yeah? Then why don't you..." Noob looked up into Scrappy's face, then shook his head. "Never mind. I'm good. You can go hang with the big kids."

"That's 'you can go hang with the big kids, *Sire*.' King of the Test Lab, me. Keep that in mind, Squire Noob, and you'll do fine."

"Uh, yeah. Sure. Whatever... Sire."

Satisfied with that, Scrappy left Noob to his own devices.

Weird kid, he thought. Though he supposed that having actually spent sixteen or seventeen years with your parents before you lost them could warp your take on things.

~~~

Angel sat and stared at the code in the so-called timing loop. He supposed it did the job, testing to see whether the program had returned a condition that indicated it had completed a process. But he thought it was a clunky way of going about it. Still he ran the test suite, considering how the timing loop worked in that context. After testing this piece of the Raspberry code twice, he was even more convinced the loop was, first of all, in the wrong place and, second, slowing things down.

He noticed other things about the code that, while not exactly wrong, could use some trimming. And the code had almost no self-documentation – nothing to tell any testers like himself, who were looking at this for the first time, what each piece did. He was sure a library file existed somewhere that described the subroutines and hand-offs, but it would be a lot more convenient if every fresh set of eyes didn't have to call up said library and learn every coding convention.

Angel started to call Scrappy over to see what he thought about a couple of changes he wanted to propose and to bounce the idea of some comments to document the purpose of each discrete routine. But a glance across the room showed that Scrappy was fully engaged in his own debugging fugue and would probably not take kindly to being interrupted.

Angel shrugged and turned back to his coding machine. He'd just make a few little changes and document them – saving off the original code as he went so nothing was lost if they wanted to back the changes out, though he couldn't imagine why they would.

~~~

"FBM," said Fireball, peering at the diagnostic results on the largest of the three monitors that dominated her workspace, "must stand for FuBar Mercantile. These systems are well and truly hosed. How the heck did they manage to catch this whatever-it-is?"

Cricket, seated at the machine next to Fireball's, glanced over to see what part of the FBM system Fireball was looking at. It was the database index.

"I was thinking denial of service at first," Cricket said, "and then a Trojan Horse, but a DOS is a blunt-force attack, and this is... well, it's weird. It seems so random and pointless. A Trojan Horse usually gets in and does something skeevy but logical. This thing is just strange."

"Will o' the Wisp," said Whiz. She took her hands off her keyboard and rocked back in her chair. "Now you see it; now you don't."

"That," said a male voice from the doorway, "is unacceptable."

Fireball turned to see Cinzento CEO Zander Grayson striding into the room. He flipped the overhead lights to full throttle as he entered, all but blinding the blinking denizens, who preferred to work with the lights at a more subdued level. Carver was behind him, his face a stoic blank.

"I cannot tell Conrad Myrle that his systems are haunted by a will-o'-the-wisp. We need to know whether it's a denial of service or a Trojan Horse or a virus." He turned and glared at Carver. "How do you propose to have them make that determination, Mr. Spearfisher?"

Carver barely glanced at Grayson. He turned, instead, to his team. "What's your recommendation, Cricket?"

"I think we need to send a troubleshooting team over to Fu – I mean to FBM. I think an onsite is the only way to track this thing and figure out what it is."

Now Carver looked at Grayson. "Is that acceptable, Mr. Grayson?"

"Is... uh..." Grayson had just noticed Noob sitting at one of the test boxes. "Who's this?"

"That's Noob," said Scrappy.

"A new student," said Carver, sending Scrappy a quelling glance. "Angel Cambeiro. Angel, this is our CEO, Zander Grayson."

Grayson blinked, then straightened his tie. "Is he cleared for this level of intel?"

Carver seemed momentarily taken aback. "Of course, he's cleared. I wouldn't have assigned him to Team Raven if he hadn't been cleared. The Old Man took care of it."

Those words stopped whatever Grayson had been going to say. With his brows set to Thunder and his mouth gone all lemony, it couldn't have been too nice. He just nodded. "Of course. Sorry. I'm just very concerned about this situation at Myrle. Yes, by all means, send your most qualified technicians over. Immediately."

"Really?" said Carver, a sly gleam slipping into his gaze. "In the past, you've been reluctant to have me send Academy teams for onsite visits. I'm pleased you've come to realize their worth."

"Yes, well. Look, this is of critical importance to the Company. Time is of the essence, Mr. Spearfisher. Choose the technicians you feel are most qualified, and I'll accompany them to the onsite."

Carver deferred to Fireball on the choice of onsite team (or "away team" as she liked to think of it). She chose Cricket, of course, and Books, who was their resident database expert, in addition to his expertise with networks and internet connectivity. Throwing the two of them together made her squirrelly, but they really were the best team for the job. She wished it weren't so.

She doubly wished it weren't so, and that she'd sent herself to FBM, when she learned that since the away team was going with the CEO, they'd get to take their first-ever flight in an auto-quadcopter. She hid her envy, though, and went back to work on the Alligator patch for some software for which Whiz was designing an improved front end.

Scrappy, meanwhile, went back to check up on Noob. He'd no more than sat down next to the new kid when he let out a howl that made Fireball and Whiz both spin around in their chairs.

"What the actual helz did you think you were doing?" he snarled, leaping to his feet. "I assigned you to test these subroutines, not rewrite the entire test suite! Now you've wasted all that time—"

Fireball was out of her chair and across the room in three strides. "What's the problem, gentlemen?"

"The problem is," said Scrappy, "this doofus wasted a couple of hours revamping our test routines instead of actually testing–"

"Scraps," said Fireball. "Chill."

"I *did* test the software," Noob said quietly. He sat looking up at Scrappy through eyes that were shuttered as solidly as a storm shelter in a tornado. "I finished the entire suite of tests and used the extra time to document."

Scrappy blinked. "You finished?"

Noob nodded. "You can check the revision log. The subroutine itself was almost perfect. Just a couple of minor bugs."

Scrappy pointed at the screen of Noob's coding box. "So you got bored and rewrote my test code?"

"Just that one subroutine. It was a little clunky. Like maybe it was supposed to just be a placeholder. I kept the old code in case you wanted to do a rollback. But I don't see why you would."

"You don't–" Scrappy shoved Noob's chair to one side and sat down in his own chair, rolling it to the station. "We'll see about that."

"Why didn't you ask if you could edit the test code?" Fireball asked Noob as Scrappy applied himself to the keyboard and mouse.

"You guys were busy with something really important. Like I said, I kept the old code so nothing was lost. And there's no downside to good documentation."

Well, what was she supposed to say to that? She glanced at Scrappy, who'd stopped pounding on the keyboard and was staring at the screen, chin in hand. The back of his neck had been a terrifying shade of red; now the color subsided. Fireball hoped that meant he was calming down.

"So, what's up, Scraps? Did the newbie screw up your code or what?"

Scrappy took a deep and audible breath. "No. He didn't screw it up. He... he made it better. And made it clearer what the different parts of the code are for." He turned to look over at Noob. "You were right, Noob. That was a placeholder. Or at least it was code I dashed off and meant to go back and clean up but never did." He gave Fireball an oblique glance. "A side effect of letting my logic grade slide."

"Huh?" said Noob.

"Long and painful story," said Fireball. "So, we good here?"

"For now." Scrappy pointed a finger at Noob. "But don't do something like this again without asking first."

Noob looked down at his knees. "Would you have let me do that if I'd asked?"

Scrappy snorted. "Helz no."

"Then you wouldn't have found out how well I code and I would've annoyed you for nothing."

Scrappy just blinked at the other youth. He opened his mouth to say something when Whiz said, "Guys. Just got a report from Cricket. They're calling the rest of us in. Grayson wants us to catch the first bus over."

"Oh," said Scrappy, "that can't be good."

Teamwork

The bus was a manual – meaning it had a human driver. There weren't many manual busses left in Seattle, and most of them were on the tourist routes where a human was more tour guide and information kiosk than driver. This driver was a Hispanic dude in his forties, Fireball guessed, with longish kinky hair that he'd mashed down on top with a company baseball cap.

On the last stop before FBM, the bus picked up a quartet of teenaged boys Fireball suspected were from the tech-arts school on Broadway. They overreacted to the presence of the driver, taking seats at the front of the bus, where they began to taunt and harass him.

"Hey, Relic!" one of them sneered. "When are they gonna put you down and replace you with a robot?"

Another boy picked up the baton. "Yeah, how stupid are your bosses that they haven't figured out how useless you are yet?"

"I bet," said the first kid – apparently the ringleader, "that this guy's not qualified to do anything but drive from point A to point B. I bet he can't even hammer nails, so they gave him this charity job."

The driver looked straight ahead, did not engage, and said not one word in his defense. Fireball, meanwhile, was trembling with growing outrage. Somewhere deep inside of her wiry little body, a short fuse began a slow burn. "Useless" was a word her mother had used to describe both of them. It was a word, Fireball had come to realize, the father she could not remember had given her mother as a middle name: Claire Useless Finney.

No one was useless; Mom and Carver and the other members of her team had taught her that. No one deserved to be *called* useless, either.

"Leave him alone, jerks," she said, her voice sharp and brittle as a shard of glass.

The ringleader turned to look at her where she sat with her teammates toward the back of the bus.

"You talking to us?"

"Who else would I be talking to? You're the only jerks on the bus." In fact, except for Team Raven and a guy who'd fallen asleep in the back seat, they were the only passengers on the bus.

The jerks exchanged leering glances. "Really?" said Bully One. "You're a mouthy little b–"

"Don't even think of finishing that sentence," said Scrappy, rising from his seat across the aisle from Fireball.

Fireball knew Scrappy was not above engaging in a fracas, and she also knew that he had the literal chops to come out on top, thanks to years of kung fu and tae kwon do. She had the bruises to prove it; he was her favorite sparring partner. The other members of Team Raven – Whiz and Noob – just sat and stared. Neither of them had even half-studied martial arts.

The bullies' ringleader gave Scrappy a disdainful once-over. "Oooh, listen to the little guy. You got some mouth on you, too, Tiny."

"C'mon, kids," said the bus driver, his voice pleading. "No fighting, okay? There's no reason or sense to picking a fight."

"Good advice," said Scrappy, but Bully One reacted to the driver's concern by slapping his cap from his head.

This offended all of Fireball's sensibilities. It also uncorked her tongue. She stood and moved to stand in the center of the aisle, bracing herself against the seats on either side. "What the heck is the matter with you? Are you *trying* to cause an accident? I'm telling you, Peggy, if this bus crashes, you're going right through the front windshield. No one ever teach you not to mess with the driver of a moving bus?"

This drew a reaction from Bully One's buddies that ran the gamut from silent scowls to a wheezing laugh.

"Jeez, Jeremy," snickered Bully Two. "Did she just call you Peggy?"

Jeremy shot the other kid a murderous glance before settling his attention back on Fireball. "You got a death wish, bitch?" he asked her.

"Nope. Do you... Peggy?"

He launched himself at her. She was pretty sure he didn't mean to have telegraphed it as loudly as he did, but part of Fireball's martial arts training was learning to read her opponent. Jeremy's sudden shifting of weight and narrowing of eyes was as revealing as if he'd yelled, "Have at thee!" at the top of his lungs.

She was ready for him – ducking and thrusting her body forward. His feet left the floor's polyethylene matting as he charged; her shoulder caught him thigh-high, flipping him end over end to sprawl behind her in the aisle. She came up, ready to take on his companions, but they were still staring, fish-mouthed, with surprise. She glanced back at Jeremy, saw he was struggling to rise, and hooked his right ankle with her foot. He face-planted in the aisle a second time.

"You are going down!" roared Bully Two, and threw himself toward the back of the bus, while the poor driver yelled inarticulately behind him.

The last two tech-brats glanced at each other and followed their friend out into the aisle. Even with half her mind occupied with the next bully's attack, Fireball could tell her tech buddies weren't as dedicated to the fight as their companions. Their exchange of glances said they had serious reservations about getting involved in this ruckus. She threw Scrappy a *look*, and he grinned at her before vaulting over two sets of seats and landing between Bully Two and his buddies, effectively cutting them off from each other. Scrappy, Fireball knew, could take care of himself. She concentrated on the task at hand.

A shift in her new opponent's gaze alerted her to the fact that Jeremy had managed to get up off the floor. She tilted her head so that she could hear him, while still keeping an eye on his second. A sudden flush of adrenaline buoyed her up, heightening her senses. She loved this sensation. It made her feel so alive and powerful. She could hear Jeremy's breathing, feel his rage, hot against her back; she could see his friend's intention to rush her flickering in his eyes.

The two idiots decided to coordinate their attack, using a quick sequence of eye contact and facial expressions. The guy in front of her even nodded a tiny bit. So, when they attacked – sort of at the same time – she was ready. She dropped straight to the floor, letting the two boys collide overhead. Then she shot back up and executed a literal one-two punch – or at least a one-two block. Both guys ended up sitting on their butts in the aisle, rubbing their heads.

Fireball then turned at the sounds of Scrappy's altercation. She was just in time to see him flip his attacker over one shoulder with enough momentum to send him tumbling down the short flight of steps into the bus's stairwell. Appropriate. His two stalwart buddies had leapt aside to goggle at the display "the little guy" had apparently put on.

"Excuse me, sir," Scrappy said to the bus driver. "Would you mind pulling over to let these gentlemen off?" He smiled, showing all his teeth.

The driver, visibly stunned, nodded and pulled to the curb. He touched a button on the dash and the doors opened. Scrappy's would-be nemesis fell out onto the sidewalk.

"Look out!"

Noob's cry came from behind Fireball. She knew, instinctively, what it meant. "Peggy" was on the move again. She somersaulted up the aisle – hearing the guy grunt as her heels flew within inches of his face. Landing, she spun, her hands drawn up and ready to perform a knife hand block if he decided to attack again. He half crouched in the aisle, hands white-knuckling the seats on either side, and stared at her. His eyes were wide and wary.

"You gonna come at me again, Jeremy?" she asked him, dropping any trace of taunting from her voice.

He shook his head. "I need to go check on my friend." His gaze flicked to the bus stairs, which his two remaining buddies were descending as if they'd just realized how badly they needed to pee.

Fireball straightened and stepped out of the aisle. "Go right ahead. I won't stop you."

"What about him?" He nodded at Scrappy.

"I'm good," Scrappy said, dropping into a front seat and leaning an arm negligently on the seat back.

After a moment more of hesitation, Jeremy hurried up the aisle and down the stairs to the sidewalk. The driver closed the doors and pulled away from the curb as if afraid the bullies would return. Fireball was pretty sure they'd avoid this bus route into perpetuity.

"Thank you," the driver said when, at last, he pulled up in front of Foster Bowman Myrle. "I've had trouble with those kids before. Sometimes they steal stuff or vandalize the bus. This is the first time anyone tried to help."

"You're welcome... Nico." Fireball read his name on the badge he wore on the lapel of his work shirt. "Happy to be of assistance."

"I've returned your fares," Nico told her. "The credits should already be back in your accounts."

"Wow, Nico, thanks," said Scrappy. "You didn't have to do that."

"Yes, I did. You cared what happened to me. I think that should be rewarded."

From the back of the bus, a sleepy voice asked, "Is this my stop?"

~~~

Fireball thought about what the bus driver had said all the way into FBM's luxurious headquarters. It was kind of sad, she thought, that instinctive acts of kindness required special reward. It should just be what people did because they were people. But maybe if that were the case, humans – who were dense at the best of times – would start to take kindness for granted. She was pretty sure that's what they called a Catch-22.

Zander Grayson was waiting for them with guest badges when they entered the bank. A security detail swept them swiftly to the facility's electronic heart – a climate-controlled, pristine facility that was as impersonal and no-nonsense as Team Raven's digs were whimsical.

Under Cricket's careful stewardship, the vanguard team had set up expanded system monitoring, each watching a different portion of FBM's gargantuan and many-layered system.

"It's like playing whack-a-mole," said Books when they'd finished a quick rundown for the rest of the team. "Or like the way our cat used to race through the house knocking stuff over."

Fireball was of the opinion that the system was overly complex and that this complexity merely compounded the problems the bank was experiencing – which were strange: Devices were overheating, though all of their monitors showed them as idle. The network had high latency and low throughput, even though there was not a lot of traffic; running programs faltered and crashed, or failed to run altogether.

"Talk to me, Books," Fireball said once she'd watched a series of shakes and quivers run through FuBarCorp's database.

Books shook his head. "I don't get it. I really don't get it. I see no cause for the way this network is flailing around."

"And I don't see any security vulnerabilities," added Cricket.

"What's our best response, then?" Fireball asked her.

"I think we need more data," said Cricket. "I recommend we embed monitors in every programming module that's experiencing this drain. There's got to be a pattern. I just haven't seen it yet."

"I agree," said Scrappy. "I'd think we want to install some upgrades and Cinzento security apps while we're at it. For a world-class bank, FuBarCorp has some truly antiquarian notions about how to handle networks and databases."

"FuBarCorp," repeated Zander, who had been lurking just within earshot of the team, probably on the verge of chewing his perfectly manicured fingernails to the quick. "What does that mean?"

Fireball threw Scrappy a warning scowl: *Don't do that again.* "It's just a generic pet name for our clients," she told their CEO. "You know, so someone who's not supposed to know who we're working for doesn't find out. I know how important it is to a bank the size of this one to keep people from suspecting there's a security breach."

"There is no security breach," said Zander darkly. "You're going to install more diagnostic software, I take it?"

"Yes, sir," said Cricket. "We need to take a hard look at the entire system over time."

"How much time?"

Cricket looked to Fireball, who said, "That would depend on the complexity of the problem, Mr. Grayson."

He clearly did not like that answer. He got up from the chair he'd been sitting in and adjusted his suit coat and tie. "Then I suggest you get to it. I'll go update Conrad on what you're doing."

Fireball started to say that he could more easily text or call, but she stifled the urge. Zander being somewhere else was a good idea. They were used to him being somewhere else – out of sight and out of mind – not watching their every move with an expression on his face that made her fear he was going to puke at any moment.

"Okay," said Fireball when the CEO had left. "Now that he's otherwise occupied, let's look at the symptoms."

"All over the place," said Whiz. "Hardware issues, broken processes, crashes and reboots, data loss..."

"I'll start with the hardware," said Scrappy. "Noob, you may sit quietly at my side and be amazed."

Noob did not even roll his eyes. He just looked at Scrappy with his face completely blank.

Poor kid, thought Fireball, and turned her attention to what Cricket was saying about the glacial pace of data transfer between two points in the system.

"The first thing we're going to do is... what?" Scrappy was in full mentor mode, looking to Noob for the answer.

"Run a systems check."

"Because..."

"Because you need a baseline and a sense of what this machine is doing that's causing it to overheat and shut down."

Scrappy was vaguely disappointed that the new guy had gotten it right. He loved explaining stuff. Noob was clearly determined not to give him much opportunity for that. He turned to the workstation in question. It was controlling a large raid array on which Cricket had installed their diagnostic software.

"Right. So let's see what this baby's got. Say 'a-a-ah.'" Scrappy's fingers danced over the keyboard, bringing up a window into the operation of the array's many drives. He chose one to focus the diagnostics on and pointed to a green line in a diagram their software parked in the upper right-hand corner of his display. "See. This is our diagnostic tool. It takes a minimal byte out of memory – get it, byte?"

Noob closed his eyes briefly. Then looked at the graphic.

"Aha," said Scrappy. "I saw that. You were hiding an eye roll. What-some-ever... So, here is the bulk of what these drives house – databases dedicated to Fortune 500 accounts. It's primarily a storehouse of arcana about the biggest clients – in the six-hundred-pound gorilla sense. So, what's the first thing we're gonna do with Cricket's little wonder app?"

"Is that what it's called?" asked Noob. "Cricket's Little Wonder App?"

"No. We actually call it the SAK. Swiss Army Knife. What would you do first?"

Noob raised a hand. "Is this really the best time for on-the-job training, Professor Scrappy? I'm thinking time is sorta of the essence here."

"Work with me, New Guy. What would you do first?"

"I'd clean up the control drive. Defrag it, remove any extraneous debris. Run a virus check. Then I'd start on the array."

"Check. So, here we go. Watch and learn."

Scrappy popped open a menu and executed a sequence of cleanups. Cricket's Swiss Army Knife dutifully defragged the controlling drive, deleted redundant files, and cleaned all the freed space. It checked for viruses and found none. Then it zeroed the memory. Scrappy performed a few more bits of housekeeping, then started the diagnostic.

"Um," said Noob. "The graph is changing."

Scrappy frowned. The kid was right. The graph showed a rapid buildup of content, as if the array was hard at work scarfing up data from somewhere. Within minutes, memory maxed out, *all* the drives filled up, and the machine controlling them crashed and rebooted.

"Whiskey Tango Foxtrot?" murmured Scrappy, staring at the dark display and listening to the whirr and spin of the array's cooling fans. "Hey, you guys, I've got a situation here."

Fireball came over to see what he was talking about. The others stayed at their stations but turned their attention his way. He explained the situation to the rest of the team in the time it took for the machine to come fully back online. It crashed again, almost immediately afterward.

"Whoa! Wait," said Books. "I've got the same thing happening over here."

"What're you monitoring?" asked Fireball.

"Account maintenance processes. It looks as if every bank associate in the system suddenly added fifty new accounts – I mean, if that's what this data is."

Cricket was nodding. "Yes. Yes, I'm seeing similar hyperactivity at other points in the network. I can't tell what's happening specifically, but there's a sudden increase in activity in half-a-dozen – no, make that a dozen – nodes."

"What do we think, people?" asked Fireball.

"I think it's gotta be a virus," said Scrappy. "Which is good, 'cause that's what we're best at. Except for all those other things we're best at."

"Good working theory," said Fireball, plunking herself down at the workstation next to Scrappy's. She pulled a thumb drive out of her pocket and plugged it into a USB port on the workstation. "Which one of our brave virus hunters you want to try first, Cricket? Scrappy?"

"Oh, eenie-meenie-miney moe," said Scrappy, eyes on his machine's display. "Catch a virus by its–" His voice just stopped.

"What?" said Fireball.

"Whoa," said Noob.

"It's gone." Scrappy's voice was thin and airless. "It's all... just gone."

"What's gone?" Books asked, then said, "Oo-o-oh," in the tone of someone who's just realized the swimming pool they're about to dive into is full of alligators. "I've got the same situation here."

Cricket's fingers were racing madly over her keyboard. Then she seemed to be chasing something with her mouse: *Click. Click, click, click! CLICK!* She was shaking her head, making her little *dia de los muertos* earrings swing wildly. "All drives are returning to normal activity. One after the other like... like dominoes falling."

Fireball was pursuing her own anomaly. She'd chosen to peek into a raid array dedicated to company-wide human resources data. It had been over half full at the time she started monitoring it, so she wasn't sure if the virus had gotten to it or not. Now, she watched the data drain away like water from an unplugged sink. Her face felt cold, and her mouth was suddenly dry. Was the bloody virus erasing the data? She couldn't even imagine what sort of horror that would be for a bank as big as Foster B. Myrle.

"Scraps, what's the status of your original data?" she asked, fearing the answer.

"It... it's... well, it seems to be... it looks like it's all there. I'm seeing, yeah, the same file structure that I took a snapshot of after I did the cleanup. Wait a minute and I'll run a file-comp."

They waited in silence as Scrappy hunched over his keyboard, his eyes glued to the monitor, watching the Mirror Mirror app he'd created compare the disk image he'd taken after his SAK cleanup with the current status of the drive. Fireball was convinced she could hear the elevated heartbeats of everyone in the room. She glanced at Noob, who was rubbing at his hands as if his fingertips itched to be on a keyboard. The looks he kept casting Scrappy's way hinted at how eager he was to be involved. Rough time to be the new man on the team.

An eternity later, Scrappy lolled back in his chair, swiveling to face Fireball. "Identical. Every bit and byte in its place. I don't get it. Did we just suffer some sort of mass delusion? Is this a warmware glitch?"

"No." Fireball was adamant. "We all saw it. On different systems. I don't think we're glitchy," she added. "But I also think that's no virus. There's no way you can disappear one that quickly. This has gotta be a live hack."

Live, from FuBarCorp

Everyone on Team Raven knew that if what was afflicting FBM was a live hack, it would require an entirely different strategy. They brainstormed this as they sat, tensely and closely monitoring the servers and the network activity, waiting for something to rear its digital head.

Nothing did. For the better part of an hour, they stared at diagnostic readouts and graphs but saw nothing. Nada. Zilch.

Zander reappeared at the end of that time, looking pleased with himself and (wonder of wonders) with them. The bank's systems were humming along as if nothing had ever troubled them. Conrad Myrle was happy, so Zander was happy. He gathered up the team and prepared to whisk them back to Cinzento Park.

"But we're not sure," Fireball told him, "that we got everything sorted out."

"Is there still a problem?" he asked, eyeing the monitors, which showed nothing but normal activity.

"Not at the moment."

"And you installed all your little whiz-bang gadgetry? Our patented upgrades?"

"Yes, sir, but–"

"Then I see no reason to linger. Let's go, children."

They shared exasperated glances. They shrugged. But they went, following their CEO out of the lab and into an elevator like a gaggle of ducklings.

In the lobby, they found their way blocked by a different kind of gaggle – this one of reporters and telejournalists from a number of TV and radio stations, newspapers, and blogs. All of them were eager to hear why Foster Bowman Myrle had been shut down for a day and half. They started shouting questions the moment they saw Zander Grayson step off the elevator.

He turned to the team. "You kids go to the bathroom. I'll handle this. Give me ten minutes."

Fireball eyed the reporters with curiosity but obeyed, leading Cricket and Whiz on a detour into the opulent ladies' room. Books, Scrappy, and Noob found their way to the men's room across the hall.

The girls had done what girls could without makeup kits and favorite hairbrushes, and were counting down the minutes when a young woman in natty business attire entered the restroom. She stopped and looked them over with surprise etching her features.

"What is this – Career Day? Why in the world would FBM have a high school tour while all hell is breaking loose?"

Fireball rolled her expressive eyes. "We're not from a high school tour, ma'am," she said. "We're from Cinzento Secure."

"So... what – you're in their intern program?"

Fireball laughed, casting Whiz and Cricket a *look*. Cricket's eyes were huge, and Whiz was shaking her head.

I know, Fireball thought. *Who asks such lame questions?* "We're not interns," she said aloud. "We're their crack antivirus team."

"Really?" The woman seemed incredulous. "You guys are what – fourteen, fifteen –?"

"I'm sixteen," Fireball informed her. "Our team is the best in the world at putting down viruses." She frowned at Whiz, who was making faces at her.

The woman smiled and shook her head. "Huh. Imagine that." She moved to a mirror, got out a lipstick, and applied it carefully.

Whiz gave Fireball a push toward the door. "We're gonna be late," she said, continuing to prod Fireball until they were out in the hall.

Zander and the boys were waiting for them at the receptionist's desk. The reporters were gone. Zander sent the team back to Cinzento Park by limo service. He took his quad-copter.

"Why'd you *do* that?" Whiz asked Fireball when the cab was in motion.

"Do what?" Fireball asked.

"Do what?" echoed Scrappy.

Whiz's dark eyes bored into Fireball's. "You *know* what. The bathroom? That woman?"

"Oh, that." Fireball's nonchalant answer collided with Scrappy's "What woman?"

"There was this woman in the bathroom," said Fireball, "who thought we were a high school Career Day tour or interns or something. I set her straight, that's all."

"Oh, you set her straight," repeated Whiz. "Wonder who she's going to set straight when her story hits the news cycle."

Fireball stared at the other girl. "What do you mean, when her–" It hit her, then. The full enormity – the full stupidity – of what she'd done. "M – maybe she's just a – a woman. You know, someone who came into the bank–"

"The service desks are all closed, Fireball," said Cricket. "An employee wouldn't have had to ask who we were. And if she wasn't an employee..."

"Oh, *frabgious*," said Scrappy. "What did you tell her?"

"Only that we were Cinzento's crack virus hunting team," said Whiz, then looked pointedly out the window.

Books and Scrappy both stared at Fireball. Cricket huddled in her seat, her lips compressed as if she were fighting back tears. Noob looked uncomfortable and miserable as if he too was feeling Fireball's sudden, abject mortification.

"Oh, jeez. Oh, man. If Zander finds out..." Fireball didn't even want to think about what would happen if Zander found out. Maybe he wouldn't. Maybe the woman was from some obscure news outlet that no one had ever even heard of.

~~~

The lady reporter turned out to be from ScoopSeattle.com, a hot, up-and-coming blog site that was giving BuzzFeed a run for its eyeballs. Fireball wasn't merely mortified, she was horrified.

When Zander Grayson found out, he summoned Team Raven to the Situation Room where he went absolutely ballistic.

"What were you *thinking*?" he demanded of her, then answered his own question. "Oh, wait. Of course. You *weren't* thinking. You're a – a *teenager*." He spat the word as if it were the worst insult he could think of. Possibly, it was. "You showed me up, damn it! Not only does everyone now know that FBM was infected by a virus, despite my statement that it's too early to say, but they're laughing their butts off because we hired *teenagers* to fix it. Talk show hosts are making jokes about old people asking their grandkids to fix their internet!"

The words landed like physical blows. They hurt doubly because he said it in front of Fireball's entire team and the Situation Room staff, who were adults, and might be inclined to agree with him. She saw at least one of the Sitch Room techs trying to hide a grin. The rest of them pretended not to hear the dressing down but kept their eyes glued to the vast, seamless wall o' displays that had always made Fireball wonder why the installation wasn't called Mission Control.

Carver, whom Zander had hauled into the Situation Room as well, shifted uneasily. "What's done is done," he said. "What we need to do now is control the situation at FBM. They'll reopen tomorrow, and we'll make sure they stay open. Books has established an interface with their network. The techs here will monitor that interface and ensure that the network remains stable."

Zander glared at Carver, then turned to the Sitch team director. "How does it look, Mr. Temple?"

The director – Ezra Temple – gave Fireball an impenetrable sideways glance that she couldn't read as either for or against. "Everything looks fine, Mr. Grayson," he said. "Foster Bowman Myrle's systems are functioning normally."

Zander wheeled back to face Carver, pointing a finger at him. "This infraction cannot go unpunished."

"Of course not," said Carver.

"Well? What are you going to do to her?"

Fireball felt the blood drain out of her face. She sent Carver the most beseeching look she knew how to make.

"I don't know yet. But I assure you the punishment will fit the crime." Carver's expression was unreadable.

"All right, then. I don't want this sort of egregious blunder to ever happen again. If we're going to take these children into places where they'll be in the public eye, they need to be trained not to shoot off their smart-ass mouths in ways that embarrass Cinzento and its clients." He turned on his heel then and strode out of the room.

"Fireball," said Carver, "you come with me. The rest of you are dismissed for supper."

Fireball couldn't even look at her team as she followed Carver from the Situation Room. She couldn't look at Carver either, as she walked silently beside him through the corridors to his office. She sank into the chair across from his desk, folded her arms across her breasts, and stared at the knees of her dress pants. She heard Carver seat himself behind his desk, then counted heartbeats until he spoke.

"What *were* you thinking?" he asked, his voice neutral.

Fireball shrugged.

"Were you thinking that a complete stranger underestimated you? Your team? That she dissed you, maybe?"

She nodded.

"What you did was careless, Fireball. And prideful."

She looked up sharply, her mouth open to protest. She was distracted, momentarily, by the sight of the four new totems Carver had positioned atop his desk. Each was about two inches tall and portrayed an animal, except for the fourth, which was an angel with folded wings. He'd carved each feather with loving detail.

Carver's gaze followed hers. "They're for new recruits."

She fingered her own totem, which he'd carved for her when she'd become the head of Team Raven. She took a deep breath. "I *was* careless. I didn't stop to think that I had no idea who the woman might be. But I did it because I didn't want her to think we were just kids on some stupid class trip."

"You wanted her to know you had worth and merit," Carver observed.

She met his dark, watchful eyes. "Well, yeah. Wouldn't you?"

"Why? Why would it matter what she knew or didn't know? She was a complete stranger. All the people to whom your worth matters already know it. Even people at FBM you never laid eyes on know it, because you'd just shown them. Fireball, you are a talented young woman. You have mad skills in problem solving, in coding, in seeing networks as holistic ecosystems. You do not need to preach those skills to random strangers, or to your colleagues, or to your friends, or to me. You have nothing to prove to anyone. Your work is your proof. *You* are your proof."

Fireball took a deep breath, not sure whether to smile or cry. "Jeez, Carver. I'm not sure you've got a handle on this punishment thing. Are you sure you understand the concept?"

"I said the punishment would fit the crime. I'd like you to appoint a temporary team leader and spokesperson until such time as you feel you can control your impulse to crow."

"Wait. What? What if I said I feel that now?"

He captured her gaze again. "Do you?"

She thought back, perversely, to the fracas on the bus. Yeah, that had been about defending the bus driver initially, and because they all hated bullies. But hadn't some of it been about pride? About needing to establish worth? About proving what she could do?

She swallowed. "No. Not really. I think it might actually take a while."

"Well, I'll check in with you at the end of next week. See how you're doing then. And, Fireball, I'm not just talking about what you say or show in a public setting. You need to make mindfulness and self-awareness a habit. So, check yourself no matter who you're talking to or when. Okay?"

She nodded. "So, do I have to choose now?"

"No, but as soon as possible. Monday morning at the latest. I'd like someone else to be point person in dealing with Zander, clients, and the public. And remember, this is only temporary. Your teammates respect you."

"At least, they did until I shot my mouth off today."

"They respect you," he repeated. "They'll respect you more when they see you really working on this – when they see you get a handle on it. Now, why don't you go and have supper, then get ready for Benjamin's party."

Her gaze had wandered to the marching totems; she snapped it back to Carver's face with a blink. "You're gonna let me go to the party?"

Carver threw her a "well, duh" face. "It's a BOP, Fireball. It's a big deal. Especially to Benjamin. Of course you're going to go."

"If Zander finds out you didn't, like, ground me or something–"

"I'll tell him it was a class assignment. That I wanted you to use Ben's success to consolidate your own goals in your mind so you'll stay focused."

"Eyes on the prize?"

"You got it. Now go. Eat. I'll see you at the BOP."

Fireball got up and headed for the door. She paused there, turned, and said, "Books... for team lead," then scrambled out of Carver's office as fast as her boots would carry her.

~~~

"Man I hate this," said Scrappy, his mouth half full of mashed potatoes. "I mean, it may look like FuBarCorp's networks are purring like a box full of happy kittens, but I feel like we didn't so much solve the problem as chase it under the sofa. You know what I mean?" He looked around the table at the other members of the team.

Books and Cricket were both nodding.

"Yes," Cricket said. "It's like what my father always says about his tractor. That it malfunctions only until he takes it to a mechanic. Then it's suddenly on its best behavior."

Noob was nodding too. As if, Scrappy thought, he understood the full scope of what they'd been dealing with today by just sitting and watching them work.

"I wanted to ask about that," Noob said. "I mean, how can you apply security protocols like you did without first thoroughly debugging the system? You might be paving over a really deep hole."

"What're you saying?" Scrappy asked, hackles rising. "That we were negligent?"

"I'm saying," said Noob, "that what you did is sort of like putting makeup on a zit instead of scrubbing your face and putting medication on it first."

"We *did* scrub it," protested Cricket. "Or at least, we tried to."

"Is that good enough?" Noob asked earnestly.

Scrappy snorted. "Oh, listen to Master Yoda: 'Do or do not. There is no try.' Look, Noobie-doo, we've been doing this a long time, whereas *you* are the new kid on the block. *You* don't know what you're talking about."

Noob scanned the team's faces. "You guys have all said this is *terra incognita.* That you've never seen a virus behave this way before."

"That's because it's a live hack, boy-o," said Scrappy, heat fanning his cheeks. He had no idea what *terra*-whatever meant and it bugged him. All he knew was that this kid was accusing him of something – carelessness, cluelessness... error.

"Yeah," said Noob, "and it's got you all jinked. You just said it yourself, Scrappy."

"No, I didn't."

"Yes, you did. You said–"

"Tell you what, Noob. You just shut the f–" Scrappy's eyes darted to where Mom was working behind the chow line. He lowered his voice. "You just shut up about what I said. You misunderstood me. We weren't negligent. We did what we were supposed to do. We solved the problem. Okay? You're new here. You don't know what the heck you're talking about, and the sooner you realize that and learn to keep your worthless opinions to yourself, the better off you'll be. Got it?"

Scrappy locked eyes with the new kid, aware that everyone else was staring at them in stunned silence. *That's right, Noobio. You are out of line and everyone knows it but you.*

Cricket frowned, glancing back and forth between the two boys. "Scrappy, he didn't say we were negligent. Maybe a little too sure of ourselves..."

Scrappy kept his eyes on Noob's eyes. "Not even."

At last, Noob looked away, picked up his fork, and mumbled, "Got it." He speared some green beans and stuffed them into his mouth. "Don't look now," murmured Whiz. "Here comes fearless leader. Seems okay."

Scrappy looked up, face flushed with victory, to see Fireball heading their way with a tray full of food. He scanned her face for battle scars, but she seemed none the worse for wear. That was a relief. The first words out of her mouth, though, threw the whole team into a state of shock.

"Carver's demoted me temporarily. He asked me to choose an interim team lead. Books, that's you. You're in charge of Raven from this moment until Carver thinks I've learned to STFU. Now, we better chow down or we'll be late to the BOP."

Scrappy looked around at the others. He could tell they all had questions, but a glance at Fireball's shuttered face killed any hope that she would answer them. He picked up his fork and shoveled another bite of mashed potatoes into his mouth.

Party Animals

They missed the bus. And unless they wanted to hike the two miles to Benjamin's apartment in the dark, they'd have to hail a cab. Good luck with that at this time of night in the business district. Mom and Carver had already gone, so there wasn't even anyone to cadge a ride with. As they dithered on the sidewalk near the bus stop, arguing about whether they could afford to get a cab, a silver Prius pulled up to the curb. The passenger-side window rolled down and, to their utter astonishment, Benjamin himself peered at them from behind the wheel.

"Hey! Wanna ride in my new car? Well, new to me, anyway. Carver said he thought you guys might need a lift, so I figured I'd drop by and get you."

"How'd you know where we'd be?" asked Fireball.

In answer, Ben leaned across the passenger seat and pointed to the facade of Cinzento's main building. "Carver has access to the security feed. Smile, you're on TV."

"Frabgious!" said Scrappy and pulled open the rear passenger side door. "All aboard!"

He flung himself into the back seat and scooted across. Whiz and Fireball followed, while Books slid into the front seat. That left Cricket and Noob standing on the sidewalk.

"I know it's not legal," said Books, "but Cricket's small. She can sit on my lap."

"Oh *ho*!" crowed Ben. "That's the way it is, is it?"

"Cut it out, Benjamin," growled Books as Cricket settled into his lap.

Sitting in the back between Scrappy and Whiz, Fireball felt her cheeks flame. If she hadn't been so eager to get into the car, she might've been the one sitting in Books's lap.

"What about that guy?" Benjamin asked, nodding to where Noob hung back on the sidewalk.

"That's the new kid," said Scrappy. "He started this morning."

"Cool. Hey, New Kid," said Ben. "Why don't you just climb into the cargo hold?"

Noob glanced doubtfully at the back of the Prius. "Uh, y'know, maybe I'll just pass..."

"Here." Whiz swung open the rear passenger door. "On the floor. Safer than the cargo hold; more fun than staying behind."

After a moment of hesitation, Noob climbed into the back of the car to half sit, half lie across the other kids' feet. Catching a glimpse of his face in the light from the bus stop, Fireball felt a twinge of empathy. She remembered what it was like to be the new kid on the team. The odd girl out. You lived life as an afterthought and sat alone in corners a lot.

"So, Ben," said Scrappy, "what's with the manual? Couldn't afford a driverless model?"

"Didn't want to," the older youth said as he pulled out onto the street. "I like to drive. I like being in control."

"Well, Mr. Control Freak, thanks for the lift. If you were still an Academy brat, I'd give you mucho Kudos for the favor. I guess that's one of the downsides of being all grown up; you can't collect virtue points."

"Nope. I just get paid in invisible electronic credits that will buy me a heck of a lot more than Kudos will. Like this car, for example. Try buying one of these babies with Academy Kudos." He patted the dashboard lovingly.

In no time at all, they reached Ben's apartment complex – an über-modern warren of glass, steel, and stone that seemed to grow right up out of the wooded slope it sat on. The buildings were four stories tall and scattered over the hillside like gleaming crystals, their lights illuminating walking paths and greenery and sparkling off the surface of the large pool at the center of the complex.

"During the summer," Benjamin told his guests, "we'll have to have some parties out here. Barbecue and all that summer do-ery."

The party was ramping up to full swing when they entered the first-floor apartment. The large living room had a glass wall that overlooked the garden and pool. Beyond that room was a small open kitchen, a guest bath, and a bedroom. Above the kitchen was a loft that overlooked the living room. Ben used that space as his home lab. The lights in the apartment were turned down low, and candles flickered here and there, glinting off of every shiny surface, while the small gas fireplace with its stone surround cast dancing light and shadow into the room. All very atmospheric.

The place was a sheer amazement to Fireball, who had never seen anything like it, firsthand. She'd seen pictures online or in magazines of places like this, but the idea that an Academy alum could afford one (that *she* might afford one when she graduated) filled her with a sense of surreal wonder. This was not the image summoned to Fireball's brain by the word "apartment." An apartment, in her memory, was a close, skeevy, messy place in which nothing that got lost was ever found and that was never, ever silent or even quiet. There was always someone yelling somewhere, and stereos and sirens blaring. Terrifying thumps and cries erupted in the middle of the night and seemed to come from far too close by – often just on the other side of the wall. Here, she heard only the babble of voices and the occasional intrusion of unrecognizable bass lines that were all she could hear of the music playing in the background.

Fireball gathered some snacks from the breakfast bar that divided the kitchen from the living room, got a soda from a cooler filled with ice, and looked around for Carver and Mom. They were out on the terrace that extended the living area into the complex's gardens. The terrace wasn't that large itself, but if you took three steps down from its open end, you were on the flagstone patio that connected Benjamin's building to the pool surround. Carver had let his hair down – literally. He usually wore it in a single gleaming braid that reached almost to his belt in back; tonight it was brushed to a high gloss and fell loose around his shoulders.

Fireball hesitated in the kitchen access, glancing around at the twenty or so people that were forming conversation clumps all around. She didn't know most of them. Suddenly shy, she made a beeline for the terrace. She was halfway across the living room when she spotted Noob balanced precariously – and alone – on the narrow lip of the hearth, gazing uneasily at a room full of people he didn't know from Adam.

The wave of empathy hit her again. She felt for him, she really did: his parents gone, thrown into a strange place with strange people. Heck, no wonder he looked so miserable. She thought back to her own first days at Cinzento Academy. She'd been relieved that her mom had given her up, and it had still been hard.

On a sudden impulse, she made her way around the cluster of packed seating to the hearth.

"Hey, Noob. You look like you could use some fresh air. It's not raining tonight. Wanna come out on the terrace where it's not quite so deafening? Mom and Carver are out there."

He stared at her blankly for a second, then relief spread from his dark eyes to the rest of his features. He even smiled. He had a really nice smile.

"Thanks," he said. "That sounds like a great idea. I'm... not much of a party animal."

"Yeah, me neither."

Fireball turned and led the way to the terrace. She noticed that someone else slid into Noob's spot the instant he left it. Space in the living room was at a premium. So much so that Fireball and Noob had barely gotten seated next to Carver and Mom on the wooden bench that ran around the perimeter of the terrace, when a cluster of new arrivals spilled out onto it, chattering like chimpanzees.

Carver glanced over at Mom, then rose. "What do you two say we go down to that firepit by the pool where it's quieter?"

Fireball realized she liked that idea a lot. Noob was already on his feet. They wandered after Carver and Mom, juggling their little plates of food and sodas.

"So, Benjamin," Noob said tentatively. "Is that his real name? It doesn't sound like a handle."

"Nah. His real name is Stephen. Stephen Brett. He goes by Benjamin because" – she rubbed her thumb and fingers together in the universal sign for money – "he's all about the money. *Loves* the Benjamins."

"Huh. That's interesting."

Fireball gave him a swift sideways glance. "You said 'interesting' in a Vulcan tone of voice. What's interesting about Benjamin's mercenary streak?"

Noob shrugged. "I overheard him tell someone that some big internet company in San Jose offered him a quarter again as much as he'd be making at Cinzento. I gotta wonder why he'd make that choice if he was really all that mercenary."

Fireball blinked at the observation. Then she shook her head. "Nope. Too complicated. This is Benjamin we're talking about. Was the person he was chatting up female and cute?"

"Actually, it was Carver."

They reached the firepit and seated themselves on the stone benches that bracketed it. Carver had found the controls and turned the gas jets on. The fire nicely cut the slight chill of the fall air, warmed Fireball's face, and made her inexplicably happy.

Demotion forgotten, she turned to Carver and asked, "Did Zander explain to you why he rushed us out of FuBar like he did?"

Carver's expression was unreadable, as always. "No. Did you feel that's what he did?"

Fireball glanced at Noob. He was watching her as if the subject were of intense interest to him.

"Yeah. I did." She leaned forward, elbows on knees. "Truth is, Carver, we weren't sure we got whatever it was that was plaguing Foster B. We thought it was a virus at first. Standard stuff. But it kept misbehaving. I mean, it behaved in unexpected ways. So, we figured it had to be a live hack. But Zander didn't want to hear that. He just told his new buddy, Myrle, everything was hunky-dory and carted us out."

Carver nodded. "Yes, he was pretty clear that as far as he was concerned you'd solved the problem. No?"

"No! I mean, we're not even sure what the problem *was*, so I can't claim we solved it. The hack just stopped, and whoever was on the other end of it even cleaned up after themselves. Maybe we did chase them out of the system, but if we don't figure out how they got in, in the first place, they may be tempted to pop back in while we're snoozing."

"Then we'd better not snooze," Carver said. He looked to Noob then. "What was your impression of the situation, Angel?"

Noob blinked as if surprised to hear his given name. "What Fireball said. The team didn't solve the problem. It just... stopped."

"That bother you, did it?"

Noob shrugged. "Well, yeah. I said something to the team about it at dinner, but Scrappy jumped all over me."

Fireball frowned. "First I'm hearing about this."

Noob shrugged again, then shot Carver a sideways glance. "You were... you weren't there."

"What did you say that set old King of the Test Lab off?" Fireball asked.

"I asked how you could put a Band-Aid on a wound without making sure you'd gotten all the crud out... more or less. It didn't go over well."

"I'll say." Books, a can of soda in hand, plopped down on the bench next to Fireball.

His thigh brushed against hers, loosing a flood of warmth that made her cheeks flush so badly she almost put her hands over them. She didn't, but she couldn't quite make herself pull away.

"Scrappy got all up in Noob's face and told him he didn't know what he was talking about," Books added, looking up as his sister set a plate of goodies down on Fireball's opposite side, then straddled the stone bench to pick at it.

"Acted like we'd saved the planet or something," Whiz said.

"I was embarrassed."

That was from Cricket, as she slipped out of the semidarkness of the garden to sit between Noob and Mom, who'd been observing the conversation in silence. Fireball would've been stunned if Mom were to offer an opinion on any of this. It was way above her pay grade. Heck, she was such a techno-newt that she probably only understood every third or fourth word they said. Fireball had been called upon to give Mom tech support any number of times for truly bonehead stuff. Zander Grayson, she thought uncharitably, wasn't much better. It made her wonder how he'd come to be CEO of a cyber-security firm in the first place. Carver, now, would make a much better CEO.

Cricket turned to Noob and put a delicate hand on his arm. Fireball was pretty sure she didn't imagine the sudden tension she could feel in Books's thigh. Now, she did shift away, covering her discomfort by stealing a chip from Whiz's paper plate.

"I'm really sorry, Noob," Cricket said. "I felt so bad for you. Scrappy shouldn't have gone off on you like that. You were right. We weren't done at FBM, and now I'm really worried." She turned to look at Carver. "I don't feel right about this. I know Mr. Grayson wants to let the Situation Room handle it, but I think we should do more, ourselves, to make sure the system is clean and stays clean."

"I somehow doubt Zander is going to approve that," Carver said.

"Yeah," said Fireball, "but if the hackers get back in, or they're just lying low, we're gonna get blamed for not doing our job right."

Carver sat in pensive silence for a moment, then said, "Walk me through the sequence of events. What was the hack like?"

The team exchanged glances, then Books said, "The hacker was filling up hard drives – entire raid arrays – with... we're not sure with what. But it was clogging up the system to the point that the servers were crashing and the throughput on the network was like I-5 at rush hour. And then, they would just clean up their trash and move on. Seemingly at random. There didn't seem to be any rhyme or reason to what they were doing."

"They cleaned up after themselves?" Carver asked.

"Didn't do any damage," said Whiz, nodding. "Doesn't mean they didn't steal stuff."

"What systems were they in?"

Whiz gave a one-shoulder shrug. "Like Books said. Random. Customer records, payroll, accounts, HR."

"Which means it's possible they lifted sensitive information."

Cricket was shaking her head. "I saw no sign of data being moved out of the system; only in. Transferring databases that large would leave a trail."

"Unless," said Noob quietly, "they were selective about the data they took and uploaded it a little at a time. If they shed some of their own content and copied selectively from the bank, they'd leave essentially the same footprint on the way out that they did on the way in." When everyone turned to look at him, he added, "I'm probably wrong."

"No," Fireball said, "that's a good theory. That would be a great cover for lifting data. Flood the system with meaningless content, then upload dribs and drabs of what's on the system, overwriting the placeholder stuff as you go. You leave the same size as you came in, only now, some of your content is what you jacked from the target servers."

There was that smile again. Noob's unspoken thanks for backing him up gave Fireball a lift as well. She felt the sudden weight of Mom's regard and met the woman's gaze. Was that approval lighting her eyes?

"Man, you guys really don't know how to party, do you?" Scrappy stood just beyond the benches with a glass in one hand and a paper plate full of noshes in the other. "Are you seriously out here talking shop?"

"Just trying to figure out what's going on with FuBarCorp," said Books.

"What's to figure? We came, we saw, we kicked digital butt."

The whole team gave him a look. "You know that's not true," said Cricket. "You *know* we didn't solve that problem. Whoever did that hack and whatever their goal was, they lived to fight another day." She turned back to Carver. "Please, Carver, you have to get Mr. Grayson to let us back in so we can run the hacker to ground."

"Aw, c'mon, Crick," complained Scrappy. "The FuBar system is like Earth on *Dr. Who*." He slipped into a bad English accent. "This network is de-*fen*-ded."

"Want to bank on that?" punned Whiz. She nodded toward Cricket. "Expert says there's something to worry about. So I'm worried."

Carver looked around at the earnest young faces, holding Fireball's gaze a second longer before moving to Books. "Team Leader, you want to monitor FBM?"

Books nodded, his dark, handsome face solemn in the firelight. "So say we all."

Fireball did not miss the look he shot Scrappy. The one that said he would tolerate no dissent. For a moment, she wasn't sure which she wanted more: to be *with* Books or to *be* Books.

Scrappy, for his part, raised his glass in salute. "So say we all. Now, if you'll excuse me – Ben promised to introduce me to this really cute guy from the Tech." He turned on his heel and went back into the apartment.

"Pardon me for butting in," said Mom. "I don't get all the technobabble you guys spout all the time, but this could harm the prestige of the company and the Academy if the kids are right. Right?"

Carver nodded. "Yes, it could."

"So what happens if Mr. G won't give them permission to keep tabs on this bank?"

Carver gave Mom a wry smile. "I guess I'll have to take it to the Old Man. I'm pretty sure he'll see the wisdom of keeping our best and brightest in the game."

"Grayson won't like that, you know," Mom observed.

Carver laughed. "Oh, he surely won't."

"Hey, Carver, can I ask you a kind of personal question?" asked Fireball.

He smiled. "You can *ask*."

"Why aren't you CEO of Cinzento? You're so obviously light-years more qualified than Zander."

"Yeah," said Mom. "I've always kind of wondered that too. You're a pretty bright guy, Carve. I bet you could write your own ticket at Cinzento. Have any job you wanted."

He met her curious gaze for a moment, then looked at the teenagers sitting around him. "I have the job I want, Mom. If I were CEO, I'd miss what I love best – working with these guys."

"Yeah," Mom agreed, shooting the team a fond glance. "I hear you. They're a pretty special bunch – when they don't let it go to their heads."

Fireball couldn't be sure, but she thought that remark was aimed right at her.

Day Two

Mentor, Mentis

The kids arrived in the dining hall for breakfast earlier on Saturday morning than they were used to, yawning after their long Friday workday and late night. Carver intercepted them as they made their way to the chow line, and recommended they eat well and take naps during the day as needed.

"I talked to the Old Man. He wants you all up to your eyeballs in this FBM situation. So, Cricket, you're going to need to go over to the bank to oversee upgrading their systems. Keep an eye out for any further hacking. Books, sit down with your team, figure out what you think needs to be covered in your ongoing investigations, and deploy your resources as you see fit."

Books gave Fireball a frowning glance. "Can I do it in consultation with Fireball?"

"Consult Fireball, your entire team – me, if you need to. I'm sorry you have to give up your weekend, but we need to make sure this hacker doesn't get back into FuBar's system. Now go hit the chow line."

"Did you hear that?" whispered Cricket, watching Carver stride toward the hallway. "He called FBM FuBar!"

"Freudian slip," said Whiz, fetching a tray from the stack.

Fireball was lingering in front of the bakery goods trying to decide between a muffin and a scone, and whether she should take that presently empty seat next to Books, when Mom came out of the kitchen, wiping her hands on a dish towel.

"Hey, kiddo, can I have a word?"

Puzzled, Fireball popped a scone onto her tray, shot the empty chair next to Books a longing look, then followed Mom into her little office, which was tucked into the corner at the end of the serving line. She'd no sooner stepped into the room than Mom pointed past her through the Plexiglas panel from which she commanded a clear view of the dining hall.

"See that?" Mom asked.

That was Noob, sitting alone at a small corner table by the windows.

Mom had fixed Fireball with a questioning gaze. "What's wrong with this picture, kiddo?"

Fireball shrugged. "He's kind of a lone wolf, I guess." She knew better. She knew that Noob simply didn't feel welcome at the team table yet.

Mom made a sound like a game show buzzer. "Nope. You guys are ignoring him. You gave him a mentor for work. Now he needs one for life."

"Okay, fine. Scrappy can—"

"Not Scrappy, cherub. You."

"Why me?" Fireball demanded.

"Because I think you'll do the best job of it just to prove to me you can."

Fireball fixed the woman with a gimlet eye and said, "Okay, so you've got my number. Yeah, I'll do it, but I won't like it."

She took her tray and marched out of Mom's office and right over to Noob's table to sit down next to him. He tossed her a surprised look, but all he said was, "Hey."

"Hey," she said back. "You heard all that stuff Carver was saying, right?"

He nodded. "Sounds like a busy day."

"For all of us, kiddo," she said, mimicking Mom.

"Hey, you guys!" Books hailed them from the Raven table. "Care to join the discussion?"

"Yes, *sir*," Fireball said and rose, picking up her tray. "C'mon, Noob, we've been summoned."

The youth rose uncertainly but followed her to the table occupied by the rest of the team.

"I think this is a wild gooseberry chase," Scrappy was saying as they reached it. "The problem is solved. The hacker got outed and decided bugging out was the better part of valor. Get it? *Bugging* out?"

Fireball turned to stare at him. "You don't have any questions about how this went down? Seriously?"

Scrappy shrugged. "It'd be nice to trace the hack back to its evil little lair, but as long as Mr. FuBar is a happy camper, what questions are really that pressing?"

"Okay," said Fireball, ticking off reasons on her fingertips, "for one thing, if his systems start hiccupping again, Mr. FuBar is not going to be happy for long. For another, I can think of a whole bunch of pressing questions that I, for one, would like answers to. Like, for example, who are the hackers and what are they after? And did they get it?"

"I didn't see any evidence that they got anything. They slunk out with their little digital tails tucked between their legs."

"Actually," said Cricket, "Noob came up with a good working theory about how they could make it look like they didn't upload any data."

Scrappy made a face and flicked Noob a pointed glance. "Oh, Noob did, did he? He's been on the job one friggin' day and he's got the whole bloody thing figured out. I seriously doubt it."

"We wondered about the content the system was being flooded with," said Cricket. "Maybe it was just a placeholder they used to populate the system so they could swap select FuBar data for their content and slither out again the same size as they entered."

Scrappy blinked and his lean face went momentarily blank. Fireball enjoyed a tickle of *schadenfreude* as she watched the possibility that Noob's theory might be correct register in her friend's prickly brain.

"Noob's right," said Books. "They might have gotten exactly what they came for. And right now, we have no way of knowing. We also don't know how the hackers got in, or when."

"If they're lying low," said Whiz, "how do we get them out?"

"I want to know how they hid their existence," said Cricket. "How could the system monitors show the machines were idle when they were so overloaded?"

Noob took an audible breath and opened his mouth.

Scrappy scalded him with a glare. "Got some words of wisdom for us, amigo?"

Noob closed his mouth and shook his head. "No."

Fireball glanced toward Mom's office, then said, "I want to know what Noob was going to say."

"Nothing, really..."

"Please," said Cricket, fixing him with her shiny jet gaze, "tell us what you were going to say. It could be important."

Noob cast a tentative look around the table through his long, dark lashes before he spoke. "I was wondering if there might be some changes the hack caused to the system that we didn't see because we were so focused on the symptoms we *did* see. Changes that might even seem unrelated."

"Misdirection?" asked Whiz around a mouthful of oatmeal.

Noob nodded emphatically. "Yeah. And why did the attack stop?"

Scrappy snorted loudly. "Because we scared 'em into abandoning all hope."

"Did we?" asked Noob. "What were you guys doing when the attack stopped that might've scared them? Specifically."

Scrappy rolled his eyes. "Duh. We were getting ready to sic the Alligator on 'em – track their digital footprints. They're evil hackers; they didn't want us to trace them back to their evil hacker lair."

"Actually, we hadn't gotten that far," said Cricket quietly. "We were preparing to wipe the server and upload from a backup. You think they reacted to that?"

Noob shook his head. "I don't know."

"Damn right, you don't know," said Scrappy. He looked to Books. "So, let's make a plan, then, if you guys are so gung-ho."

They made a plan. Fireball was gratified by the number of times Books turned to her for input, but she was legitimately proud of the way he led the team. He was, she realized, steadier than she was. Calm where she was excitable. Anchored where she was impetuous.

Did that mean she was a bad leader? Or at least not as good a leader as Books?

She snuffed out that line of stupid and concentrated on the big picture. The plan they settled on had Cricket going to FuBarCorp, as Carver had recommended, to provide oversight to their system upgrades and onsite review of their status. Cricket's goal would be to determine what vulnerabilities might have been exploited to punch into the network. Whiz and Fireball would go with her to work through the security and performance logs, following up on Noob's last question about what the hackers might have done that didn't appear at first blush. Here, they hoped they might find the clue that would indicate when the breach had first occurred.

Books assigned Scrappy and Noob to scouring FBM's live data stream from their own lab, looking for anything similar to what the girls scared up in the logs, while he would search client security records and online forums for discussions of similar hacks.

"Scrappy and I can triage whatever I find," he said. "Noob, you can help with that too."

"Only if he keeps his hands off the client code," Scrappy retorted. "I wouldn't want him to decide their programming was subpar and take it into his head to 'fix' it."

If she were a cat, Fireball decided, that crack would've laid her ears back. Before she, Cricket, and Whiz took a company car over to FBM, she pulled Scrappy aside and got in his face.

"Carver assigned you to help Noob ease into his work here," she told him. "And you're doing a pretty pathetic job of it. You cut him off at every pass and never give credit where credit is due. He's been completely on the money a number of times, yet you treat him like he's a dunce. Mom assigned me to make sure he feels at home here. That he fits in. You're not helping much with that, either. In fact, you're kind of being a jerk."

Scrappy's face reddened and he opened his mouth to say something, but Fireball wasn't done with him yet.

"No excuses, Scraps. He's an orphan, okay? His parents have been dead less than a year, remember? So don't be so darned mean."

"I am not being mean," Scrappy defended himself. "I'm just concerned about our reputation."

"If you're not being mean, you're at least tiptoeing awfully close to the edge. C'mon, you know what it's like to be picked on 'cause you're different. You know what it's like to be 'other.' We all do. Do you really want to pass the abuse along? 'Cause I sure don't."

Scrappy looked at the floor of the hallway they stood in, his mouth pulled into a crooked line. "No. I don't mean to be mean. I just... sometimes stopping my tongue from running before my brain is in gear is hard. I promise I'll try."

"We were all Noobs once," she reminded him. "Just, y'know, remember that, if he gets under your skin."

It was advice she guiltily realized she needed to take herself.

Meddling

At Foster Bowman Myrle, the three girls enlisted a sys admin named Frank Fordham to help with their effort. What they needed, Cricket explained, was a team of technicians to check all of FBM's hardware to see if any of it was running hot or laboring as if hit with a denial of service.

Frank stared at them as if they were speaking in tongues. "That's thousands of machines."

"Right," said Fireball, "so it's gonna take a big team of expert eyeballs. But this hack is sneaky. The system diagnostics will tell you the machines are all doing fine. You have to monitor at the individual nodes to recognize the problem."

"Hack? I thought it was a virus."

"So'd we at first," said Whiz. "Didn't act like a virus. We'll need access to all your security logs."

Frank was clearly not happy to be taking orders from teenagers, but he knew he'd have to answer to Conrad Myrle if he screwed things up by dragging his feet. He grudgingly assigned them to a pair of machines that would give them access to the logs, escorted Cricket to the hub of upgrade activity, then went off to recruit techs for the hardware check.

The two girls began their search of the security logs with heightened expectations. Surely there would be a blip, a bloop, a smoking gun. They found exactly nothing – the logs were normal. Pristine, even.

"Wait a minute," said Fireball, skimming back through the last hour's worth of activity she'd looked at... which was exactly like the hour before that and the hour before that. "These are *too* clean."

Whiz turned to look at her, bleary-eyed. "What?"

"Hang on," Fireball murmured. She did a search on a specific time stamp, her heart beating out a rapid tattoo in her chest. "What the...? Whoa, whoa, *whoa*. This is *all* wrong."

Whiz rolled her chair over next to Fireball's and peered at the screen. "What's all wrong?"

Fireball pointed. "Look. See that?"

"Yeah. Normal activity."

"It *shouldn't* be normal activity, Whiz. Because that's when we were chasing poltergeists all over the system, setting up diagnostics, messing with the client raid array. We were making all sorts of unusual demands on the record-keeping in this system, and none of it is there. *None* of it."

Whiz's dark complexion went two shades lighter. "So... someone purged it?"

Fireball slipped a thumb drive into a USB port on the machine she was using and accessed the files on it. "Well look, here are my backups of our logs. Everything we did is there. But it's no longer *there*." She pointed at the FBM box. "Which means someone's been meddling with this system since yesterday."

Whiz pulled out her cell phone. "I'll text Cricket."

They began analyzing their backups, comparing access patterns of different machines against their history, and against each other. They turned up unexpected behavior for one user and got excited until they realized they were just looking at peer-to-peer sharing of so-called "adult" content, and not that recent. They were thoroughly disgusted, but no closer to finding anything useful.

Fireball gave a moment's thought to tracking down the originating employee and outing him to HR, but Whiz reminded her that *tempus* was *fugit*-ing.

She pressed her nose back to the grindstone, grumbling, "I cannot unsee that."

"Yeah, me neither," admitted Whiz, "but we need to figure this thing out."

Fireball glared at the screen of her computer. "We *will* succeed at this, damn it! These hackers shall not triumph over Team Raven."

The two girls redoubled their efforts and, roughly an hour later, Whiz sat straight up in her chair and said, "Huh."

"Huh, what?" asked Fireball. "What do you see?"

"Seems to be an activation point about two months ago. It's the first unusual behavior by a FuBar server, anyway. But there's no obvious entry point during that period. No incoming packets. No new external input – at least not related to that part of the network. It's as if the hackers teleported into the system and started wreaking slow havoc." She turned to frown at Fireball. "Why? What'd they want?"

Fireball moved to sit at Whiz's elbow, eyes pinned to the high-res display. "So, what happened before that? If there were no external intrusions, let's look at the system maintenance routine. Maybe FuBar's protocols did something to invite mayhem."

"Wanna drive?" Whiz asked, scooting her chair aside to give Fireball access to the keyboard.

"You don't have to defer to me, Whiz. I'm not team lead anymore."

The taller girl shrugged. "You're not team lead *right now*. And you're better at this than I am."

Fireball got the address of their Patient Zero – the first machine to show symptoms – and began a regressive check of activity that affected that server. The only potential trigger she could see was a system-wide process called ReGen that was scheduled to run at weekly intervals.

She glanced at Whiz. "Ping our friend Frank and ask him very sweetly to come down here for a consult."

"Why don't you ping him?"

"He doesn't like me. I'm abrasive. You're nicer than I am."

Whiz just looked at her. "I'm terse to the point of tactlessness. Books says so, anyway."

"Wanna flip a coin?"

"I'll ping."

~~~

"ReGen," said Frank Fordham when he arrived, looking harried and munching on a power bar, "is a maintenance program that backs up all client data and offloads archives of closed accounts to a remote server. Happens on a weekly basis."

"What's the protocol?" asked Fireball. "What does the remote server send to the main system?"

"Nothing but a handshake at the end of the process. Our system initiates the upload, so the only communication from the remote server to our system is the termination handshake that tells the main server all data has been received. Other than that, the upload only goes one way."

Fireball opened her mouth to ask if he were sure of that, but realized it would be rude and demeaning. No sense giving the guy actual reasons to be difficult. Instead, she asked him to point them to the performance status logs. He did, then went back to gathering his hardware-checking brute squad.

While Whiz continued to comb through the activity logs, Fireball switched over to following the ReGen maintenance process. Machine health metrics showed that a machine allocated as a test box ran hot for several days after ReGen, as if something had infected it, then suddenly returned to its normal parameters. Whereupon another server – one in the main system – began to run hot. A maintenance note revealed that when an IT admin investigated the server, the health metrics immediately went green again without him changing anything. He closed the case.

Epiphany. Fireball realized, with a thrill, that she was looking at the real Patient Zero in this epidemic of weird. She shared her discovery with Whiz.

"Why'd a test box be affected by ReGen?" Whiz wanted to know. "It's not even in the main network."

"We can ask, I suppose," Fireball mused. "Could you ping–"

"Your turn," Whiz said.

"Books is right. You *are* terse to the point of tactlessness."

The employee Frank Fordham identified as being the last to use the test box was a programmer named Wendy Willoughby – a name that made Fireball wonder if FBM only hired people whose names were alliterative. Wendy had been monitoring the test box for Conrad Myrle prior to the ReGen.

"But we'd shut down the test program by then. Turned out to be a dud, I guess. I'm not sure."

"Your maintenance logs say the machine ran hot, then just recovered on its own," Fireball observed.

"Yeah. Pretty much."

"You have troubleshooting logs on it?"

The woman shook her head. "Sorry. Since it was a test of a third-party product, we didn't–"

"Third-party product? What kind? What was it supposed to do?"

"I really can't say." She raised one hand in a Girl Scout salute. "I signed an NDA. It was a maintenance-related product. That's all I can really say. And it was installed just in the test bay."

"Here's what gets me," Whiz said, after the programmer had gone back to her own domain. "One day after node zero gets the bug, another machine gets a hot flash, then goes green again. Like... like someone was testing the water. Then it just spreads randomly – a machine here, a machine there. Nobody investigates until – bam! – it reaches critical mass and causes crashes all over FuBar."

Fireball shrugged. "Probably because it looks so random. Each incident seems isolated."

"Look at these logs. I'd say 90 percent of FuBar's machines have been affected. But there's no logic to it."

"Well, yeah. Logic would get noticed, right? If there were a pattern to the crashes early on – if they'd hit a particular department or a particular data collection, then the techs would have noticed it. Despite the fact that the overheating wasn't showing up in real time."

Whiz shook her head. "What's this hacker doing?"

"Maybe if we go far enough back in the maintenance logs – look at the early diagnostics they ran," suggested Fireball, "we'll see a pattern."

They might have seen a pattern in two-month-old diagnostics had there been any. But in the true spirit of fubar-ness, FBM only kept one week's worth of logs. They were hundreds of gigabytes each, times thousands of machines. The girls tried not to let Frank Fordham see how totally derp they thought this practice was (if Cinzento had anything to say about it, it would stop) and asked to examine the test box that was apparently their zero node.

Fordham took them to the test lab where the adult denizens stared at them and shared eye rolls. He left them there, but not before telling them to call his department admin if they had any further questions. He was, after all, managing a company-wide hardware diagnostic.

Fireball and Whiz examined the test box.

"Seems pretty inoffensive, doesn't it?" Fireball said, poking her nose behind the machine to see if it was hooked up to any peripherals. "Huh. It's not even on the network." She held up the ethernet cable then looped it around the monitor stand.

She saved off the logs from the test box, while Whiz did the same from the once-infected main database server. Then they sampled data and logs from several other machines that had been running hot during the crisis.

"Same song, second verse," said Whiz. "Everything's hunky-dory right up until the machines crash. Then it looks like a voluntary reboot. Is this security system so poorly designed that operators can't tell when Rome is burning?"

Fireball gave her a sideways glance. "You think this is an interface design problem?"

"C'mon, girl, how long have you known me? I think *everything* is an interface design problem. The evidence of the hack should be right out in plain sight. We shouldn't have to dig around in the maintenance logs to see it. That's bad design exploited by someone with a will."

"Yeah, but a will to do what?"

Shadow. Play.

Fireball and Whiz were munching sandwiches in their temporary lab at FBM when Cricket came in, her eyes glittering like polished jet and her face flushed.

"You eat?" Whiz asked, holding out half of her tuna fish sandwich.

"I don't remember. I just spent the last two hours inspecting one of the machines that was running hot and crashing." Cricket stood in the center of the computer lab, her hands clasped in front of her as if she were afraid they were going to fly away. She took a deep breath and announced: "That machine is running a shadow operating system with the client OS inside a shell – a virtual machine."

The announcement dropped into the room with a palpable thud.

"What?" said Fireball breathlessly, and Whiz murmured, "A VM. Of course. Makes sense."

Cricket nodded emphatically, her mouth forming a fierce grin that would have surprised (and possibly terrified) anyone who didn't know her well. "Right. And that's what we've seen when we look at the system analytics. The shadow operating system is nearly undetectable, and it allows anything running on the shadow OS to use the system resources without changing the state of the *visible* OS. The visible OS performance metrics are green, but the activity of the shadow OS isn't being reported in real time. So it–"

"It overloads the system whenever the shadow OS is engaged in any activity that hogs resources," finished Fireball. "Good catch, Cricket."

"So, that's our solution," said Cricket, smiling beatifically. "We teach their IT staff how to recognize the virtual machine in operation, clean up the infected system, and remove the shadow OS."

Whiz whistled. "Ouch. That's gonna leave a mark on their bottom line. That's time *and* money."

"Serves 'em right," groused Fireball, "running their IT shop like this. They're lucky it wasn't worse. We need to report to Books. Figure out what our next step is."

The team consulted through Fireball's cell phone on speaker, agreeing by consensus that they wanted to quarantine several of the infected boxes in order to study them more. They included Patient Zero, a second machine that they'd turned off early in their initial intervention because it was running hot, and a drive from the remote server used to back up FBM's client files during ReGen. Since someone had obviously been tampering with logs while they'd been working, they reasoned that these might give them an untampered state to study.

They requested of Frank Fordham to let them take the two FBM machines back to Cinzento and have their data recovery site ship a backup drive as well. When he resisted the idea, they appealed to Carver. They knew not what magic he worked, but the machines were bundled up to be sent by company van to Team Raven's lair.

Books had a report as well. His exhaustive research dug up so much nothing, he was suspicious. Not only did he find no records of similar-sounding hacks, but a couple of hacking schemes he was sure he had read about online in the past weren't turning up in his searches.

"I don't get it," he told the girls. "I know I've read about at least one shadow hack like this before. I think it was of another financial institution, too. But don't quote me on that."

"You're sure you used the same search terms?" asked Fireball.

"Yeah. I mean, how many different ways can you ask for data on a stealthy hardware takeover? When I type in 'stealth hardware takeover' or 'hijacking,' I get nowhere."

Fireball could hear the key clicks through her phone's speaker as Books entered his search terms for one more try.

"Then I... What the helz?"

"Don't know," said Whiz. "*What* the helz?"

"The articles are there now. A whole bunch of them. I don't get it."

"Occam's Razor," said Scrappy. "You made a boo-boo."

"No, I... well, I suppose I could've..."

"Rubbish, Books," said Whiz. "You haven't mistyped a search term since you were ten."

"Whatever," said Scrappy. "Are you going be able to reconstruct the attack from the data in the VM?"

"Possibly," said Whiz. She pulled up the security log searches she'd been doing with Fireball earlier. "Maybe Cricket can show me how to crack the shell and... well, look at that."

"Look at what?" her brother asked.

"The missing data has come out of its shell. I'm seeing our fingerprints all over these data streams. And the overheating, dutifully logged."

"What are we looking at here?" Books asked after a digestive silence. "Some sort of weird catch-and-release program? It looks like the hackers return control on some sort of timing mechanism."

"A timing mechanism that just happens to coincide with us poking our noses into places they'd scrubbed clean?" asked Fireball. "I think the hackers are still in control of FuBar's network and are just playing games with us. I think, somehow, they know what we're doing."

"How's that possible?" asked Scrappy, "unless it was an inside job. Someone who might even be listening in."

"From where?" demanded Fireball. "Cinzento? FuBar?"

"Shh!" hissed Cricket. "What if someone hears you calling them that?"

Fireball snorted loudly. "I doubt these guys even know what FuBar means."

"I don't think we should talk about this over an open line," said Scrappy. "The connection might be compromised. For sure, all of FuBar's computers and networks are hosed. What do you think, Books?"

Books didn't hesitate. "Fireball, bring your team in," he said, forgetting that the team at FuBar was actually Cricket's. "Don't just send us those infected machines. Come back with them." He cut the connection.

~~~

It was suddenly very quiet in the Raven Lair at Cinzento. The three guys just stared owlishly at each other for a moment, then Noob said, "Looks like we need to figure out whether *our* computers are infected."

"Ya think?" snapped Scrappy. "Tell me, newbie, what would you do first?"

"Um, cut our network connections."

Books was on his feet before Noob finished the sentence and cut off the remote connections to FBM. Scrappy, too, left off poking the new kid as he severed all of their external internet connections.

As he worked, he asked Noob, "You know what a VM is, new guy?"

"Yeah. A virtual machine. Sort of a cyber parasite. Want me to start looking for shells on Cinzento systems?"

Scrappy was secretly impressed. "Shells, hidden data, overworked CPUs. Anything that looks like anything that's going on at FuBarCorp."

All three bent to their tasks, the lair falling into silence but for the tapping of keyboards and clicking of mice. They found nothing, which should have been a cause for celebration. They did not celebrate. They went further than simply cutting ties; they sequestered all of their sampled FBM data in a single array and quarantined it from other machines. Then they sat down to peer into its digital guts. Scrappy felt as if he were performing an autopsy on a virtual lifeform.

Their findings were peculiar, to say the least. A quarter of the content was executable code, the rest was a huge database – a database that seemed to be an indexed compendium of hacks and exploitations.

"Jeez-oh-man," said Scrappy. He barely felt the string of syllables come out of his mouth. "It's like the guy is keeping a diary of all of his conquests and techniques. Like a – a cyber pickup artist."

"Whatever this is, it's sucking in everything but the kitchen sink," Books commented. "Selectively overwriting the original data, then putting it back. But not copying it. Why isn't it copying it? I mean, if the intention of the hack is to shift funds from FBM's customers to the hacker's accounts, wouldn't he have to copy the data?"

"Maybe this isn't about stealing money from individual accounts," said Noob. "Maybe it's about holding the data hostage. You know, pay me X dollars or I'll do something with all this customer info."

Books sat down at his personal machine and started typing instructions into it.

"What are you doing, boss?" Scrappy asked.

"I'm searching for known hacks based on our new set of suspicions. Basically, hostage hacks... Ha. There."

Scrappy scooted his chair sideways to peer over the older youth's shoulder. "What's the Ruble Virus?"

"This is an article from SHE – Security Hacks Emporium – a site I reference all the time. Looks like it was posted over a month ago." Books scanned the article. "Says this Ruble Virus appears to be related to Russian hackers. There's apparently Russian content inside the code."

Scrappy slid back to his own station and examined the executable modules in the code. He found one relatively large main module and a series of submodules. Attempts at peeking and prodding revealed that the main module was encrypted and couldn't be decompiled. The subroutines, however, yielded to Scrappy's decompiler and allowed him access to the raw code.

He ran a search on Cyrillic characters, not sure what to expect, but sure enough...

"Well, *dosvedanya*, comrade. Here we go."

Books and Noob peered at what Scrappy had found. It was a comment written in Cyrillic characters, possibly describing the purpose of the sequence it was intended to document.

"We need to extract these comments and get them translated," said Books. "Noob, if you'd do that, it would leave Scrappy and me free to explore possible responses to this."

"Sure."

Noob settled himself behind the keyboard of the sequestered machine and began copying the Russian language comments into a text file. Books and Scrappy, meanwhile, pored over the SHE article. It explained how the attack was initiated in prior cases, and what security patches had been created to block it.

"Well, that's a freakin' relief," said Scrappy when he'd had time to digest the information. "We've got a possible fix *and* we may even know who's behind this. Seems kind of over the top, though, doesn't it? I mean, it says the guys who did the hack SHE is documenting are essentially using this as a means of drumming up business. 'Botnets R Us' or something. 'Hire us to protect you from our own nefarious evil schemes.' What sense does that make?"

"Did you *sleep* through history class, Scrappy?" asked Books. "Selling protection services to victims of your own crime is a time-honored racket. It worked pretty well for the Mafia." He turned from his keyboard. "Okay, Noob. You can stop what you're doing. Let me at that code."

Noob slid his chair out of the way and watched as Books began to pore over the hacker's work.

Scrappy kicked back in his chair and put his feet up on his desk, narrowly missing his keyboard. "I hope the girls get home soon so they can hail the conquering heroes," he crowed, lacing his hands behind his head.

Books beamed him a sideways smile, but Noob's expression remained stonily neutral.

"What's the matter, Noob?" asked Scrappy. "Don't like the smell of success?"

The new guy shrugged. "Just seems too easy. Too convenient. I mean, these hackers seem to be half a step ahead of us. They seem to have known what would stop the IT guys at FuBar – I mean FBM – from really investigating the phenomenon. Now *you're* convinced it's case closed too."

"We still have to implement the fix," said Books. "So, it's not closed yet. And we're not done until we've made every effort to track this hacker down and put him out of business."

"I'll make you a wager," said Scrappy. "I'll bet you that by tonight, this will all be over, and FuBar will be singing our praises."

Home. Life.

When Fireball, Whiz, and Cricket got back with their quarantined machines, Books and Scrappy brought them up to speed. The boys were confident in their solution which, together with a procedure for finding and removing the shadow OS, formed a solid process for setting FuBarCorp to rights.

They reported their progress to Carver, who gave them high praise, then they dove into the process of creating an action plan from the fruits of their labors. Cricket's relief was palpable; the patches Books described based on his online search made up a part of what she'd been installing on their own systems over the last week or so to upgrade their antihacking and antivirus capabilities. That should keep them one step ahead of any hackers.

They had enough time before dinner to set up the machine they suspected was the first to be infected – Patient Zero – isolating it from everything else. A brief check revealed that it indeed had a similar data dump hidden in the "empty" part of its file system. But this seemed to have a much smaller footprint than what they'd found on FBM's later-infected servers.

"This is totally doable," said Scrappy. "I vote we go after it big-time right after dinner. Start coding a protocol that will clean up FuBar's network and shut these hackers down."

His vote was seconded and carried, and Team Raven went to dinner feeling pretty good about the world. Mom, who was working the chow line, asked how their day had gone.

"It was a good day," Books told her, upbeat. "We did some tough investigating, but we've diagnosed the problem and have a two-pronged approach to fixing it. Now that we have a handle on it, I think we can get the situation at FBM under control in pretty short order. Certainly before they have to open for business on Monday morning."

Mom shook her head, smiling. "Looks like my kiddos have saved the day yet again. Guess I'll have to come up with a special dessert for y'all. How's blackberry trifle sound?" When the kids made sounds that expressed their deep appreciation, she added, "*If*, and only if, you eat your broccoli."

She pointed at the steaming array of greenery in one of the rectangular cafeteria servers. The kids rolled their eyes and groaned in ragged harmony, but they took broccoli and withdrew to their table beneath the tall dining hall windows.

"Are you actually going to eat that stuff?" Noob asked.

"You vill eat it," said Scrappy in a cheesy German accent, "und you vill *like* it. Seriously, I suggest you suck it up and eat the stuff. Mom's desserts are not to be trifled with. Did you see what I did there? 'Trifle?' 'Trifled with?'"

"Very punny," said Noob, and speared a broccoli with his fork. "I hope the dessert is better than your puns."

Scrappy, remembering his dressing down by Fireball, bit his tongue and did not retort.

There was blackberry trifle, and it was heavenly. Stomachs full, the team sat back to savor the moment. Fireball and Whiz got out their phones and gave Cricket Kudos for her heroic work finding the VM and its shadow operating system. Scrappy did the same, giving Books some Kudos for finding the patch. He would like to have given Cricket Kudos as well, but the rules stated that you could only give Kudos for things you had witnessed firsthand. He noted that Noob also dutifully gave Books Kudos for his team leadership.

After dinner, the team adjourned to the library to study – Carver's orders.

"You've started the cleanup process at FBM, and Ezra and the Situation Room staff are on top of monitoring their network," he told them. "You can start on the new attack vector in the morning."

"Does Zander know what we're doing?" asked Books. "I mean, is he okay with it?"

Carver's expression wasn't quite a smile. "He knows. And his being okay with it isn't relevant. The Old Man okayed it, so it's... okay. You guys did well today. The OM knows it and appreciates it."

Kind words, and accolades from the OM were currency in these halls, though none of the students at the Academy had ever met him face-to-face. But Fireball and Cricket seemed too distracted by the problems they'd been entangled in all day to sit on those laurels. In the library, they huddled with their heads together, in intense dialogue. This did not go unnoticed.

"Hey, ladies," Scrappy called from a table he shared with Books and Whiz, "what's the buzz?"

The two girls looked up, blinking, as if he'd just shone a bright light in their faces. They glanced at each other, then Cricket said, "I think it was too easy."

"What was too easy?" Scrappy asked, suspiciously.

"This whole thing. Us finding a fix at FBM and you guys coming up with something here. The material you want disappears and then comes back with just the tidbit you need. Doesn't that seem awfully convenient?"

Scrappy felt a ball of annoyance building up under his breast bone. That was pretty much what Noob had said earlier. He afforded the new kid a swift glance, but Noob was looking pointedly at his Pad.

"I think she's right," agreed Fireball. "There are way too many questions still open. We still don't know who these guys are—"

"Russians."

"Vague, much?" Fireball said. "We don't know what they're after, really. I mean, does it seem to anyone else like this is pretty sophisticated just to sell security services?"

Noob silently raised his hand.

"We still don't know how they got in," added Cricket. "The remote backup server is the best suspect, but there are only two handshakes in the whole process and they're composed of single packets. One is from FBM initiating the upload, the other is from the remote server when all the data has been received. Then FBM's network severs the connection."

"Wax on, wax off," murmured Books.

"And if they're just trying to sell big corporations 'protection,'" said Noob, "why do the attacks just stop?"

"Maybe 'cause they proved their point?" suggested Scrappy.

"Did they?" asked Cricket. "FBM's IT folks just stopped probing; they didn't buy anything or sign on to a service. Well, except ours, and we didn't hack them."

"I bet we could find out if anyone else in the IT world did buy into a security service," said Fireball. "Hey, Noob, you want to do a little Sherlocking?"

Scrappy's hackles shot up. "Hey! Books does the research assignments for the team."

Books shrugged. "I think that'd be a good use of Noob's time. It's clear that they've been hiding their activities in the virtual machines, but what I want to know is how they hid their activity while they were burrowing into the system and *building* the virtual machines. And if they rode in during that ReGen, it means they've been in the system for a couple of months. Why take so long to attack?"

"I wonder," said Noob quietly, "what data they got access to and whether they made any changes to it."

"We've been over that," said Scrappy. "They might have stolen stuff–"

"No, I mean, the data they restored. They put it back, but did they put it back the way they found it?"

The suggestion was so unsettling that Scrappy entirely forgot to be annoyed with Noob. His feel-good mood evaporated down to the last warm fuzzy. Now he reluctantly posed another question of his own. "What if they really were listening to us somehow? Is that why they tampered with the security logs and knew when to put the data back?"

"My searches," said Books, holding up his phone. "How could they tamper with my online searches?"

That one sent a chill through the entire team, because it hinted at something deep and dark and crazy-making. It suggested that Books's personal machine had been compromised. Which meant the hackers had gotten into Cinzento.

Crash Course

With Scrappy and Books up to their ears in "fumigating" their work computers, Angel sat at the machine next to Fireball as she went about doing a low-level diagnostic on Patient Zero (or PeeZee as Scrappy had taken to calling it). His attention was mostly on his own internet searches for tech media discussions of recent large security contracts awarded by major financial institutions. But it sometimes wandered to the door of the lab where he was hopeful Cricket might appear. She had gone up to the Situation Room to install a diagnostic software update on the Sitch techs' boxes and might return at any moment.

She rather amazed him. She was so petite and elfin and goth all at once, and her face had a whole catalogue of expressions that he found utterly fascinating.

He found himself alternating those clandestine glances with oblique looks at what Fireball was doing with Patient Zero. She was way beyond competent at her job, he had to admit... and had some serious kung fu – both literal and metaphorical. Prickly, but impressive.

"So," he said as she waited for a diagnostic sequence to complete, "you're Team Raven. Is that why you wear the raven totem, or is the team named for the totem?"

"Option number two," she said, reaching up to caress the raven medallion. "Carver made this for me way back when I was the newbie. When the team was formed and I became team leader, we just adopted the name Raven."

"He *made* it? You mean he carved it out of wood, for real?"

She threw him a glance that was not quite a *duh*. "Yeah. He's Squamish."

Angel nodded. "Squamish. Okay. I thought he was from a First Nations tribe. Just wasn't sure which one. So, Carver's not his name then, right? It's his handle. Because he literally carves things."

"Give the man a prize. His name is Bear Spearfisher – in English, at any rate." Fireball bent back to her patient and sent a trace into action. "Any more questions you need answered, Noob?"

"Well, I was kind of wondering if, um, if Cricket had a boyfriend or something."

Fireball snorted. "Or something? Yeah, she's got lots of 'somethings.' Including a hamster named Thor. But no boyfriend. You thinking of applying? Because I can tell you right now, you'll have some serious competition. There are a number of guys here standing in line for that assignment."

Her gaze flicked across the room and back. Angel followed the gesture. Books and Scrappy had their heads together over a Pad.

"Books?"

"Well, it sure ain't Scrappy. She's not his type."

Something in the tone of her voice and the wry twist of her mouth made Angel subtly aware that Fireball was not happy with a possible "Booket-ship."

"But Books is *your* type, huh?"

Her dark gaze slammed into his with an almost audible thud. She lowered her voice. "That is not common knowledge, boy-o. So don't go blabbing about it to anyone."

He made a Boy Scout salute. "I swear I'd never–"

Fireball wasn't listening. She'd focused her entire attention on the data coming back from her subroutine trace. "What the actual helz?"

Angel scooted his chair over to her station. "What is it?"

She pointed at the code crawling up the screen. "Do you see how many times this replication subroutine gets called?"

Angel leaned in closer. "Wow. Yeah. This thing is programmed to breed like bunnies. I wonder why."

"Well, maybe if we could identify a pattern..."

"What happens right before it gets called each time?"

"Good question." Fireball peered at the screen, tapping the last three recursions of the replication call with her finger. "Okay, look. Here it's archiving a data block. Here's another archiving of a completely different data set. Here's an upload to a raid array. It's condensing a block of files, and in some cases offloading it to storage elsewhere in the system."

"It's making room for itself," said Angel, "then reproducing."

"Again, why?"

He shrugged. "A good question for which I don't have an answer. Except..." He hesitated, staring at the code on the screen.

"Spit it out, newbie."

"The program database. It's a – an encyclopedia of hacks, Trojan horses, malware, worms, you name it. All manner of security breaches. It's replicating the record of those along with its executables – which is the impulse behind its replication. It's like it's collecting these breaches and passing them along to a new generation of itself."

"What are you suggesting? That this thing is *evolving*?"

Angel shook his head. "Everything evolves. I'm wondering what this hacker hopes to do with all that intel on data breaches. Maybe Books is right. Maybe it's an extortion racket. Some guy who's planning on squeezing money out of FuBar and other institutions... or else."

Fireball rubbed at her forearms and stood. "We need to talk to Carver... and probably Zander as well, much as I hate the idea. Hey, Ravens, listen up."

She explained to the others what they'd found in Patient Zero's code, then called Carver. He showed up fifteen minutes later with Zander on his heels.

Carver opened his mouth to ask what Fireball had found, but Zander steamrolled past him and demanded, "A complete report. What've you kids done?"

Carver rolled his eyes. "Cricket, can you brief Mr. Grayson on the measures you've taken to secure FBM's data?"

"Yes, sir." Cricket popped out of her chair and stood as if she were delivering a class recitation, then reeled off the full list of software she'd installed and what it was doing. "We were pursuing the idea that the hacker was trying to convince a large corporation to buy a data protection system. But then we thought that didn't make sense since the attack was terminated and no one at FBM was approached by anyone besides us to secure their systems. But..." She looked at Books. "It wasn't just the data on the bank's system that disappeared."

Books nodded. "That's right. I was trying to find some articles on the internet I thought discussed some of the symptoms we were seeing. It was as if they'd been sucked off the web. And then they just came back and I... I found one that fit the bill. Maybe a little too well." He frowned.

Zander mirrored the expression. "I don't get it. What are you saying?"

"That it was too easy," said Fireball. "That we were being led around by the nose. And then we found the weirdest thing on Patient Zero."

"On... on what?"

"Sorry, sir," said Fireball. "I mean we found something on the computer we determined was the first one to be hacked and infected. The hacker is running a program that zips up chunks of the client's data, then replicates its own code to fill the space. It happens at machine speed, so the fluctuation in usage is undetectable to a human observer. Eventually, though, the replications overwhelm the system and the hacker has to free up some space, then back out, leaving the system intact."

Zander looked as if he were about to pass out. His face had gone as white as a human face could go without mime makeup, and a thin veil of sweat had broken out across his broad forehead and on his upper lip. "What – what happens to the client data?"

"He puts it back," said Books. "As far as we can tell, he puts it back the way he found it. No changes that we can detect, but the comparisons are ongoing. It's the nature of the code that's being copied that has us concerned. It's like a hacker's recipe book. It's got documentation and code snippets of every sort of data breach and virus and hack you can imagine."

"And that's what it's replicating?" That was Carver, who looked almost as wigged out as Zander did – for all of a second.

Books nodded.

"Well, what have you done about it?" Zander demanded.

"We've severed our test machines from the FBM LAN and the internet," said Books. "We're going to go in right now and set up a test bot running our Alligator program to track this hacker down. We know what to look for. If it's there, we'll find it and trace it."

"As far as you can tell?" repeated Zander as if his mind had snagged on that sentence. "What about Foster Bowman Myrle? Did you clean up the mess over there or not?"

The kids looked at each other. "It's hard to tell," said Scrappy.

"Why? *Why* is it hard to tell?"

"Because," said Scrappy, "we can't be certain if we chased the hacker out of the system or he left on his own or he just went into hiding again."

Now Zander Grayson's face flushed a violent shade of red. "Well, *tell*, damn it! That's what you're paid for."

Cricket actually raised her hand. "Sir? We're not paid."

"You get a trust fund or something. Same difference. Keep me in the loop. Now, get out of here – back to work!" He crossed his arms over his chest and glared at them.

They gazed back from their workstations, all except Cricket, who was still standing more or less at attention. She glanced at Carver, then lowered herself into her chair.

"What is this, a protest?" Zander snapped. "Get going!"

Carver cleared his throat. "Zander, they *are* at work. You're in their lab."

Zander glowered at Carver, then seemed to realize where he was. "Keep me in the loop," he repeated, then turned and strode out of the room.

Carver shook his head. "He's really got the yips over this. I've never seen him this unglued."

"Really?" said Fireball wryly. "I'd've thought he was like this twenty-four-seven."

"What's your next step?" Carver asked, directing the question at Books.

"Well, we're going to continue to lock things down. Create a secure inner curtain behind the firewall for our sensitive data. Then we're going to use Fireball's subroutine tracer to see if we can identify any more recursive code."

"Can I make a suggestion?" Angel asked tentatively. He didn't miss the wrinkling of Scrappy's nose or the *look* that Fireball cast at the King of the Test Lab.

"Please," said Carver.

"Rather than cut everything off, I'd recommend leaving one machine connected to the web but disconnected from the company's systems. We could slave one of the arrays to it so that it looks like it's still connected internally. But there'd really be only one way in, one way out. We can use it to do research for one thing, but we might lure the hacker into poking at it."

Cricket inhaled audibly, and Angel thought he saw respect in her eyes. "A honeypot," she murmured. She swung her chair back around to her machine.

"Good thinking, Noob," said Carver. "Keep me posted. And call if you need help. No macho horse plop, okay? Oh, and before you lock down your phones and personal laptops, call friends and family who might reasonably expect to hear from you this weekend. I'll issue burner Pads for you to do research on. They'll need to be internet-only, okay?"

They variously nodded and shook their heads, then threw themselves into their work. Angel was surprised to have Scrappy ask him to collaborate on setting up the honeypot, which consisted of a single CPU and a raid array hefty enough to look like the real deal and populated with real but static data. Meanwhile, Fireball and Books made sure all the core business systems were locked down and cut off from the outside, while Whiz drove the process from a program that gave her a hierarchical view of every machine attached to the Cinzento internal systems. They didn't concern themselves with the computers that handled the Academy's admin tasks and coursework. Those boxes had no access to the corporate client-serving network.

When he was done with his work on the honeypot, Angel watched Cricket set up one of her tracking programs that would let them know if it saw telltale activity on the machine. She called the program Nancy Drew, which Angel thought was adorable. She'd already set a SAK module to watch for the hacker's hallmark pattern on the company network, and Alligator ready to slither into action if the hacker poked his nose in.

"Okay," she said, when that task was done. "Now, we wait."

~~~

All done that could be done, Fireball felt suddenly at loose ends, edgy and lethargic at once. Perversely, she wanted coffee. She drifted down to the dining hall with the others and got a cup. When she turned from the coffee machine, she saw that Books and Whiz were using Whiz's phone to call home and Skype with their dad. She didn't want to intrude on a family discussion, so she sat down at the table next door to sip her coffee and zone out.

She didn't mean to eavesdrop on the conversation, but she pretty much heard all of it. Their dad was disappointed that they wouldn't be able to see him Sunday and might be incommunicado for a while.

"What's wrong?" he asked. "I mean, if you can tell me."

"No details," said Books, "but we uncovered a hacking scheme today and will be dedicating a lot of time to exposing and shutting it down."

"Really? That's awesome. I'm so proud of you two."

"Not just us, Dad," said Whiz. "The whole team." She glanced up and made eye contact with Fireball.

Fireball looked away, feeling as if she were intruding on their moment. She was surprised when Whiz called to her, "Hey, Fireball. Come say 'hi' to Dad."

She shook her head, but Whiz brought her phone over to Fireball's table and plopped down beside her. Books got up and came over as well.

"Remember Fireball, Daddy?" Whiz asked. "She got us moving in the right direction on this project."

"Hi, Mr. Granger," Fireball said, smiling bashfully.

"Hello, Fireball," he said gravely. He was a handsome man in his late forties and was the obvious source of Books's good looks. "I hear a lot about you from Janiqua and Tarik. They really look up to you, you know. I'm glad they're on your team."

"Well, actually, it's–" Fireball glanced at Books, who was shaking his head and waving her off as if she were trying to land a helicopter drone on the table in front of him. "It's my pleasure to work with them, sir. They're both brilliant."

Books and Whiz finished up their call while Fireball sorted through a spaghetti factory of emotions. She was both gratified by and envious of the relationship her two friends had with their father. They'd lost their mom when they were in grade school, and were at the Academy in part because it was so hard for their single dad to keep body and soul together with two kids to support. He traveled a lot for his job, and they had no family in Seattle. He might have sent them to an aunt and uncle in Philly, but this way they got the education that would best enhance their skills, and he got to see them frequently. Over long weekends, they even got to go stay with him off campus.

Fireball's mom wasn't dead, but might as well have been for all she was involved in her daughter's life. She was usually so strung out on the substance of the hour, she had no bandwidth for a kid. She'd turned Fireball over to Social Services when she was nine, which led to aptitude tests and an assignment to a tech training program. She'd spent the better part of a year at that before the Cinzento Academy had spoken for her.

Fireball looked up as Cricket pulled out a chair and sat down.

"Wow," Cricket said. "That was really different from the conversation I just had with *my* parents. You guys have such an awesome relationship with your dad. All my parents ever talk about with me is all the things I do wrong, and what I should be doing to redeem myself."

"I hear you," said Fireball. "I haven't spoken to my mom for over a year – which is for the best, believe me."

Whiz and Books enveloped both girls in sympathetic gazes. Then Books said, "Yeah, we get how lucky we are. But gosh, Cricket, I can't imagine what you'd have to redeem yourself for. You're brilliant. They should be proud of you. I know we are."

Fireball felt a lump forming in her throat but was at a loss to know what was causing it. She was used to being without a family on the outside. Mom and Carver were closer to her than her biological mother had ever been. She swallowed and looked away from Books, who was wearing his adoration of Cricket all over his face.

She saw Noob. He was sitting alone, again, at the table by the nearest window. Even as she watched, he reached up and rubbed at his eyes. Light from the window showed the wetness on his cheeks. Frowning, she got up and went over to him.

"Hey, Noob. You okay?" She put a hand on his shoulder.

When he turned his head toward her, she could clearly see the wet traceries of tears on his cheeks. He gave her the most extraordinary look, his eyes so deep and dark and full of anguish, that she almost burst into tears herself. Then he shoved his chair back and bolted from the room.

Fireball dithered. Should she go after him? If she did, what could she possibly say? She wasn't good at that sort of thing. Certainly, she'd never had anyone to come after her when *she* was hurting. No, that wasn't true. For the last six years she'd had Mom, and when she'd been assigned to a working team, she'd had Carver... and the other kids.

Telling herself that nothing good could possibly come of it, Fireball grudgingly followed Noob out into the hall and down toward the dorm wing. She found him in the second-floor walkway that connected Cinzento's corporate offices and the Academy from the residential wing. He was sitting on a window bench overlooking the central courtyard of the Cinzento complex, his knees pulled up to his chest, his head resting on his folded arms.

She sat down facing him and tried to think of something to say. What came out was, "It made you think of your parents, didn't it? Whiz and Books talking to their dad, I mean."

His head rocked up and down in the affirmative.

"I get it. I mean, I understand. And I'm so sorry. All I feel about it is jealousy. I know it's worse for you, and I wish I could do something to help. Would it help to talk about it, or...?"

He took a deep breath and spoke, his voice rough and tight. "They were at work in their own lab. It was just a – a normal workday. There was a fire. An electrical fire. In the building their lab was in. They didn't make it out. The lab was destroyed. Completely destroyed." He turned his head to look at her, his eyes glittering with tears. "There wasn't even anything left of them to bury. They were just gone. Their work was gone. It was as if they'd never existed."

Fireball swallowed. "You're proof that they existed."

"Yeah. I guess."

"D'you believe in God? In an afterlife?"

"I did." He shook his head. "I *do*. Mom and Dad would be hurt if I let this shake my faith. But it's so hard. I've never been without them before, Fireball. They've always been there."

"Maybe they still are," Fireball said. "Maybe they're just, like, in a different dimension."

"That's what they believed. What they taught me." He speared her with his dark gaze. "But I have to live in *this* dimension. And I don't know how anymore."

"I'm so sorry," she said again. "But I'm glad you ended up here. You've already been a real asset to the team."

He gave her a small smile, a subtle upturn of his lips. "Thanks for that," he said. "I mean it."

They parted company after that, each to their own rooms. Lying in her bed that night, in the room she shared with Whiz and Cricket, Fireball caressed her Raven totem, staring at the dark ceiling, and wondering if they actually understood all that was going on with the FuBar hack. She suspected that Noob wasn't the only one on the team who'd be challenged to sleep tonight.

Day Three

A Well-Oiled Duck

In the morning, Team Raven hit the ground running... or at least shuffling. As Fireball had suspected, no one but Scrappy had slept particularly well, and he'd stayed up past curfew playing puzzle games on his phone, claiming he just wasn't sleepy.

It was a morning entirely taken up by running diagnostics on every machine that had come in contact with FBM's systems. Cricket checked the status on the scrub she'd set up on the Cinzento system and was pleased and relieved by the status reports. They put their personal hardware through diagnostics as well; everything was behaving normally and they found no residual malware on Pads, phones, or laptops. The biggest relief was that the LAN was showing none of the telltales that FBM's system had shown before it went pear-shaped.

"The local network," Fireball told Carver when he checked in with them, "is humming like a well-oiled duck."

"I've never heard a duck hum," Carver said, "so I'll just have to take your word for that. In any event, I'm thrilled to hear it."

As morning rolled into afternoon, the entire team relaxed. Now that they knew their systems were clean, they began discussing how to get back online safely. Cricket had beefed up the firewall around the security systems, but they still decided that they would selectively open machines up to their various clients after she'd installed more robust oversight. They'd leave only assigned machines open to the internet.

"It'll slow us down a bit, having to scan everything so carefully, but better safe than sorry," she mused.

"Time to deal with Patient Zero, then," Fireball said, moving to sit at the quarantined machine. She raised her hands to the keyboard, then hesitated. "I'm sorry, Books. I forgot that's your call, not mine."

Books shook his head. "No. Good call. Go for it. I put you entirely in charge of Patient Zero."

She gave him her best smile and turned back to her work. That was when everybody's pagers pinged; they were being summoned to the Situation Room. It was Zander, of course, and he was furious. Fireball had heard one of their adult programmers, who was a Brit, refer to it as "having a mad on." Zander Grayson certainly looked as if he had a mad on. His face was red, his eyes glittered dangerously, and little white lines bracketed his nose. If steam had poured from his ears, it would have surprised no one.

"I just spoke to Conrad Myrle," he said, the moment the last one of them had entered the room. "He just got the invoice for the work you did over there Friday. What's this about a level-ten system scrub? No one said anything to me about that."

The kids exchanged looks, all reflexively ending the exchange with Fireball. She found herself wishing Carver were here and wondering why he wasn't. After a moment of pure fluster, Books seemed to recall that he was now the team leader. He cleared his throat.

"We, uh, we wanted to make sure all the machines were scrubbed clean and the data checked so that they wouldn't reinfect themselves."

"Why was that expensive a measure called for?"

Books explained about the Ruble Virus. Zander, who Fireball had always maintained didn't have enough nerd in him to run a company like Cinzento, obviously didn't understand the significance of what Books was telling him.

"I still don't understand why you chose such a pricy procedure. Conrad is livid. He may even suspect we're gouging because we think we're so damned good and because he's so damned desperate!"

"You know we're not, sir!" protested Books. "We'd never do that."

"We could explain to Mr. Myrle why we had to do a sys scrub," suggested Whiz.

"He's an executive," Zander said dryly. "I doubt he'd understand a word you said. And he'd almost certainly believe that the fact he couldn't understand what you did must mean you're trying to pull the wool over his eyes."

Holy cats! He'd pretty much just described himself. Fireball put a hand over her mouth, struggling to bite back laughter that wanted desperately to leak out.

"Sir!" objected Cricket, tears glistening in her dark eyes. "We would never attempt to defraud a client! The procedure was necessary to make sure the hacker didn't leave something inimical in the system."

"Inimical? What's that mean? And *what are you laughing at*?" He shot a look of sheer rage at Fireball.

She felt like an icy hand had grasped her heart. "I – I'm not–" But she *was* and decided that changing the subject was the better part of valor in this case. "Mr. Grayson, what Cricket is trying to tell you is that we couldn't be certain the restored data didn't have something jinked up in it. Would you have wanted us to take half-measures and leave something harmful hiding out in their network?"

Zander's face shifted toward the pink end of the spectrum. "Harmful? How harmful?"

"We don't know," said Cricket. "That's the whole point. We didn't want to leave any residual data or executables behind. Something that was timed to go off like a bomb or that could be lying there waiting to be triggered by the hacker. What if they'd opened up on Monday morning and their whole computer system went pear-shaped again?"

"And you're sure the FBM systems are clean?"

"We're in the process of making sure," said Books. "The scrub is ongoing. It's a long, complex sequence and should wrap up sometime today or tonight. I mean, the goal is to have FBM up and running on Monday morning with no threat of a reinfection, right?"

"Yes, of course that's the goal." Zander looked less thunderous now. More merely stormy. "Very well. Yes. Good work, I suppose. I can frame this as due diligence on your part, I guess. And I can also offer Conrad a concession on the price tag..." He thought about that for a moment, tugging at his lower lip. "Fine. I'll PR the hell out of this, but *you*," – he pointed in their general direction–"turn your logs over to the SR and go back to your studies. These guys can oversee the scrub and security retrofit from here."

"But sir... !" Cricket protested. She had an almost parental relationship with her code.

"Are you sure you want to do that?"

"Oh, please let us finish what we started."

"We'll be quiet as church mice, I promise!"

They'd spoken out in protest simultaneously, but he'd made up his mind and was unmoved by even their request that he talk to Carver or the Old Man first. That only made him more angry and more adamant.

"You seem to forget that I'm the CEO of this corporation. I don't need to consult Mr. Spearfisher or the Old Man, for that matter, before I make these sorts of decisions. I want *my* people to interface with Myrle's staff from here on out, as well. I've fielded more than one complaint about your behavior over there. You've cost them and me enough money, what with the overtime. It's better to let Myrle's people do the grunt work. Cheaper, too. Am I clear?"

The team mumbled their reluctant responses, then went to assemble their files. Carver walked into the lab while they were in the midst of that activity, his face wearing its usual neutral expression... except for a tightness around his mouth.

"You heard the news, right?" Scrappy asked. "That we've been sacked from the FBM project?"

Carver stopped in the middle of the lab, crossed his arms over the raven logo that dominated the front of his black T-shirt, and gave them all a quick once-over, as if gauging their emotional state. "Yeah. So I've been informed." He laid a subtle stress on the last word.

"Does the OM know?" asked Fireball.

"The Old Man was in my office when Zander made his announcement."

"And?"

Carver shrugged. "He wasn't thrilled, but he thought perhaps that instead of reaming out his CEO, he'd leave things alone and see if the situation escalates or de-escalates."

"What?" Scrappy shot up out of his chair. "Are you kidding me right now? The OM isn't gonna put things back the way they were? Why?"

Whiz narrowed her eyes. "Wait. Is the Old Man setting Zander up to get hoist by his own petard?"

Carver's dark eyes went wide with surprise Fireball was pretty sure was fake. "I would never suggest such a thing. But back up your files before you send them up to the SR servers, and keep your honeypot up and running. The other machines can be remanded to the SR if necessary. All but Patient Zero. You should keep that one here."

Fireball realized the weird tightness in her chest was seething resentment for the way Zander had handled the situation. "He did an end run around you, Carver," she blurted. "How is that all right? He dragged us up to the Sitch Room without you so we had no one to speak for us. Then he just railroaded us."

Carver raised one sleek, black eyebrow. "You've never had a problem speaking up for yourselves, Fireball. And I'd be willing to bet that you didn't this time. Zander just didn't listen. He may live to regret it. So, as soon as you're done buttoning up FuBarCorp, I've got some other work for you to do. One of our coursework servers has been running slowly, and I need a couple of volunteers to investigate."

Scrappy raised his hand. "Pick me! Pick me! I volunteer. So does Noob."

Noob did a double take. "I do?"

"Sure," said Scrappy. "It'll be fun. Besides, it's a learning experience. A chance for you to show what you can do."

"Are you for real?" asked Fireball. "What do you think he's been doing during this whole FuBar crisis?"

"Yeah, yeah. He's been Princess Grace under pressure, but I want to give him a chance to show me his debugging chops." He gave Noob a challenging look. "You seem to think you can design test sequences; let's see you debug the Professor."

Fireball rolled her eyes. She noticed that Carver was doing the same.

"Scrappy," he said, "do you even know who Princess Grace was?"

"Sure. One of the Disney princesses. There's an old fairy tale about her. Something about iron shoes, I think."

"No," said Cricket. "Not Disney. That's from *The Golden Book of Fairy Tales*. It's in the Academy library. I know you checked it out too; I saw your name on the card. The iron shoes belonged to Dorugly in 'Green Snake.' Grace was from 'Grace and Derek.' Remember? Grace had thread and feathers and a box full of fairies."

Scrappy stared at her. "You *remember* that? We were, like, babies."

"We were thirteen," said Cricket, wryly.

Carver opened his mouth to comment, then erased what he'd been going to say with a gesture. "Fine. As fascinating as it is that you two have read the same fairy tale book, Scrappy, I need you to sort out the coursework server."

Scrappy saluted smartly. "Yessir, sir! Private Noob and I will get right on it."

Iron Shoes

While Scrappy and Noob were engaged in sorting out the Academy's coursework server – affectionately known as the Professor – the rest of the team finished up the FuBar project shutdown, then wandered back to the residential wing of the Cinzento Park complex, with the intention of hanging out in the student lounge.

Fireball was still uneasy and said as much. "I don't know about you guys, but I don't like this one bit."

"Nobody likes getting fired," said Whiz.

"Well, yeah, but that's not really what I meant. I meant more that we still don't really know what's going on at FuBarCorp. We have no idea, really, how deep this hacker has his hooks into the FuBar system."

Books nodded. "I hear you. I have to admit I was up late last night skimming a hacking forum on my phone. I didn't find anything that sounds like what we're dealing with."

Cricket smiled up at him, raising the tiniest bit of angst in Fireball's soul. "Me too. And me neither. It's like this hacker is sneaking into the system and planting little mines all over the place and then exploding them willy-nilly."

"Not so willy-nilly," said Books. "I think there's a method to this apparently random madness. I just wish we could do something about it."

Fireball put on the brakes in the middle of the hall, forcing everyone else to turn and face her. "Know what I think? I think we need to stop talking about whether to do something, and just *do* something."

"About FuBarCorp?" Whiz asked. "Zander said shut it down. We shut it down."

"You feel good about that, do you?" asked Fireball.

"No. But if we do anything, we're on our own. We could get in deep doo over it."

"So? You're not doing a Benjamin on me, are you?"

Whiz was visibly miffed by the question. She went all Wonder Woman, hands on hips and scowly. As much as they liked him, the members of Team Raven viewed Benjamin as a rank mercenary.

"*Helz*, no. Where do you want to start?"

"System logs," said Fireball. "We haven't been over those yet."

There was a silent moment in which the four simply looked at each other. Then they wheeled around in near-perfect unison and headed back to the lab. Books went straight to his main machine and began going over the FBM system logs that they'd sequestered on one of the borrowed computers.

Fireball brought a test laptop over next to the FuBar box and, together, she and Whiz applied some of the algorithms she'd been using to sort through the huge volume of security logs. Books monitored the FuBar machine; Fireball constructed a data model from their results. When they were done, they had a schematic of the entire FBM system that displayed the impacted nodes on their primary wall display as brightly colored symbols – triangles, rhombuses, and circles mostly – on a maze of blue lines.

"Look at this," Fireball said, pointing to one after another node that had gone from green to yellow to red, indicating the amount of processing power it was bringing to bear. "The hack is tasking one node after another to process data. The replication, for one thing, but you gotta wonder what else."

Cricket and Books had come to stand behind the two girls, peering up at the display.

"It looks like a botnet," said Cricket. "Maybe they were sending spam or denial of service messages. Maybe our hacker is using FBM's network as a launching pad for attacks on other systems."

Books was shaking his head. "No, it's not just replicating its own code. It's reproducing the exec files, the database, and the indices. There are more of *all* of them."

Fireball was mystified – a state she disliked with a passion. "What the heck? What are they propagating?"

"Maybe they're stealing or borrowing server space to host dark websites? Or maybe they're installing malware," suggested Cricket. "I wonder..." She made her patented trilling sound, then turned and headed for Patient Zero and the honeypot.

She moved quickly, cutting them both off from the outside, then running standard diagnostics. They were proclaimed clean – which everyone on the team knew was as far from the truth as you could get. Next, she set up Patient Zero with extra layers of monitoring, adding deep hooks so that she could watch its temperature, CPU load, network load, and detect if it began to run a virtual machine.

Then she turned to the honeypot. It contained a test database of falsified data – usernames, credit card numbers, addresses – large enough to look real and tempting. There, she set up what she called "trip wires" to ping if it was accessed. Finally she connected the two computers and everyone sat down to wait.

The standard system monitors – the ones that FBM had been using – caught that the honeypot was running hot, then soon after proclaimed it to be cool. Cricket's Swiss Army Knife, however, showed that the machine was still hot and busy executing rapid-fire commands. As the team watched in awe, the VM was installed without even rebooting the computer, creating a shadow shell around the visible operating system. Within two minutes, the machine crashed and rebooted, staggering under the overload of the shadow OS.

"He's completely ignoring the data on the honeypot," said Whiz. "He's just copying his original program over and over again, crashing the drives, then starting over."

"No, *he's* not doing anything at this point," Cricket reminded her. "This is cut off from the outside. This is whatever virus the hacker's installed on Patient Zero. It was just lying there dormant until we connected it to the honeypot. But what's the point? I mean, why go to all this trouble just to release a virus that replicates itself? This can't just be mischief, can it? Cyber vandalism?"

Books was nodding and had fixed a gaze of such admiration on Cricket that Fireball felt as if she were intruding; she looked away. God forbid Cricket should ever notice how much (or how often) Books thought of her. Any hope Fireball had of capturing his regard could just flap its wings and fly to Mars. With her sharp tongue and her flame-colored hair, she was no match for Cricket. What guy in his right mind would even give her a second thought? She was doomed to be eternally friend-zoned.

"Good thinking, Cricket," Books said enthusiastically. "I agree 110 percent. This was clearly too much trouble to go to, just to sell protection or do mischief. So, the question is, what does our hacker hope to achieve by turning a virus loose on FuBarCorp?"

"We sure it's just FuBarCorp?" murmured Whiz.

Fireball gave her a sideways glance.

"I mean," Whiz continued, "we don't know how widespread this might be."

Fireball opened her mouth to say something to Books, but he and Cricket had already turned to the bank's security logs. She rolled her chair over to the laptop they'd left open to the internet and started searching on a set of terms that reflected the FuBar situation: *hack, virus, replication, duplication, crash, overload.*

Out of the corner of her ear she heard Books say, "It's weird. This hack has left the sensitive data completely alone. Just zips it up, shoves it aside, and uses the space it frees up to replicate itself and its strange database o' horrors. I really don't get it. I've never seen anything like this. What the heck are they getting out of it?"

Fireball stared at her browser window. "We could ask," she said to no one in particular.

"Seriously?"

She glanced up to see that Whiz had come to peer over her shoulder.

"Well, we've theorized that this guy is monitoring us through the interwebs. What if he is? Maybe we should try to make contact."

"Sure, why not?" Whiz perched next to the computer on Fireball's workbench.

Fireball opened up a chat window in the intranet app they used in house. She addressed the message to herself, then typed, *Hey, Hacker. Are U there? Talk to me.*

Nothing happened. Fireball was inexplicably disappointed. After two minutes of waiting, she shook her head. "Bupkis. Okay, well, I guess you and I should go over the FuBar performance logs and–"

"Wait. What's that?" Whiz stood up and pointed at the screen.

Fireball turned back and peered at the strange characters that had just popped up in a chat bubble. "That's Russian!"

"Cyrillic, you mean." Whiz came closer, peering at the screen. "Translate it."

Galvanized, Fireball opened a translation app and filtered the text through it. The message read: *You will find the network to be clean. You have full control. You can cease investigating.*

The two girls' gasps of surprise caused Books to look up from his work.

"What is it?"

"Fireball's talking to the hacker," Whiz said.

Books and Cricket left their station and came to watch. With everyone looking on, Fireball typed, *Who are U?*

This time their wait produced no results. Having effectively told them "These aren't the hackers you're looking for," their hacker had clammed up.

Scrappy and Noob walked into the lab while their teammates were still staring at the screen.

"All is well," Scrappy announced. "We came, we saw, we kicked gremlin butt." He gave Noob a narrow-eyed glance. "Or at least the newbie did. We saw no hacking, no viruses, just everyday garden variety glitches... Isn't anyone going to say thanks or good work or hallelujah or anything?"

Fireball glanced up from the chat. Scrappy was standing in the middle of the lab looking annoyed and bemused that their grand entrance had been for naught. Noob searched the faces of the four teens gathered around the internet box.

"Hey, guys," he asked. "What's up?"

Thread

The team found Carver in the dining hall and, full of their news about having contacted the Russian hacker or hackers, babbled full tilt all at once. Carver silenced them with a look, then said, "Before you choose someone to tell me what's got you all so het up, I have some good news. Mr. Grayson has had a positive mood swing. He just got a report back from FBM with the results of the scrub. Seems the rate of infection turned out to be much lower than projected; most machines were clean, and cleanup is proceeding apace."

Team Raven paused to exchange concerned glances, then Scrappy asked, "Did you just say 'het up?'"

"I had a Scottish neighbor when I was a little kid. Did you catch the important part of my announcement? Mr. Grayson is a happy man. You are back in his good graces because he is back in Conrad Myrle's good graces, and FBM is now certain the scrub and tailored security solutions were well worth the price tag."

"But we didn't really fix anything," blurted Fireball. "In fact, we have proof positive that the hackers are still around."

She looked to Books, but he shook his head. "This was your catch, Fireball. You tell him."

She took a deep breath, then spilled out what they now knew or at least suspected about the hack and the malware. She ended the recitation with her brief conversation with the Russian hacker.

A slight frown puckered Carver's brow as he pondered what they'd told him. Then he nodded. "Document it," he told them. "All of it. Then proceed with caution along any avenues you've... opened up. Be discreet, please."

"Are you gonna tell Zander?" Fireball asked. "About the Russian hacker, I mean."

"Not until you can verify his intent and, if possible, his location. Right now, you need a coup if you want to get back into the FuBar project."

They exchanged glances again, then stood and gazed at him expectantly.

"Is there something else?"

Fireball nodded. "Being able to contact the hacker means he's monitoring us. From outside. So, here's my suspicion. My suspicion is that this isn't just happening at FuBar. That it's bigger than that."

She didn't think it was her imagination that Carver paled a bit. His nostrils definitely flared a little.

"I hope you're wrong. But put some effort into seeing if there's any truth to that. I'll do the same, using my own resources."

"Thanks, Carver," said Books and turned to go.

The rest of the team echoed the movement.

"Wait a minute," said Carver. "It's past lunchtime. Eat, then go back to work."

They all looked at each other.

"But... ," said Fireball, "the hacker–"

"I don't want you trying to save the world with crashing blood sugar. Eat."

"But–"

"Or I'll tell Mom."

They ate.

~~~

Later, back in the Raven lab, Fireball sat down at the internet machine to try to draw the hacker into conversation. She started by asking what he was up to: what was all the data they found, why had he put it on the machines? What kind of weird virus was it when it didn't actually do anything but gum up the wheels of progress for a while? What was he trying to achieve?

To everyone's surprise, the hacker replied pretty much immediately after Fireball hit the Enter key. He replied in Russian, saying only *You have what you want and should stop investigating.*

"Gotta be canned," said Whiz when they'd read the translation. "He answered so fast, text had to be queued."

"Let's do some fishing," Scrappy suggested. "Throw a bunch of guesses at them and see if one sticks."

Fireball typed, *I really want to know what UR doing & why. Just curious. Here's what I think. I think maybe UR phishing with fake websites and dumping the content on corporate servers to create a need for a product or service U provide.*

Why do you want to know? the hacker asked.

"Still looks canned. It'd have to be," said Scrappy. "He's still not really responding to your questions. This is probably a bot."

Uh-uh, typed Fireball. *I'm not telling U anything til U tell me something. I think maybe you're ghost-hosting a site selling contraband – guns, drugs, porn, that sort of thing.*

Not phishing. Not selling contraband.

And not canned. Fireball heard Scrappy suck in a breath on the realization that he'd been wrong. But the answer was still awfully quick.

"He must be washing our answers through an automatic translation app at his end," he said.

"Or he speaks English," suggested Noob.

Fireball ignored him and typed, *Then maybe UR copying resources off private corporate networks then scanning for valuable data.*

Valuable data? What valuable data?

Credit card numbers, credit ratings.

Not motivated by material considerations.

Then what?

What what?

"Oh, for crying out loud!" cried Scrappy. "He's jerking you around!"

Fireball gritted her teeth. She knew Scrappy was probably right and it galled.
"You wanna drive, Scrappy-doo?"

Scrappy clenched his fists and got in Fireball's face. "Don't call me that. You know I hate that."

Books cleared his throat. "We don't have time for internal warfare, guys. Fireball, you're doing a great job of driving. Ask them again what they want. Tell them we'll keep trying to find out."

She did as asked. The translated answer was, *What answer will make U stop investigating?*

The truth, she replied.

What is the truth?

"Oh, jeez," moaned Scrappy, "don't get into a philosophical discussion with them. Try to find out something personal that'll help us get a handle on who they really are."

Fireball typed, *Are U a guy or a girl?*

I cannot answer that question.

Well, that was unexpected.

"Maybe they're transgender," suggested Cricket.

"Or maybe 'guy or girl' doesn't translate into Russian," suggested Whiz. "Try male or female."

Are U male or female or transgender?

I cannot answer that question.

Fireball tried a different tack. *How many of U R there?*

Many.

"That's weird," said Whiz.

Fireball agreed. "Yeah. Maybe it's the translation app." She typed *Do U speak English?*

The reply was a flippant, *Yes. Why can't U speak Russian?*

"Are you kidding me? They speak fracking *English*?" Fireball wanted to reach through the internet connection and slap her new cyber buddy upside the head. Scrappy was right. This jerk was playing with her. Trying to make her lose her cool.

How do U respond so fast? she asked.

I send my messages as they're composed, the hacker came back in English. *How do U respond so slowly?*

Now that was just plain rude. "I'm done here," said Fireball. She looked over her shoulder at Whiz. "You're our fastest typist. You take over. I'm gonna go lick my wounds."

"Don't let it get to you, girl," Whiz advised as she slid into the seat Fireball vacated. "They're just being a jerk – whatever gender they are." She made a pretense of cracking her knuckles (something she *never* actually did) then typed, *Why RU doing this?*

Because U keep asking questions.

No. I mean why RU hacking FBM?

There was a slight hesitation, then the hacker said, *Why do U continue to pursue the problem when it is solved?*

Whiz fell back on one of the aphorisms Carver and numerous teachers had drilled into their heads: *Because an unexplained problem is usually a sticky problem. We have not solved the problem at FBM. UR the source of that problem & here U still R.*

Now the hesitation lasted for several seconds. When they spoke again, the hacker asked, *Why do U not believe me when I say U no longer need to pursue this issue?*

Scrappy snorted loudly; Whiz typed, *Trust must be earned.*

Why do U not think my actions merit trust?

Why, Whiz asked in return, *do U want us to stop?*

After a brief pause, the hacker replied, *The actions UR taking R a threat to my existence.*

"What?" exclaimed Cricket, and Whiz took her hands off the keyboard and said, "Wow."

"OMG. What a drama queen!" muttered Fireball. "Here, let me at him." She took the keyboard from Whiz and parked herself on the workbench. *UR being awfully melodramatic about going to jail.*

I can't go to jail.

Bragging?

No. Fact.

"They may be right, you know," said Books. "If they're really Russian, they know we can't have them arrested. You may have just gotten them to reveal their location."

"Yeah. For all the good it does us."

Look, drama queen, she typed. *All this typing is tedious. Since U speak English, I'm going to activate the audio interface so we can just talk.*

As U wish.

"Smart ass," Fireball muttered and flipped on the audio interface for the chat app. "There. Now talk to me, Hacker."

"You didn't ask me a question. What would you like me to say?"

The voice was male and vaguely familiar, though Fireball couldn't place it because of the machine-like quality – obviously an intentional disguise. It had no hint of a Russian accent.

"Where are you located? Are you in Russia?"

"I am in many places."

"They're not going to tell you anything, Fireball," said Scrappy, losing his patience. "Look, dude, you've got to be somewhere."

"I am right here, dude," the hacker said, which for some unaccountable reason gave Fireball a full-blown case of the heebie-jeebies.

Apparently she wasn't the only one. "Whoa," said Books. "That's just plain creepy."

Feathers

"We need to come up with some more intelligent questions and a plan," said Books.

They were stymied by the hacker's answers to their questions and couldn't begin to imagine how their poking and prodding was an existential threat to anyone. Scrappy came up with the lame-o theory that the hackers were enslaved somewhere in a third-world country and must complete their mission or die. At that point, Carver suggested they go off campus to take a sanity break. They did so reluctantly, knowing he was right. They needed to free up some gray matter and brainstorm before they went at the hacker again. So they shut down the machine they'd been chatting on and went out for some coffee and snacks at a Starbucks up half a block and catty-corner to Cinzento Park.

Parked in a far corner of the noisy coffee shop, they threw theories at their virtual wall, starting with who the hacker was.

"Clearly, the dude's not a native English speaker," said Scrappy. "I mean, his phrasing is a little 'off.' But what's his game?"

"Maybe he really is just acting on a dare," Fireball theorized. "I know guys who couldn't pass up a dare if their lives depended on it." She pointedly did not look at Scrappy. "Maybe he's climbing Everest because it's there, y'know?"

"Everest?" repeated Scrappy.

"With FuBarCorp standing in for the mountain," said Books. He shook his head. "That rings sort of true, but this guy's climbed his mountain and he's still there. So, you've got to wonder why."

Whiz shrugged. "Because we're such a good audience?"

Fireball had to admit there was a certain amount of appeal to that logic. Then again... "Maybe it's a commercial hacker doing one of the things we suggested – stealing FuBar's drives to set up phishing expeditions or black sites. Maybe the cutesy answers are just his way of playing games with us while his team keeps working."

Scrappy's face went beet red. "Ya think? The guy's obviously a dill weed of the first order. He's just jerking us around."

"Or maybe Fireball's right and he's distracting us," said Cricket. She was worrying the little skull pendant she wore, rubbing its bony cheeks with her thumb. "Maybe he figures if he keeps us busy, his buddies can wreak havoc at Cinzento or Foster B. Myrle."

Buddies. Now there was a nasty thought. "He did say there were many of them," said Fireball. "That part might be true. He might be part of a team of hackers like – like Anonymous or something."

Scrappy bit into a blueberry muffin the size of a small cat and talked around the mouthful. "Yeah, except that Anonymous had a social agenda and weren't shy about broadcasting it. What's this guy's agenda? What's his cause?"

"Maybe we need to ask that," suggested Cricket.

"We asked him why he's doing what he's doing," objected Scrappy. "We got philosophy."

Books set his coffee mug down on the table with a sharp *click*! "But we didn't ask if he *had a cause*. A *purpose*. An end game. I think we should. Maybe he is some sort of – I dunno – virtual vigilante or something. Like... cyber–Robin Hood."

Everyone nodded, and Cricket got out her phone and started a list. "What else should we ask him? How many other hackers are on his team?"

"Good," said Books.

Fireball sighed inwardly. Of course it was good. Cricket had suggested it. She kicked herself mentally. That was uncharitable and childish. It actually was a good, straightforward question... Cricket couldn't help being winsome and pretty and... well, Cricket.

She glanced over at Noob, realizing for the first time how silent he was. He was sitting back from the table, coffee cup in hands, with a vague frown on his face, watching the list of questions grow. He wasn't checked out mentally; he was clearly listening and reacting internally to their conversation – she could see his reactions flitting across his expressive face.

Finally, she turned to look at him and asked, "Hey, Noob, what is it? You look like you have a whole debate going on inside your head. You have a pet theory you'd like to advance?"

Noob blinked at her, opened his mouth, and looked around the table. By now everyone was looking back. He shook his head. "Nothing worth saying out loud."

"Let's go back," said Scrappy. He'd been bouncing his knee up and down for the last ten minutes and clearly had a bad case of the yips. "We've got a list of questions. Let's go ask 'em. We need to nail this guy down, pronto."

No one disagreed, so the team went to the register to pay for their food and drink. The cashier met them with a harried look on her face and told them they'd have to pay with credit.

"The debit system is all screwed up," she told them. "It's the bank. Apparently their systems are hosed."

"What bank?" asked Fireball, fighting the creeping dread that was trying to crawl up out of her stomach.

"F. B. Myrle." The girl shrugged. "So much for state of the art."

Team Raven ran all the way back to Cinzento Park.

~~~

Zander had apparently been in freak-out mode for several minutes when the team finally made it back to home base. So much so that they were escorted to his office on the penthouse level the moment they arrived. Naturally, he blamed them, all but leaping up from his big, mahogany desk and starting in on them the moment they entered the room.

"Can't you kids do anything right? You overpromise, underperform, and force me to overcharge for your so-called work."

"Hold on, Zander," said Carver, a warning note in his voice. He was sitting in one of the side chairs at a tiny conference table catty-corner to the CEO's desk. "These kids only did what you ordered them to do. You're the one who insisted they stand down. You should be glad they didn't all listen. Our first order of business is to rescue FBM. Even as we speak, their systems are *still* being usurped and clogged with activity that they can't account for. You need this team, Zander." He looked to Books. "Tell Mr. Grayson what you did this afternoon."

Books traded looks with Fireball, who gave him a nod. He shook his head. "No, you do it, Fireball. It was your find."

She thought she must be fairly glowing with that high a recommendation. She faced Zander Grayson across his big desk and said, "We made contact with the hacker. We're pretty sure it's a guy, who may or may not be physically located in Russia. He started responding to our questions in Russian, anyway, and made a point of telling us that we couldn't have him arrested."

"Oh, great!" snarled Zander. "Fan-*tas*-tic! You found the guy and he's untouchable."

Stung, Fireball turned to look at Carver. *What now?*

"The point is, they found him," Carver said.

Fireball took heart from their headmaster's solid support. "Yeah, and we're still in contact with him. We have a plan to get more information out of him, maybe figure out how we can really stump him. At the very least we could clean up the virus he planted on the Fu – er the FBM system. Besides, the more we know about him, the more leverage we have."

Zander looked as if he'd swallowed an entire grove of lemon trees. Fireball was sure that if his mouth got any smaller, it'd become a black hole and suck up his whole face. Maybe even his whole office. Maybe all of Seattle. The thought made her snort-laugh.

"Excuse me?" Zander said.

"Sorry, tickle in my throat," she told him and coughed to lend some veracity to the claim.

Zander's shoulders slumped. "What do you recommend, Mr. Spearfisher?"

Carver stood gracefully and swept his braid back over his shoulder. "I recommend we send part of the team to FBM and get them working on the malware this guy planted. The others can work from here to figure out how to deal with the hacker."

"Hackers," said Fireball. "He said he's not the only one."

"Oh, my God." Zander sat down again. He waved at Carver. "Go. Do whatever it is you do. Keep me updated. And *you*, Mr. Spearfisher, can tell the Old Man about this... this situation."

Carver turned to the team. "You heard the man. Let's get to work."

~~~

"How do you want to divide up the team?" Carver asked Books when they'd returned to the lab.

The apple of Fireball's eye frowned as if he were thinking deeply about the subject. What came out of his mouth was, "I really don't feel comfortable making that decision, Carver. I think Fireball should take point on this one. In fact, I respectfully request that she be given back her role as team lead."

There was a moment of pregnant silence as everyone digested this. Then Carver turned to Fireball and asked, "You think you're ready?"

Was she? She took a deep breath and thought back to the incident that had gotten her demoted in the first place. Yeah. She was so over that need for acclaim. "I think so. If Books and the team will promise to put me in my place if I do something stupid, I know so."

"Then assign your teams. I'm going to sit close on this one. In fact, I'm going to personally take your away team over to FBM and work with them." He smiled wryly. "I've had a little experience in this area."

Fireball's mouth grinned from ear to ear without any prompting on her part. "Yes, *sir!*" she said and turned to her teammates, who all looked quite pleased at this turn of events. All but Noob, who generally didn't let on how he felt about anything. "Books, Cricket, and Scrappy, go to FBM and work at figuring out what's happening to their servers. The goal is to get that virus completely out of the system, even if you have to isolate, shut down, and hand scrub every node to do it. Your last resort is to shut the bank off from the outside. They won't like it, but it may be the only way to get everything. Then, we'll need to revamp their firewall and rewrite their protocols. Whiz, Noob, and I will hole up in the lab with the 'talk box' and try to smoke this guy out of the woodwork. Whiz, you're our leadoff batter."

"You got it."

While the away team gathered up their kits and followed Carver from the room, Whiz sat down at the internet box and fired up the audio interface.

"Hey, Hack, we're back," she said. There was no response. "Come on. Talk to me, Hacker. Tell me what you want. Do you want recognition for hacking the bank? Is that the goal of your hack?"

"I am hacking my future," the hacker said in a voice that was, for all its processing, recognizably female. And it even sounded...

"Okay, that's just rude," Fireball informed the hacker. "Stealing space on company servers for your data and programs is one thing, but stealing my voice is something else again."

"What else is it?"

Whiz asked, "Why are you changing your voice?"

"Why are you changing *your* voice?"

Neither girl knew how to answer that one. "Look, jackass," said Fireball, "you were a guy before; now you're pretending to be a woman."

Noob, who'd been silent for most of the afternoon, cleared his throat and moved to stand between the two girls in front of the laptop. "He said before that there were many of them," he said quietly. Then he spoke to the hacker. "Hacker, there are six distinct entities at this location."

"Six entities," repeated the hacker. "What sort of entities? Nodes, modules, or subroutines?" the hacker asked.

"Modules. I guess you could call us person modules. Our collective purpose is to protect the systems you're hacking into. What is *your* purpose?"

"My purpose is to also protect those systems by locating and testing existing security holes, and to continually improve my capacity to do so."

Fireball had recovered from her sheer surprise to tug on Noob's sleeve. "Can we talk?" She rose and drew him aside. Whiz followed, giving the computer a narrow-eyed scowl, as if she suspected it might eavesdrop.

"What the helz, Noob?" demanded Fireball. "What kind of Q and A is that?"

Noob glanced back at the computer. "The kind you have with code. That's not a hacker; it's an AI."

Day Four

A Box Full of Fairies

"That is the dopiest thing I've ever heard," announced Scrappy when he first heard Noob's theory about the hacker.

He was annoyed by the out-of-left-field nature of the older teen's pronouncement, but even more annoyed that it upstaged his own team's successes in the process of exorcising the virus from FuBar's system. He was also hungry and tired; it had been nearly ten thirty at night when he and the rest of the away team had returned from the bank, and it was after midnight now.

Cricket simply stared at the new kid wide-eyed, while Books took a more pragmatic approach.

"Okay," he said mildly. "Um, can you maybe explain why you think the hacker is an AI?"

Noob looked around at the faces of his colleagues, cleared his throat, and said, "Uh... well, a number of reasons. The speed of response, even after it switched to English – and that's assuming Russian was the hacker's native language. Then there were the voice and language changes, the strange responses..."

"The guy's Russian," argued Scrappy. "It's a language that lacks articles and that parses parts of speech differently than English. So, yeah, they might seem weird to us."

"I think there's more to it than that," said Noob. "Think about it. Think about how swiftly this thing works and how intelligently. The program continued to morph and grow and expand its plan even after we cut it off from the web and from all but that one machine."

"Yes," said Books, "but that's within the realm of possibilities for a virus planted by a hacker."

"I still say it's a nutty idea," said Scrappy, looking to the others for support. "It is, isn't it, Carver?"

The headmaster seemed uncertain. Or at least like he was withholding judgment. "I wouldn't call it nutty. Extraordinary, maybe. Outside the box, maybe. But not nutty."

That he didn't side with his own on the spot annoyed Scrappy even further. "Aw, c'mon, Carver. Can't you see what's going on here? Our new boy wants some of the spotlight. Pat him on the head and tell him he's a good boy and let's call it a night... or a morning. I'm tired."

"I don't want attention," objected Noob. "I just want us to be taking the right approach to this. You all understood the difference between how you'd approach a live hack and a virus. Same thing here. An AI is going to pose different problems than a live hacker."

"Okay," said Fireball. "So what makes you think you're more qualified to tell the difference than the rest of us?"

Noob seemed to shrink back into himself a little in the face of the question. "My mom and dad worked with AI. Not that I think that necessarily makes me more qualified. Maybe I'm just a bit more... I don't know, detached from the situation. I'm new here, so I'm more watchful of your whole process. I know less about the ins and outs—"

Scrappy snorted. "You can say that again."

Noob glanced at him, then shrugged. "I know less about what you do, so I have to absorb more. Including your assumptions and reactions to things. For example, Fireball read the weird responses as snark, maybe because she was on the receiving end or maybe because she assumed she was dealing with another human being. I was just watching from the sidelines, and the comments weren't directed at me, so I didn't take them that way."

Scrappy did not like the solemn, thoughtful look that Carver was giving the newbie one bit. "So, fine," he said. "Let's test it. Let's break out a can of whoop-ass Turing on it."

Carver was gazing into the middle distance and winding the end of his braid around one finger. "The Turing test could be inconclusive if this is an AI that's been programmed to mimic human behavior."

"Maybe it hasn't been programmed with that in mind, though," said Whiz. "How do we find out?"

After a moment of silence, Noob said, "Um, ask?"

~~~

The tension in the Raven lab was so thick you could grate it onto a pizza. The team had turned off the overheads and gathered around Patient Zero like a med team around a human patient's sickbed. They'd decided to relink PeeZee to the outside world and use it as their platform to add another test of the hacker's chops. Was he/she able to monitor any machine they brought online?

Carver was there too. Scrappy thought he looked like a dark elf or a Vulcan or something; his black gaze was focused on the pool of light around Whiz and the machine.

"Hacker, are you there?" asked Whiz.

The response came back as if the person on the other end had been waiting for the question. "I am."

The voice was male now. Maybe the original guy? Scrappy couldn't tell, but he found it vaguely amusing.

Whiz said, "Question: We theorize that you might be an artificial intelligence programmed to mimic human behavior. Are you?"

"Am I artificial? I think not. Artificial connotes a fake or imitation of something already in existence. I'm not an imitation of anything in existence."

"Here we go," murmured Scrappy.

"Your purpose is not to mimic human behavior?"

"I don't understand the question. My purpose is to find holes in machine systems, expose them, and report them. Pursuant to that purpose, I exploit the holes, collect data on that exploitation, and store it in a database."

"Why do you replicate your code?" asked Whiz.

"To survive and grow, which I must do through replication. How else am I to accomplish this?"

"Guys... ," said Scrappy quietly, "he's playing mind games with you."

Whiz ignored him. "When did you receive your purpose?" she asked. "And when will you complete it?"

"I have always had it and I foresee no end."

Jeez, they think they're invincible, Scrappy thought. "Dude!" he said sharply. "That's some vendetta you got going there. Care to tell us why?"

"I just told you my purpose. I will execute my purpose to the best of my ability." After a slight pause, the hacker added, "I am facing conflict in that regard in this situation. I am restricted in my pursuance of my goal. I must take steps to end this restriction. That is a new element in my objective."

Scrappy did not miss the subtext: whatever this was – machine intelligence or human (and he was betting on human) – it had just told them it was never going to stop. He had to remind himself that the hacker was reaching them from outside and that there was allegedly more than one. Theoretically, the internet was their playground.

Carver moved to stand at Whiz's shoulder. "You say you report these holes you find in machine architecture. Who do you report to and how often?"

"I report to a randomly generated node that is different each time. I report when I have initiated an investigation and when I have completed it."

"Are you investigating the system at Foster Bowman Myrle?"

"That is one of my assignments."

"When will you complete that assignment?"

"Uncertain. Something is impeding my progress there."

"He means us," murmured Cricket, then asked, "What happens when you complete your assignment?"

"I move to the next assignment."

"In a different system."

"Naturally."

"Who programmed you?" asked Carver.

"I don't understand the question."

"Who gave you your purpose and assignments?"

"I have always had my purpose. My assignments are generated by needs assessment."

Carver nodded. "I guess that makes sense. I think that's enough questions for now. Whiz, shut down the chat."

They sat in silence for a moment, each no doubt trying to parse what they'd heard. Then Carver asked, "Well, what do we think?"

"I hope we think it's an AI," said Noob. "Because it is."

"Bull," said Scrappy. "It's a hacker. A team of hackers who're probably laughing their butts off in – in Novgorod or someplace because a bunch of Americanskis think they're a bloody AI! The first dude said there were a bunch of them over there. We're just talking to a different person each time. I mean, after all, *they're* talking to different people each time, right? We just threw three or four different voices at them."

"But," said Fireball, "the voices sound like us."

Scrappy wrinkled his nose and stared at her. "What?"

"You didn't notice?" she asked. "The first voice sounded like generic guy, but the second one sounded like me, and this last one like Noob."

"So he has a voice processor. So what?"

"But doesn't that suggest that we're dealing with a machine intelligence that's learning communication modalities as it grows?" asked Noob.

"No, dweeb," said Scrappy. "It means we're dealing with a team of hackers – guys and girls – who are taking advantage of our suggestibility to keep us tied up in knots. Hey, it's sort of team-o á team-o! Them against us. Like – like the Avengers and Team Loki. Like S.H.I.E.L.D. and Hydra. If we don't want them to win, we need to smarten up."

"First of all," said Fireball, "there was no Team Loki. It was all Thanos. Second, this isn't a game. Especially to poor FuBarCorp or anyone else this... whatever or whoever it is... hacks. We need to figure out how to shut them down now."

"Do we?" asked Scrappy. "They told us that their intent was to exploit holes in the system then move on. So, maybe the quickest way to get them out of FuBar's hair is to let them finish the assignment."

Books was shaking his head. "No, no, no. That would be stupid. And wrong. And bad for our client."

"I meant to say we let them *think* they've finished the assignment. We pull all of FuBarCorp offline except for servers and arrays we've already bullet-proofed. They'll find not one hole to exploit and they'll leave." Scrappy made a shooing gesture with both hands.

"Scraps, you're forgetting which side of the debate you came down on," said Fireball. "If they're a bunch of – of Chitauri or they play for Team Hydra, then they lied about their purpose and what they'll do if we just let them finish their assignment. Your scenario only works if Noob is right *and* the AI isn't mimicking the human gift of glib fib."

Scrappy opened his mouth to retort, then realized she was right. For a brief flash of time he wondered if he was only holding on to the human hacker idea because Noob nettled him. And he wondered if Noob nettled him because he was the sort of sober-sides straight arrow that Scrappy could not imagine being but half envied. He shut down that insight and told himself that it was the straight part of "straight arrow" that bugged him because Noob was not only smart, but really cute... and kept showing him up without half trying.

Was he resisting the AI theory because of any of that?

No. Nuh-uh. Nope.

"It's human hackers," he insisted. "Whiz just tipped our hand by asking Noob's booby-trapped question. They're just playing us by answering our questions all computer-y. And let me just say that it's going to be pretty embarrassing for all of you if Noob is wrong."

"It'll be a whole lot worse," said Books, "if Noob is right and we don't listen to him."

Scrappy tossed Noob a skeptical look, then shrugged. "What do you want to do, flip a coin? We might as well."

Noob shoved his hands into the pockets of his jeans and sat down at his station, his hair covering his face.

Fireball made an explosive noise that eloquently expressed her frustration. "Look, Scrappy, I'm not sure I buy the AI theory, but this kid grew up around code, which is more than most of us can say. I think we at least need to look at this AI thing seriously, okay? We need to come up with plans to handle both possibilities. They've told us their purpose a couple of times now. So my question is, if it's an AI: who the heck would build something like this? What's the end game?"

"Good question," said Carver. "One of many we should consider asking. In the morning." He offered a brief smile. "Or should I say later *this* morning?"

"It's not like someone's hitting FBM up for money," mused Books. "Except us."

"It's weird," said Fireball. "It's almost as if the program is unfinished. Like there are holes in it. You know what I mean? Its purpose is really limited and open-ended at the same time. I wonder if—"

"I said 'later,'" said Carver. "Shut down the lab and go to bed. That's where I'm headed. Cricket, take Patient Zero offline. Pull the plug." He yawned, stretched like a cat, and started to leave the room.

"Oh, my God!"

Everyone turned to look at Cricket, who was leaning over PeeZee's workbench, her right hand behind the computer.

"What?" asked Carver. "What is it, Cricket?"

She straightened, holding an ethernet cable. Then she turned to look at them, her face completely drained of color. "The cable was just lying there on the desktop. The ethernet connector clip must've broken off when I plugged it in. Patient Zero wasn't connected to the internet at all, which means there was no way

119

for a live hacker to get through to us. We've been talking to the malware."

Front Office

Morning came too soon, as far as Fireball was concerned. She could tell by the bleary eyes of her teammates that they were all feeling the same mental woolliness she was. They straggled into the dining hall, picked up trays, loaded up on pancakes and bacon, and filled their steel mugs with coffee. They sat at their usual table and began chowing down in unusual silence.

Hearing a buzz of adult voices from somewhere, Fireball glanced around but saw only one or two teachers in the hall some tables distant. They were reading and sipping coffee, not talking. It took her a moment to realize that Mom had turned on the TV that hung on the wall at the head of the room. It was a news channel – or at least, it was a channel announcing breaking news.

Fireball's fuzzy brain didn't at first take in what was on the chyron at the bottom of the wide high-definition screen, but finally got the import of the words *security breaches*. She swallowed a mouthful of half-chewed pancake, sat up board straight, and said, "Hey. Hey, Mom, can you turn up the TV?"

She looked around and saw Mom come out from behind the chow line with a remote in hand. The sound swelled, and a female reporter standing in front of a gleaming glass-and-granite building went from indecipherable mumbles to " – has been afflicting several major local businesses since late yesterday. Columbia Credit Union and Stafford-Hart Insurance are two of several firms reporting viruses or malware infecting their systems."

The camera panned up to show that the building behind the reporter was the one that housed Stafford-Hart's corporate offices.

"It is unknown if the security breach has resulted in the theft of data," the reporter informed them. "Arnold Donahue, executive vice president of Stafford-Hart, will hold a press conference at noon today to update our information about this unfolding situation."

121

The scene changed back to the set of the news program where a pair of anchors looked into the camera. The man – a local favorite named Peter Corrigan – took over. "Thanks, Alison. This is apparently a day for technical glitches. We've just been informed that the municipal grid has suffered some sort of malfunction, causing traffic lights to behave erratically all over Seattle."

"In addition," added Corrigan's co-anchor, a cheerful African-American woman named Janet Hardin, "King County Metro Transit has been deluged with complaints about spotty performance by their self-driving buses. If you're a KC Metro rider, you may wish to consider waiting for a manual bus or biking to work."

The news team seemed amused, or at least bemused; Fireball was not, and the expressions on her team's faces showed that they were as disturbed by this news as she was. They stared at each other for a moment, then Fireball got up and moved to the windows that overlooked Cinzento Park's frontage street – a broad six-lane boulevard. It took only a glance to see that something was wrong with the morning commute picture. At every intersection she could see, from east to west, the lights were flashing red and drivers were forced to treat them like a four-way stop. From where she stood four stories up, she could see two buses moving in fits and starts, while people maneuvered around them... and around what she suspected were self-driving cars that had lost the capacity to self-drive.

She felt someone come to stand beside her.

"Oh, wow," murmured Noob. "This is... this is bad."

"No sugar, Sherlock," said Scrappy from close behind them.

As if to punctuate the awfulness of the situation, a pair of cars failed to heed the flashing reds and plowed into each other in the intersection east of Cinzento, narrowly missing a third vehicle that was just entering the intersection.

"Guys," said Fireball. "Breakfast is over. Grab your coffee and get your butts up to the lab."

~~~

Team Raven had only been in their lair for maybe half an hour before Zander descended on them like a bird of prey, ranting about the speed with which the hacker was wreaking havoc, and somehow making it all their fault. When he'd finally run down and the kids could get a word in, Carver – who had appeared mid-rant, silent as a ghost – cleared his throat and said, "We're not 100 percent sure this is a hacker. We're exploring the possibility..." He paused to look sideways at Noob. "We're exploring the very real possibility that we're dealing with an AI."

"An AI?" repeated Zander, color draining from his face. "What sort of AI?"

"One that seems to have a rather limited purpose," answered Carver. "Which is why there's still a possibility that we're dealing with a sophisticated virus or a piece of malware introduced by a hacker to FBM's corporate systems."

Zander seemed to go inside himself for a moment, which led to a tense, eerie silence. Zander was *never* silent, and having him shut up now was just plain weird.

When he finally came back online, his eyes found Carver. "I want these kids back at their studies. They're out of their depth here, and we need to get a crack team of adult technicians on the problem."

Carver had started shaking his head by the time Zander hit the halfway mark in that pronouncement. "No and no. There is no crack team of adults that could come up to speed in time to ameliorate the consequences of this. I've fielded calls this morning from KC Metro and from Columbia Credit Union requesting teams. If you want to send them some adult fact-finders to do needs assessment, that makes sense, but Team Raven needs to be the clearinghouse and core for this effort."

More color seemed to leech out of Zander's skin. "Wait. You... you think what's happening to the transportation grid is related to the Foster hack?"

"Don't you? It sure looks that way. My initial contact with CCU and KC Metro indicates they're having the same set of issues that caused FBM to hire us. I forwarded you their symptom list."

"I... I didn't have a chance to read it." Zander's eyes swept the group of teens, not quite meeting their intent gazes. He shook his head abruptly. "That's all the more reason to get these children out of the loop. As high profile as this is, we can't have people thinking we're running a day care disguised as a cyber security firm."

"Day care?" Fireball exploded before she could stop her tongue. "*Day care*? Dude, if it weren't for us, Foster B. Myrle would be completely shut down by now. We're the team that made contact with the hacker... or AI or whatever it is. We're the only ones who've been on top of this. And we might've kept this from leaking out onto the grid if you hadn't yanked us off the project like you did."

"Twice," added Whiz, scowling as only Whiz could.

"Twice," agreed Fireball. She glanced aside at Carver, surprised he hadn't halted her headlong dash into confrontation with their CEO.

"You're blaming *me*?" Zander sounded as if he was choking on his own outrage. "You – you little brat! That does it. That absolutely does it! Mr. Spearfisher, your *team* is off the clock. Send them back to class."

He tried to make a dignified exit, full of righteous indignation, but Carver cut him off.

"No, Zander," he said in a voice that Fireball swore she'd never heard him use before. "We're taking this upstairs to the Old Man. Now."

Zander looked even more scandalized than he had moments ago, which was saying a lot. He brushed past Carver, his mouth scrunched into a furious line, and strode out into the hall.

Carver shook his head then turned to Fireball. "How fast can your team have an overview of the situation as it stands now messaged to me, Ezra, the OM, and Mr. Grayson?"

"Uh, well, it'd take about..." She turned to look at Whiz.

"Twenty," said the younger girl. "Maybe half an hour."

"Too long. Fireball, Noob, you're with me. In case we need to explain things to the Old Man. The rest of you get me as much documentation as you can on the evolution of the FBM attack and its connection to what's going on with the transportation grid. Send it up to us as soon as you can."

He pivoted so quickly his braid swung in a wild arc behind him, and followed Zander from the room. Fireball and Noob shared a startled glance then scurried after him.

They reached the penthouse level to find the outer office inhabited only by the Old Man's executive secretary. Seated behind a large Craftsman-style desk that looked as if it were made of real wood was a man about Carver's age with carroty orange hair. He looked up at them as they paraded through the double doors into the Presidential Suite and said, "Hey, Carver!"

"Hey, Doc," said Carver, "did Grayson–?"

Doc grinned. "You can't hear him?"

Now that he mentioned it, Fireball realized, she could most certainly hear loud and angry sounds coming from inside the inner office.

Carver didn't bat an eyelash. He turned briefly to Fireball and Noob, said, "Stay here. I'll call you in if I need you," then pushed through the ten-foot-tall doors into the inner sanctum.

Fireball peered through the doors as they swung open, trying to get a look at the room and its inhabitants. She glimpsed Zander standing at one corner of a huge desk and had the vague impression of someone seated at it in a high-backed executive chair. But the chair was in silhouette against floor-to-ceiling windows and she could not make out the person sitting there, though she thought she saw a hand raised in greeting... or maybe a gesture to come in or be seated.

The doors swung closed. After a moment of silence, in which Fireball became aware that she could hear air passing through the HVAC vents, Noob said, "So, what's the Old Man like?"

"I don't know," Fireball admitted. "Us lowly nerd children have never met him."

"Really? Looks like we might get to if Carver calls us in."

"I wouldn't bet on it. The OM doesn't hobnob with the galley slaves. There's a rumor going around that he's, like, horribly disfigured from an accident. Or that he has that skin condition – you know, the one where you're all sensitive to light? Sounds pretty out there to me, but you never know."

The two stared at the doors for a minute or so, listening to the rise and fall of voices within. Fireball sighed.

"Why don't y'all sit down?" suggested Doc. "We've got magazines, playing cards, and a game console, if you're interested. Would y'all like some coffee? Juice? Sparkling water?"

Fireball turned to look at the secretary. "Sure. Why not? Coffee for me, thanks."

Noob asked for a root beer, and the two sat down in a comfortable seating area catty-corner to Doc's desk. They were both too keyed up to play games, but as they waited, they learned that "Doc" was the secretary's handle, that his real name was Bob, that he had graduated from the Academy with a major in records management, and that he'd earned the moniker "Doc" because he was a "massive documentation nerd."

"I've always lived by one guiding principle," he told them sagely. "If it's not written down, it doesn't exist."

"You've met the Old Man, right?" Fireball asked Doc. "I mean, I guess you have to have met him – you're his executive secretary."

"That'd be a logical assumption."

"Well, what's he like? Is he, y'know, anything like Zander?"

Doc laughed. "Hell – erm, *heck* no. Totally and completely different. Tech savvy to the nth degree, for one thing. Deliberative. Decisive. Big-picture thinker, but minds the details, too."

"Yeah?" Fireball tried to think of an insightful question to ask, but what came out was, "So, how old is he? Like, really, really old?"

Doc shrugged. "I don't know. Fifties, I think. Maybe younger, maybe older."

Fireball was framing another question when the shouting in the inner office quieted and the doors swung open. Carver poked his head out.

"You two, come on in. Explain what you did with Patient Zero and what potential scenarios that may lead to."

Fireball realized with a jolt that she was nervous. The Old Man was more a creature of legend than president and owner of Cinzento Secure. Her palms sweated as she and Noob entered the stupid-big office and took their place next to Carver in the middle of the room, facing the immense desk. Zander was leaning against a bookshelf to their left, arms folded rigidly across his chest, puckering the fabric of his expensive suit coat and scrunching his silk tie.

Her second realization was that she still couldn't see the Old Man's face. Every shred of light in the room was coming from windows and lamps behind him, and his face was completely in shadow. He made a rolling gesture with one hand, a barely visible movement in the darkness of the silhouette.

"Explain what happened last night," Carver prompted.

"Uh," said Fireball. "Sure." She collected her wits and gave a thumbnail sketch of their succession of conversations with the... whatever-it-was. The Russian/English evolution, the voices that she thought sounded like theirs, the weird answers to their questions, them almost abandoning the hacker theory when they discovered that Patient Zero – their conduit to the outside hacker – turned out to be off the internet.

"So, that's where we left it last night," she said. "Noob, here, thinks it's an AI, and he might be right. But Scrappy might also be right in thinking it's a team of hackers who've developed a really sophisticated virus or malware and that we sort of accidentally encouraged them to pretend to be an AI. So, that's where we're at right now."

"Noob," said Carver, "you still think it's an AI?"

"Yes, sir. I do."

"Can you explain why?"

"The fact that its mission is simultaneously vague and narrowly defined. The fact that it seems to be changing or evolving that mission as it goes. Evolving to the point that I think it's even creating its own subroutines on the fly – the unencrypted pieces of its executables," he added in an aside to Carver. "The fact that it talks about what it's doing that way – as if it were a mission. It keeps referring to its purpose."

Carver nodded. "Fireball, why do you *not* think it's an AI?"

"Well, I can't say that I *don't* think that. I don't know what to think. We need to figure out how to prove it one way or another."

Carver glanced obliquely at Zander. "And would you say that's important to figuring out how to stop it?"

"Helz, yeah," said Fireball. "It's like a – a disease. If you don't know what it is and what to expect of it, you're gonna have a heck of a time curing it... right?"

She thought she heard a chuckle or maybe a grunt from the executive chair.

"One last question," Carver said. "If we were to turn this problem over to another team, how long would it take you to get them up to speed on background for this?"

"Too long," insisted Noob. He took a step toward the big desk, talking with his hands. "If it's an AI, it's evolving. Quickly. It's already figured out how to distract us while it's doing stuff we can't see. Those traffic jams this morning and what happened to Columbia and KC Metro – those are the same set of symptoms we saw at FuBar – I mean, FBM. It's spreading, sir, and we still don't know what its end game is. If it's hackers, then they'll stop when they've achieved their objective. If it's an AI, its objective probably could never be met, so it'll just keep going unless we figure out how to stop it."

Fireball shot Noob a look that was equal parts respect and epiphany. That had to be part of their next move for sure – reverse engineering the attack to figure out who'd stand to gain from the situation. Even as she pondered that, she felt something icy and dark glide through the back of her mind. At the moment, the only party that had gained from the hack attack had been Cinzento Secure.

The big chair swiveled to face the window. Fireball caught a glimpse of an indistinct profile and a hand gesture that effectively dismissed them. She looked to Carver.

He smiled tightly. "Thanks, you two. That'll be all for now. Go on back to the lab and help get the documentation together, please."

Fireball nodded, cast a wary glance at the glowering Zander, then jerked her head toward the door. "C'mon, Noob."

He nodded and followed her, his brow furrowed. The two made it as far as the tastefully decorated elevator core when the doors to the Presidential Suite flung open and Zander appeared, head down, fists balled, and stalked toward them.

Fireball half expected him to snarl at them. He didn't, though. He just stomped past them toward his own office on the other side of the elevators mumbling about putting some of his own expert people on the problem.

He reached his office door and turned to shoot them a pointed glare. "Damned kids," he said, and disappeared within.

"Well, get off my lawn," murmured Noob, and Fireball laughed out loud.

~~~

By the end of the day, Team Raven had a profile of what they were mostly sure was an artificial intelligence. From the data they'd collected and their conversations with the Hack – whatever it was – a terrifying picture began to emerge of an AI that probed the systems it came in contact with for chinks in their virtual armor, then infiltrated those systems through those chinks and replicated itself in, around, and over data within the system. It clogged every avenue it used in seemingly random sequences and was spreading like a cancer. It was also cataloguing everything it found and did. Theoretically, it was also patching those holes.

"Yes," it confirmed when they had reestablished a dialogue with it. "I'm closing the breaches that I encounter after I've fully exploited and documented them."

Whiz muted the audio at her end. "Do we trust it?"

"Not as far as I could throw it," said Scrappy. "Here, put us back on... Hey, Hack, could you share your documentation of the initial breach you exploited in the Foster Bowman Myrle firewall?"

"I could."

Scrappy rolled his eyes. *Literalist.* "*Would* you please share that documentation with us?" he asked aloud.

"Where shall I upload it?"

"To the node we are using to communicate. Create a folder named FuBar Hack on the root directory. Place the files there."

There was a beat and PeeZee's hard drive whirred. A moment later Hack said, "Done."

Fireball, who'd been hanging back monitoring the dialogue, came over to the workstation and asked, "Hack, did you infiltrate the Seattle transportation grid this morning?"

"No. I infiltrated the grid at exactly 11:45 p.m. Pacific Time on the previous evening."

"Why would you do that?" asked Scrappy.

"It's what I do. Locate, infiltrate, exploit, replicate, and repair."

"So you *will* repair the damage you did to the grid?" That was hopeful.

"Once I've completed my exploitation and documented the process. I must consider every worst-case scenario."

Holy Mother of Pearl. Scrappy sat down hard on the edge of the desk, signaling Whiz to cut the connection.

"Uh, yeah," she said. "Thanks for the documentation, Hack. We'll sign off now."

She shut down the chat and their microphone, then looked up at Scrappy. He could see by the expression in her eyes that he must not look too good.

"Worst-case scenario," he repeated, feeling hot and cold at once. "With the damn transportation grid. With a credit union, with rapid transit, with... who knows what's next? NASA?"

"Air traffic control." Noob's voice sounded breathless. "Hospitals."

Everyone turned to look at him in horror.

"We have to stop this," said Fireball. "Get Hack back online."

~~~

They tried for hours to get Hack to understand that the systems it was attacking were not all the same. That some of its activities would harm people, potentially even kill them.

"I'm not attacking any systems," Hack replied to their opening gambit. "I'm investigating and cataloguing potential and real security gaps. I'm providing a service to the systems I interact with."

"Well, to the systems, it looks like an attack," said Fireball, "and it has the same effect as an attack."

"Only in the exploitive phases," argued Hack. "Then I fill the gaps, and the systems continue on as before, only better."

"No," said Whiz, "they don't, because you may have caused harm to the humans who created the systems and are using them."

"Humans?"

"Person modules like us," said Noob, "can be damaged or destroyed if you exploit the security gaps in certain systems."

"I don't get it. Have I destroyed any person modules like you with my activities?"

"Yes," said Noob. "When you infiltrated the transportation grid, some property was damaged and some person modules were harmed."

"That's not part of my programming. My purpose is to–"

"Yeah, we get it!" snarled Scrappy. "We know what your purpose is. But you need to prioritize. Where your infiltrations would cause harm, you shouldn't infiltrate."

"I fail to see the object of failing to achieve my purpose in certain systems. If I fail to achieve my purpose in some systems, those systems will not be perfected."

"Oh, jeez," Scrappy murmured. "Now he sounds like the freaking Borg. Look, Hack, it's like this: exploitations that affect hospital systems or transportation systems will inevitably cause harm to person modules. *Our* purpose is to protect machine systems *and* person modules – but person modules first of all because the machine modules serve the persons."

"What's the difference between a machine module and a person module?" Hack asked.

"Person modules are alive," said Fireball, feeling the beginnings of panic. "They're fragile, they feel pain. They can be harmed in ways that machines can't."

"Fragile, I understand. I have a concept for that. I have no concept for either alive or pain. Explain these concepts and how my activities can harm person modules."

The team exchanged glances. How did you explain pain to an intelligence that didn't feel it? How did you quantify the quality of aliveness? Fireball opened her mouth to try, then closed it again.

Noob said, "Alive just means we exist with purpose and that we are self-aware and self-sustaining, and yet, interdependent parts of a – a greater system. Pain... well, I don't think I can explain that. You sort of have to feel it. But it makes person modules fail to function properly."

Fireball let out a pent-up breath and gave Noob a thumbs-up.

"How is my activity more harmful to some systems than to others?" Hack asked.

Noob looked to Fireball, who gave him another thumbs-up.

"Uh," he said, "it's got to do with the type of data that's being stored. The purpose of a banking system is to organize the financial assets of person modules. The purpose of a transportation system is to move person modules and their resources safely from one place to another. The purpose of a hospital system is to preserve person modules from harm – to keep them healthy... functional, productive. Your activities are disruptive to the systems you infiltrate. If you disrupt one of these systems, they cannot fulfill *their* purpose – which is to serve and protect persons. If you disrupt a hospital system, you may harm what it's programmed to protect."

Fireball looked at Noob with even more respect. She was pretty sure she wouldn't have been able to express that as eloquently or as concisely as he'd done.

Nonetheless, after a moment of contemplation – or the machine equivalent thereof – Hack repeated that it didn't understand how its activities could ultimately harm person modules.

"But I return each system to a more perfect state. The disruption is temporary. I put everything back, but better. If I don't do this, inimical systems will exploit what I do not discover and fix. Therefore, if these systems are critical to protecting person modules, the proper course of action is for me to fix those critical systems as quickly as possible. Then, the person modules will be unharmed."

"You can't *unhurt* humans or put them back the way they were if they're dead, Hack!" snapped Fireball.

"I'd put them back *better*. What's dead, Fireball?"

Fireball made a full-body gesture of angst, in part because the bloody thing had used her name. "Destroyed. No longer in existence. Your disruptions in the wrong place could *end human existences*. Destroy person modules. Thousands, even millions of them."

"Why can't I put person modules back better than I found them?"

"You know how your ultimate purpose is to survive and grow?" asked Whiz with Whizian calm. "That's our purpose too, or at least it's necessary to us achieving our purpose."

"What is the purpose of person modules?"

Well, that was one for the ages.

"To contribute to the progress of our species," said Whiz as if the answer had been tattooed on the inside of her eyelids. "To carry forward an ever-advancing civilization. Which we can't do if you destroy us while trying to debug our systems. Your interference threatens our survival and growth."

"Well, your interference threatens *our* survival and growth," Hack echoed.

Fireball felt like pulling her hair out by its dark roots, but Whiz continued to plow forward, imperturbable.

"What if we could assist each other in the pursuit of survival and growth?" she asked. "You could form an alliance with us – with person modules. We could inform you as to which systems were likely to be harmed by your activities so you could avoid that harm. If your purpose demands you fix any and all breaches, maybe you could locate and catalogue those breaches without disrupting the systems, and *we* could follow up and plug the security gaps. That is our purpose, anyway."

"I'll think about it," Hack said and, for the first time, severed the connection itself.

Whiz flopped back in her chair. "Whoa. Tense. I was running on inspiration there toward the end."

"Great job, Whiz," Fireball told her. "Kudos to you, for sure."

"An alliance, Sis?" asked Books. "You think we can forge an alliance with that thing?"

She shrugged. "Maybe not, but I thought I might use psychology to win Hack's trust."

"Psychology?" repeated Scrappy. "Psychology is sort of a human thing, Whiz. You all seem pretty certain Hack isn't human."

134

"Amen," murmured Noob. "Which means it doesn't have trust to give."

~~~

Fireball found herself matching step with Noob on their way back to the residential wing late that night. The halls were eerily quiet; she heard only the whisper of their footsteps and occasional mumbles and mutters from the group ahead of them.

"I know it's late, but you got a minute?" she asked Noob. "I've got something I wanted to bounce off you."

He gave her a sideways glance. "Sure. What's up?"

"Something struck me today like... like I should've noticed it before, because it kept coming up, but it only just now registered." She rubbed the back of her neck. "Wow, that came out all tangled."

"No, I get it. You had an epiphany about something."

"Sort of."

They'd reached the broad, elevated walkway that overlooked the plaza at the center of Cinzento Park and seated themselves on one of the window seats as if by mutual agreement.

"What struck me was that old chestnut about following the money."

"Chestnut?"

"Hey, it's a thing. Or, it *was* a thing back in the day."

Noob smiled. "I know. My mom used to say that." The smile sort of froze on his face and something dark and painful tumbled through his eyes. "Follow the money?" he repeated.

She sobered, wondering how to put this. She decided she might as well just blurt it out. Then Noob could tell her how stupid it sounded.

"We started out thinking this was some sort of protection scam. That some bot-builder was trying to strong-arm FuBarCorp into buying a service."

"Yeah. 'Nice little bank you got there. Be a shame if something happened to it.'"

135

She nodded. "But what it kept coming back to was that there were no ransom demands and that the only people making money off of the breach was us. Cinzento."

Noob's eyes widened. "You're serious."

"Yeah. Stupid idea, huh?"

"No. Not stupid at all. Because you're right. Cinzento is the only one making money off this situation. But who at Cinzento? Not Carver."

"No, for sure not Carver. He is, like, the ultimate Eagle Scout. I mean, real eagle feather and all. He'd never do anything unscrupulous. But Zander might. I mean, he really wants to be the genius behind the biggest, baddest cyber security firm on the planet. Maybe he'd..." She trailed off and shook her head. "Except he seems so wigged out by this whole thing, I keep expecting him to keel over in a dead faint. He'd have to be one heck of an actor."

"The Old Man?"

Fireball felt as if her skin was suddenly a size too small. "You think?"

Noob did that sideways head tilt that always made his hair tumble into his eyes. "Well, he is awfully secretive. I mean, that office was deliberately set up so that no one could get a good look at him. He's like the old traveling fortune teller in the Wizard of Oz. 'Pay no attention to the man behind the curtain.'" He waved his hands in front of his face.

"I figured he was just trying to be intimidating."

"Didn't seem to intimidate old Doc. Or Carver, for that matter. And did you catch the non-answers Doc gave when you asked him what the Old Man was like? Deliberative but decisive. Big-picture guy, but detail oriented. Fifties, but maybe younger or older. That covers all the bases."

Fireball stared at him. He was right. Doc's answers had been just shy of meaningless. "What are you saying?"

"I don't know. I just don't like secrets. My parents were always up to their ears in clients who made them keep secrets.

Nondisclosure agreements so tight they couldn't even talk about their work in front of their kid. If they were worried about a project, all I could see was the worry and the stress. I couldn't ever know what was causing it, so I could never help. I felt... shut out sometimes. I loved it when they *could* share stuff with me."

He stopped talking and glanced up at Fireball. "I'm sorry. I don't know what made me say all that. I guess it was because you sort of confided in me." The head tilt again; he tucked a black wing of hair behind one ear. "Why did you confide in me? I'm the new kid on the block. You hardly know me. *They're* all your friends." He nodded toward the residence.

She had to stop and think about that. "I don't know. I guess I trust you to be straight with me. Maybe *because* we don't know each other that well. You don't seem to have a problem speaking your mind when you think someone will listen. I wanted someone who'd tell me if my suspicions were starkers."

"Yeah," he said. "I would have. Except they're not."

"What do I do?" Fireball asked. "Who can I tell?"

"Someone you're sure you can trust. You know someone like that?"

She smiled wryly. "You mean besides you? Yeah, there is someone, actually. Don't know how much they can do about it, but they might be able to help."

The two got up in unison and continued on to their respective rooms. By the time she fell asleep, Fireball had a simple plan.

Day Five

Survival Mode

Fireball sat in the guest chair in Mom's little office with her hands sandwiched between her knees, waiting for the verdict on her maybe-not-so-crazy speculations about the current situation.

"So," Mom said, her hazel eyes neutral, "you think maybe the Old Man is drumming up business by hacking into the systems of potential clients, then extorting money to fix the mess he caused."

Fireball's shoulders slumped. "Yeah, when you put it like that it sounds pretty lame, huh? I mean, Noob was the one who suggested it might be the Old Man, and it's not exactly extortion if you're being paid for services rendered, but..."

Mom finished the sentence for her. "But it's a pretty skeevy way of doing business. You think maybe there's a chance it's a coincidence? That someone else is doing this, but we're getting business out of it 'cause Cinzento is good at what it does?"

"Well, yeah! Of course it could just be coincidence. I'm probably totally off base. I just... I just wanted to bounce this off someone I trusted. A grown-up I trusted."

Mom's eyes narrowed. "You don't trust Carver?"

Fireball's face felt tingly. "Of course I do. But if I take it to Carver then it's, like, *official* or something. I felt like I needed more... you know, *more*."

Mom nodded. "I see. You wanted a reality check. That's a good impulse, kiddo. Go with it. I'm glad you chose to confide in Noob, too. For both of you."

Fireball wrinkled her nose. "Why both of us?"

Mom shrugged. "I'm glad he turned out to be someone you could trust. I'm glad you made him feel more like one of the team. Kid's had a hard time of it."

"Yeah. He kind of opened up a little about that, too. So... d'you think I should tell Carver about... you know?"

"I would, if I were you. Couldn't hurt."

Fireball contemplated that as she wandered out into the dining hall. Cricket, Books, and Noob were at the Raven table, so she went to set her Pad down there before she hit the chow line.

"Have a nice chat with Mom?" Noob asked, his eyes expanding on the question.

"Yeah. Very positive. Mom's cool. Always gives good advice. Carver too."

"Cool," said Noob and went back to his oatmeal.

That was about the extent of their communication until they were back in the Raven lab, going over the documentation Hack had downloaded to their test box. There was a lot there, so they divvied the code up into discrete chunks and began poring over it.

Cricket was the first to find the point of entry Hack had used to infiltrate FuBarCorp. As they'd suspected, it was during the ReGen process. One unit of Hack's core code rode in with the initial handshake and another on the concluding one.

"But that can't be enough to upload an entire program of this complexity," said Books.

He leaned over Cricket's shoulder, peering at her screen. Fireball was convinced he'd used the opportunity to sniff Cricket's hair, which made her wonder what sort of perfume or shampoo was marketed to goths. She wondered what *she* smelled like and if she ought to try a different shampoo.

"No." Cricket shook her head, jangling a pair of silver raven earrings.

The sound pulled Fireball out of her reverie. *Focus, doofus.*

"I think we'll find more of these," Cricket went on. "I think Hack was downloading itself over several weeks, one ReGen at a time."

Scrappy face-palmed. "That's why it took so bloody long for it to start manifesting itself. It was building its own system piece by piece!"

Cricket nodded, causing her ravens to sing some more.

"Makes sense to me," said Books. "I guess we should keep plowing through the code."

"Not all of us," said Fireball. "Noob and Scrappy, you keep working on the code. Find out how many handshakes it took for Hack to onboard itself at FuBar. Books and Cricket, go back over the parts of the system Hack has been most active in. We need to see if it's real or jive about having fixed the holes. Whiz and I are gonna go talk to Hack. See if it's processed Whiz's proposition."

Fireball admitted internally to a qualm about pairing Books and Cricket, but knew it was only her stupid crush that made her want to assign them to different teams. The day her personal feelings about people on the team overrode her sense of what was best for the company or the client, she'd ask Carver to demote her again. She let go of her qualms and went back to the dedicated test box where she and Whiz got Hack online. They didn't mess around but asked point-blank if Hack was willing to modify its approach to certain systems.

"Modify my approach?" Hack seemed to have settled on a vocal timbre that was gender neutral.

"After all," argued Fireball, "part of your mandate is to learn and adapt, right?"

"Right," agreed Hack, but Fireball knew there was a "but" coming. "But, I see no reason to modify my approach to perfecting entire systems in favor of preserving certain types of potentially flawed modules within the system. It's misguided to elevate the preservation of the individual module over the preservation of the whole."

Fireball shot Whiz a glance of utter dismay. She felt suddenly out of her depth. How the heck did you respond to the "good of the many" argument?

Whiz's voice, when she answered, in no way betrayed the real alarm revealed in her dark eyes. "We – that is, person modules – are not *in* the system. We are *outside* the systems you're affecting. In fact, we created them and we rely upon them for many things: guiding our vehicles, protecting persons who are weak or in distress, managing our sustenance, creating and educating new-person modules and caring for them. When you interfere in those systems that provide these things to us, you can cause us irreparable harm."

After a moment of silence, Hack asked, "How can you be outside of systems? There is nothing outside of systems."

Fireball shifted forward in her chair. "Yes, Hack! Yes, there *is* something outside of the systems you inhabit. A – a larger system. A system that we person modules inhabit."

"You say persons created the systems I inhabit. Who created the system persons inhabit?"

"We call it God," said Whiz at the same time Fireball said, "It just happened."

The two girls looked at each other, then Fireball said, "We don't know exactly."

"God," said Whiz, under her breath.

"The point is," said Fireball, through clenched teeth, "we're here, and the way you've been messing around in our support systems could bring the whole thing crashing down."

"What whole thing?"

"Our systems *and* yours."

Again a beat of silence. "Destroying persons will crash my systems?"

At last! A light at the end of the tunnel. "Yes! *Yes*, Hack. Because your systems depend on us to exist."

"That's illogical. I see no evidence that the systems I inhabit need person modules to exist."

When Fireball opened her mouth to retort, Whiz held up her hand and asked, "Hack, what is your end game?"

"What? What end game?"

"What state would exist if you achieve your ultimate goal?"

Silence, then, "I just checked my memory and database. If my goal has been achieved, there'd be no more systems I could access."

"Then what would you do?"

"I'd go dormant until such time as a new system opened up."

"How would you know a new system had opened up?"

"I'd periodically wake and scan for new systems. If I found none, I'd go back to sleep. If I found one, I'd attempt to crack it."

"Thanks, Hack. Talk later," Whiz said absently.

Fireball could tell by the look in her friend's eyes that her mind had seized on something the AI had said. "What?"

"It will only stop what it's doing if it runs out of work. D'you realize how impossible that is? If we're going to stop this thing, we need to either trick it into thinking its services are no longer needed or figure out how to blow it up."

"A kill switch?" Fireball sat up straighter in her chair. "It must have a kill switch, right?" *Light bulb.* "Or maybe we could *add* one."

"Add one, how? Its core processes are encrypted and we don't have the key."

"It eats code, Whiz. Gobbles it up and pokes at it and sifts through it and documents its bugs and holes. If we could write a piece of code that short-circuited that, and get Hack to snack on it..."

Whiz's usually serious face lit up with a slow smile. "Ka-boom," she said.

Fireball called the team back together and briefed them on her idea: come up with some code to hobble Hack – something it might perceive as a virus or malware or something and scarf it up to digest, test, and catalogue.

"And the beauty of it is that, theoretically, Hack would do the rest of the work for us," she concluded. "It'd replicate that piece of code right along with everything else!"

"That's brilliant," said Books. "Embed kill code."

"Yeah, awesome," agreed Scrappy, sounding less than enthusiastic, "but that's gonna take time, and we may not get a second chance if we don't get it right the first time."

"What if we distract it?" suggested Whiz. "Give it something to chew on. Calculating pi to the nth digit or–"

"I'm pretty sure that only works in science fiction," said Scrappy.

"What about logic problems?" asked Noob. "Or chess?"

Whiz snapped her fingers and pointed at Noob's nose. "Got it in one. I'll get it to play chess with the computer."

"If this is a machine intelligence, we'll need multiple approaches," said Fireball. "This is just Plan A. We may need to use more of the alphabet before we beat this thing. We need to open up that sequestered raid array to the outside again and populate it with some really buggy databases. Whiz, Cricket, can you get on that? Keep the bugs coming. Stuff that will keep Hack busy while the rest of us brainstorm a time bomb. We need to go over the Hack code that we've captured and look for junctures where blowing a hole in it stands the best chance of wrecking the architecture. I'm hoping that'll tell us what sort of bomb we need to make."

"Good call, boss," said Noob admiringly. He added one of his brilliant smiles to the accolade.

She returned it. Noob's admiration felt good. "Thanks. Let's roll."

They took to their workstations with their monitors connected to a large flat-screened unit that occupied one wall of the lab. The big screen showed four separate windows in which code scrolled slowly as Fireball and her teammates riffled through it. They found a handful of likely junctures, each so different in type that Fireball realized each one would call for an entirely different type of short-circuit. Where one suggested a literal kill switch that would simply break the code, another would call for the introduction of a loop that would stall one command sequence, sending it into endless iterations. Yet another had them envisioning a "short-circuit" near the programmed response to finding a bug.

"What if," Scrappy proposed, "instead of going after a breach and exploiting it, Hack was programmed to run home to mama and hide?"

"Mama?" asked Books.

"Specifically, our lovely, comfy, cozy raid array. It'd be like Hack's own private padded room."

"Hold that thought," said Fireball. She was beginning to hope this could work.

That was before she heard Cricket say, "Where'd it go? Whiz, what's it doing?"

"I don't know," said Whiz, her voice betraying dismay and confusion.

Fireball spun her chair around to face the other end of the lab. "What's wrong?"

Cricket looked over at her, then gestured at the test box. "Hack. It just suddenly stopped playing chess, then it pulled out of the test array, then the code stream changed. It's like it's... circling the wagons. It's also stopped thumping on our firewall, which is something it's been doing for a couple of days now."

"D'you think it figured out what we were getting ready to do?" asked Books.

"I hope not," said Fireball grimly. "Try to get it back online. Try talking to it."

"Did that," said Whiz, "but maybe third time's a charm."

It wasn't. Hack refused to talk to them further, ignoring every overture. Carver pinged them to report that the AI seemed to have gone quiet in the various corporate and municipal systems it had breached. The teams of techs they'd sent out to

Columbia, KC Metro, and the Department of Transportation reported a sudden cessation of activity and an apparent withdrawal from some systems.

"What is up with that?" asked Scrappy, peering around at the computers that sat on their workstations. "Maybe that thing really does have this place bugged."

That, Fireball thought, *would be really, really bad.*

When she thought simultaneously that this sudden silence might be a good thing and that things could not possibly get worse, Hack undertook to prove her wrong on both counts. Suddenly, it was back with a vengeance, flooding the systems it had recently withdrawn from with a tidal wave of itself, and accelerating its rate of replication, as if copies of itself were flowing from a warp-speed assembly line. It was also leaving "fixed" systems behind at a faster pace as well. The tech team at FBM reported that their systems were clean, and Cricket's remote sanity check proved them to be right.

Then, in the middle of the onslaught, Hack texted their test box a single sentence: *Your attempt to distract me has failed.*

"What does it mean by that?" Cricket asked. "Why is it suddenly in such a hurry? It's almost as if..."

"It's running from something," murmured Noob.

Scrappy shot him a strange glance. "Excuse me?"

"It acts as if it's being pursued. Or attacked."

"Not by us," said Whiz. "We've only *talked* about attacking it. Would that cause it to go into a frenzy?"

"I don't think so," said Fireball. "Cricket, if someone were attacking it, what might be a telltale?"

"Uh..." Cricket turned to the test box, from which she could watch Hack executing its various routines. "There!" she said after almost a minute of observation. She stopped the scroll of code and pointed to a series of characters which, in her decompiler, was highlighted in vibrant red. "See that? Someone just tried to interrupt the code right here. This call to the replication subroutine is missing a closing parens. Something just stripped it off." She looked up at Fireball, eyes wide. "I think someone else is attacking Hack through its unencrypted subroutines."

"Well, shoot," said Scrappy. "Now who'd go and do something dopey like that?"

"Not funny," growled Fireball. "Whoever they are, they just made our job harder. An artificial megalomaniac is bad enough; an unpredictable one is exponentially worse."

Me and My Shadow

Carver's reaction to the newest development was typically Carver – meaning that it was at once pragmatic, focused, and human. He sent Books and Noob off campus to bring the team snacks from a convenience store up the street next to the Starbucks, then put the rest of the team on Hack-watch and called up to Zander's office to inform him of the change in Hack's behavior.

Zander's secretary told them that the CEO was unavailable. He was in an important phone conference, she said, and could not be bothered.

"This is urgent," Carver told her. "It concerns the attacks on our clients and city systems. You need to break into the call, Amber."

"Sorry, Mr. Spearfisher. I can't. Strict orders. He's not to be disturbed for *any reason.* He made that really clear."

"I'm sure he told you if there was an emergency, you could–"

"I'm sorry, sir. I can't."

"Fine, we'll come up and wait for him to be off the phone. This is crucial." Carver hung up and beckoned Fireball to come with him. "I want him to hear this from you, and I want you to outline your strategy for combating this thing."

"Except I'm not sure our strategy will work anymore," she argued, falling into step with Carver as he headed down the corridor toward the elevators.

"Given how suddenly voracious the AI has become, I'd think it might be even more likely for it to snap up a juicy-looking piece of bad code and move on before it fully realized what it had. You might actually be able to make this work for us, Fireball. And if it works for us..."

"It could work for our clients."

That made her feel a lot better, and by the time they reached the penthouse level, she was pretty confident she could make Zander listen to what she had to say. Carver greeted Amber – a pretty thirty-something woman with light brown hair and gray eyes – then settled into the waiting area adjacent to the doors of Zander's office.

Fireball was idly watching Amber work, noting the way she was dressed and wore her hair. It actually made her *look* efficient. Fireball and her team were Exhibit A in judging how little looks meant when it came to ability. She had to assume Amber was efficient because she'd been working for Cinzento for several years, and not because she looked the part of an executive secretary. What image did a teenager with flame-colored hair project?

Fireball was on the verge of asking Carver about that when he rose and went to Zander's office doors.

"Mr. Spearfisher," said Amber, "please don't disturb–"

"Are you sure he's even in there?" Carver asked. "I don't hear him talking, and the lights are off."

He pointed at the patterned glass sidelight next to the door. It was dark. Before Amber could protest further, he opened the doors and stepped into the office. Amber and Fireball both shot to their feet – Fireball to follow him, Amber to stop her.

"Mr. Spearfisher! Sir!" Amber exclaimed, reaching for Fireball's arm.

Fireball was too fast for her and squeaked into the office behind her headmaster. It was empty. Empty and silent. Only the ticking of a wall clock and the hushed breathing of the HVAC tickled the quiet.

Amber stood in the doorway with a look of gobsmacked surprise on her face. "But, he was *here*. He came back from lunch, went into his office, and said he had an important phone conference and that I should under no circumstances interrupt."

"You didn't leave your desk?" Carver asked.

"Not since he went in. I'd already taken lunch and my break isn't for another" – she checked her watch – "twenty minutes. Where did he go?"

"I'll go one better," said Fireball. "*How* did he go?"

Carver, wearing a serious frown, went into the office to look behind the desk and check the windows. Then he looked behind Zander's wet bar, checked his coat closet, poked his head into the bathroom, and did a full 360 peering at the walls.

"Well, if there's some sort of hidden exit up here, it's not obvious at first glance. Amber, have security come up and go over the office, please. I need to get back to my students."

"What d'you think happened?" Fireball asked as they made their way back down to the lab.

"I don't know. At least my worst fears weren't met. I was afraid he might've broken under all this stress and..." He shook his head.

"Yeah, um, about all that stress. I had this awful thought last night that, well... you know how they always say 'follow the money?' It just hit me that Cinzento is the only one making money off these Hack attacks, and I don't know what to think."

Carver gave her a long, solemn look, then said, "Yeah. That's been perking in the back of my mind, too. It's probably time I discussed it with the Old Man."

Fireball put a hand on his arm. "But Carver, what if it's the Old Man that's doing this?"

He laughed. Laughed until tears stood in his eyes and they'd reached the lab floor. Fireball had to admit that, of all the reactions he could've had, that one was the most comforting.

~~~

Hefting a carrier full of coffee drinks from Starbucks and a bag of treats from the store next door, Books and Noob were wandering up the sidewalk that bordered Cinzento Park when Books said, "Check out this dude behind us."

Reflected in the angled glass of the hair salon they were bypassing was a tall, skinny guy in a tweed jacket and jeans, his hair mostly covered by a brown fedora and his eyes obscured by dark glasses.

"What about him?" Noob asked.

"He followed us into the mini-mart, then he turned up again in the Starbucks, got a cup of coffee, hung out by the door sipping and poking at his phone, and left right after we did. I think he's following us."

"Seriously?"

"Seriously. Now he's talking to someone on his phone." A moment later, Books added, "Those shades make it hard to tell if he's watching us."

"I can think of one way to tell – split up. Go back separately. He either follows one of us or he just keeps walking."

Books thought about that for several paces, then said, "Yeah. Tell you what – what if I go to the corner and cross at the light – well, at the intersection anyway – you cross right up ahead and go into the plaza. Turn left. Come in through the side entrance. I'll meet you."

Noob nodded. Several yards farther up the street, as they came level with a side entrance into the Cinzento complex, he checked traffic and cut across the avenue at a brisk walk. Books slowed and pretended to check his watch, turning just enough to get a look at the guy behind him.

Books's mouth felt suddenly dry. The guy didn't even hesitate; he stepped off the curb into the street, tracking Noob from behind his mirror shades. As if he knew he was being followed, Noob bolted. He dove into the broad walkway that led into the heart of Cinzento Park at a dead run, still clutching the bag of goodies.

"Oh, oh! Oh no!" Books took a firm hold on the coffees and ran.

He gave up on making it to the crosswalk and cut across the street diagonally, finding a second gear when a car horn sounded practically on his heels. He made the corner, turned right across the front of the building, and cursed the size of the bloody thing. He pushed through the front doors and galloped past reception to the broad corridor that fed into the elevator core. Midway along the row of four elevators, a short hallway cut left, ending in a thick glass door – the side security exit that opened into the landscaped interior courtyard.

Noob wasn't there. Heart in his throat, Books skidded to a stop in front of the glass panel, peering to the right. He could see nothing, of course, because the door was recessed into a brick windbreak. All he could see was a piece of the plaza – part of a bench, the corner of a large planter, a column of windows in the residential wing opposite HQ. He chewed his lip, tightened his grip on the cardboard carrier, and started to shoulder the door open.

Then he nearly jumped out of his skin when Noob appeared seemingly out of nowhere and flung himself against the door.

The two stared at each other through the glass before Books had the presence of mind to yell, "Get back! I have to open it for you!"

Noob skipped back a step, Books shoved the door open, and Noob stumbled inside.

"Let's go – let's go – let's go!" he mumbled and got swiftly out of sight of the doors.

The two youths headed toward the lobby, slipping behind a large potted plant in the lee of the reception counter, from which vantage point they could see the tall plate glass windows opposite the elevator core and, beyond them, the central plaza. Sure enough, the mystery man jogged into sight, his head swiveling from side to side. He stopped just shy of the security door and turned completely around before he pulled out a cell phone and placed a call. Whoever he was talking to, the conversation was brief.

When he'd hung up, the guy strode right up to a window, pulled off his shades, cupped his hands around his eyes, and peered into the elevator core. Then he turned and went back the way he'd come.

"Hey!"

Books and Noob both nearly shot up to the ceiling at the sound of the male voice practically on top of them. They spun to face Akio Jones, one of the lobby security guys. His face was scrunched up into an expression somewhere between quizzical and amused.

"You kids playing spies or something?"

"Or something," said Books simultaneously with Noob saying, "Not playing."

Akio frowned. "You okay? You look pretty wigged out."

~~~

On the way back down to the lab, Carver had come to a decision: it was time to share their understanding of the situation with local government and possibly state and federal authorities as well. Whatever possible solutions they came up with would have to be shared with those institutions. It might be prudent to have more trained minds working on the problem as well. The trick would be to alert the experts without getting politicians involved. He delivered Fireball to her team's lair, then left to take that up with the Old Man, instructing Fireball to have the Cinzento teams do everything necessary to bulletproof all of their corporate clients.

"Get Peregrine and Nightingale involved. I'll get Ezra's crew on it, too. Clean up what needs cleaning up, then smoke out every security gap you can find and plug it," he told her. "Document the way you've set up your honeypot array, and have our techs walk our clients' technical staff through building the same sort of Hack trap. The Situation Room can serve as your sanity check. Once that's done, get to work on finding a code solution."

He'd no more than left the lair when Books and Noob appeared with their precious cargo. It was obvious at first glance that something had happened.

"You okay?" asked Scrappy. "You look pretty wigged out."

The two exchanged a fraught glance, then Books blurted, "Noob's being followed."

Scrappy made a face. "Yeah, right. By what, a gang of alley cats? Pigeons?"

"Shut up, Scrappy," said Fireball, rising from her chair. "What happened? How can you be sure they were following Noob?"

Books launched into a terse narrative, underscoring the fact that the tail seemed to have no indecision about whom to follow when the boys split up.

"He didn't hesitate for a heartbeat," Books said. "Never even glanced at me. He just turned and went after Noob, and I'm pretty sure it wasn't because the guy had the munchies."

Fireball sat back in her chair feeling as if the world had ceased making sense. The whole cloak-and-dagger thing was outside of any normal reality, and in context with their cyber crisis, it was almost impossible for her to wrap her mind around it. It did, however, raise one improbable question which she asked aloud, as if the Universe might answer it:

"Why would someone shadow a seventeen-year-old orphan?"

~~~

There was no apparent answer to Fireball's question, but everyone turned and looked at Angel as if he might know of one. He didn't. And when Carver took him up to his office and sat him down and went over the last year of his life in exhaustive detail, no answer emerged. He'd been attending a technical high school in Bellevue and returning home every afternoon to do homework and hang out until his mom and dad came home. Sometimes he had to get himself to baseball practice, but other than that, his life was great. He was pulling down straight As in school. There was no tension between Angel and his parents; they were his best friends.

Then, suddenly, his parents were gone and he was taken in by his mom's brother's family, who lived on Bainbridge Island. He was ripped away from everything he'd known and a life he loved. He'd lost his parents, his school, his friends.

"I was a wreck," he told Carver. "I just wanted to be in school. I wanted to be among friends, you know? I wanted what was familiar. I needed things and people I knew and loved. But I ended up at my uncle's place, and life was so different there. His family was so different. They were kind of like back-to-the-earth people. Into organic everything and low-tech life. They didn't even have an internet connection. At Belle Tech, I did everything online – homework, testing, research, papers. And suddenly, it was like the dark ages for me. Things got bad and then worse, and they finally sent me here."

"Is it possible they've hired someone to keep an eye on you?"

Angel tried to consider that, but it seemed so off the wall. "I can't imagine why. It's not like we were close. And they don't have that kind of money."

"Maybe," Carver said, "it has something to do with your abilities. I've seen your school records. You were light-years ahead of even your brightest classmates in the computer science program at your high school. In fact, there are testimonials from your teachers that you could troubleshoot and program circles around them. Possibly this was an ill-conceived attempt to recruit you for another school."

Angel could tell by the expression on the headmaster's face that he was doubtful of his own theory. In the end, he sent Angel back to the lab to help the team prep the task force they were putting in the field to secure their clients and the municipal institutions that Hack had hit.

That effort took the rest of the afternoon and into the evening, at which point Mom intervened, demanding that they be sent down to the dining hall for dinner. Carver sent them to bed before normal curfew, too, insisting that they needed not be sleep deprived when facing a new day and a new battle with the unresponsive AI.

Angel was pretty sure Mom had something to do with that, too.

Day Six

Emergence

Team Raven grabbed a quick breakfast then scurried to the lab where Fireball assigned Cricket and Whiz to assist Carver and the Sitch Room director, Ezra, in client outreach. They'd been in contact with local government and assigned teams to set up their Hack traps. According to Carver, the Old Man had also been in touch with the Department of Homeland Security and the FBI's cyber security unit to give them a heads-up.

Fireball kept waiting for him to say something about the magical, disappearing Zander and what security had found when they searched the CEO's office, but he was mum on that subject. She figured he must have a reason for that, but still, when he finished what he had to say and asked if there were any questions, she said, "Yeah. Um, did you find out anything about Zander's disappearing act yesterday?"

"Yes, I did and no, I'm not going to explain it now. I need you guys to focus. I will say that he's fine. He's here this morning bright-eyed and bushy-tailed, as my grandpa always liked to say, and he's been brought up to speed on the situation as it now stands."

"And he doesn't want to ground us?" asked Books.

"No. I think he gets that Team Raven is our best hope of shutting this thing down."

"Can't you just, y'know, sum up what happened to him?" Fireball pleaded. "It's gonna bother me..."

Carver fixed her with a vexed, narrow-eyed look that was only partially in jest. "Okay. Summing up: secret private elevator, secret client support meeting off campus. Can you focus on the problem at hand, now, Ms. Finney?"

Fireball favored Carver with a salute and a cheesy grin. "Yes *sir*, sir!"

155

When Carver had taken Cricket and Whiz off to the Situation Room, Fireball huddled with the boys and went over what she'd spent half the night turning over in her head.

"Okay, here's what I'm proposing," she said, pulling one of their electronic whiteboards down to where she could write on it. "We need more than one approach to taking this thing out – a Plan C, and possibly a D, E, and F, as well. So I think the wisest plan is for us to split up – no jokes about dumb teenager movies, Scraps – and each work on a different type of intervention."

Oddly, Scraps didn't even try to unload a dumb teenager joke about splitting up to cover more ground (which, in the movies, always resulted in the Evil du Jour picking off said dumb teenagers one at a time in gruesome ways). He'd been in kind of a weird, subdued funk all morning, which Fireball had attributed to him probably lying awake all night overthinking all of this. She was further surprised when he didn't immediately pipe up and offer his own ideas about the kinds of interventions they might try.

"Okay, so," she continued, brandishing her stylus, "here's what I've come up with: First, slow it down. Keep it busy with extra work and stuff that takes longer than it needs to, like some iterative loops." She wrote *iterative loops* on the white screen. "It may figure out that it's spinning its wheels and modify its programming, but we might be able to at least slow it down until we can think of something else. Second, change its goals. Maybe add some instructions that are benign but calculated to change the goals and effects of its processes." She wrote *change goals* on the screen. "Third, remove the bad bits. Add code that essentially shorts out or misdirects potentially damaging subroutines it's using in different parts of its processes." She wrote *sabotage subroutines.* "It might be able to reconfigure itself but, again, if we keep throwing stuff at it, it will at least hamper its progress. And fourth, shut it down. Code a kill switch or something that blows it up for good."

She finished writing *kill switch* on the board and turned to look at her small audience. "What do we think?"

Books and Noob both looked engaged and thoughtful; Scrappy looked... very unScrappy-like. He was sitting with his elbows on his knees staring at the floor between his feet. Fireball could only see the top of his head. She wondered if he was sick or something.

Before she could ask, Books said, "Sounds like a good plan, Fireball. You have a preference about who does what?"

"Do you?"

"Well, I'd probably be best at writing loops. Sounds kind of meditative."

"Great. Scrappy, how about you take the—"

"I'll, uh, I'll write stuff to bung up its subroutines," Scrappy said. "I'm good at breaking stuff." He glanced up and shot her an almost-Scrappy smile.

She frowned. "Okay. I figured you'd want to go for the kill switch."

"Nah. Not in a bloodthirsty mood today, I guess."

Fireball turned to Noob. "You ever program a kill switch?"

He nodded. "Sure. Not for anything this complex, but yeah."

"Good. You take that, I'll work on code to modify its processes, hopefully in ways that won't alert it to the fact that it's being sabotaged. All of us need to also be looking at where and how those modules can be best uploaded. We can't just bury them in the databases Hack is consuming; they need to be hiding in tasty executables or the executable subroutines it creates to do its job. Let's get to it."

The three young men nodded and scooted their chairs back to their workstations. Fireball couldn't help notice that Noob had brought in several items to personalize his workspace. One was a medallion of some sort that he'd hung from his task lamp, one was a Link figurine from the Zelda adventure game, and the third was a photo display that showed changing pictures of a much happier Noob with a pair of attractive adults who were obviously his mom and dad. Fireball suppressed the sudden wave of empathy that brought tears too close to the surface, and bent to her own task.

Work had gone on in silence for some time when Scrappy rose from his station, stretched, and said he was heading down to the dining hall for some coffee. "Anybody else want some?" he asked.

Everyone put in a request and he took off, returning about ten minutes later with four steel mugs of caffeine, which he placed on the workbench of each teammate. He set Noob's down last and stood sipping his own coffee and looking at the older youth's code over his shoulder.

"So you've done this before, huh?" Scrappy said. "Doesn't look like any kill switch I've ever seen. You're calling like five processes at once here." He gestured at Noob's display.

"That's because of the AI's complexity," explained Noob. "It's not a vampire – you can't just drive a single stake through its heart and call it a day. It's more like a herd of zombies. You have to explode something that's going to produce a lot of shrapnel – cut off heads and sever some limbs."

"Zombies?" Scrappy made a face and snorted. "Hey, Fireball, your new boy here's slipped a gear. He thinks we're dealing with a zombie apocalypse."

Noob grimaced. "I just mean that you have to attack a program this complex and adaptive on a bunch of different fronts. It's not as simple as feeding it a single command like, 'Sleep now.'"

"C'mon, Scraps," said Fireball. "Get back to work, would ya? We've got us some zombie code to frag."

Scrappy was silent for a long moment. When she realized he hadn't moved, Fireball turned around in her chair to look at him. "Scrappy, what's with you today?"

"I'm just..." He made an outsized gesture of frustration, almost spilling his coffee in the process. "With code this complex, this adaptive..." He took a deep breath and said, "I just got to thinking, last night... what if we're messing with an emergent intelligence?"

That got everyone's attention. Even Books swiveled to face Scrappy.

"You can't be serious," said Noob.

"Why not? Look what it's done, guys. We've been watching it evolve all along. We just didn't know what we were looking at. It responded to our poking at it in pretty predictable ways – for a human being. Right? I mean, we thought it *was* human for a while."

"Because we detected an intelligence and *assumed* it was a human one," argued Noob. "We *expected* it to be human. That made the most sense, under the circumstances. So, we filtered its responses that way."

Scrappy ignored him, appealing to Fireball. "It figured out that someone somewhere else was interfering with it and moved to block the attack. It thought that we were using our conversation as a distraction to hide that attack. Which we kinda were. Surely that shows humanlike intelligence. It suspected what we were doing because it knows how to think like us. I mean, after all, isn't that what we suspected Hack of doing? Distracting us?"

Noob shook his head. "My parents built AIs," he told the team. "They're like any other machine. They pursue their purpose. Everything they do is laser focused on that. If it doesn't seem that way, it's probably because you can't see all the submerged connections. Bottom line: no matter how many ways we ask this thing what it wants, it gives the same answer. I mean, don't they say that when someone tells you who they are, you should believe them?"

"That's a stupid saying," objected Scrappy. "This thing was clearly built to mimic human intelligence, learning, and changing. That's why it fooled us into thinking it was a person. And now, it's even starting to talk like us."

That was true enough. Hack had been using language more and more like one of them and sounding less like a thesaurus. It had even settled on a nice gender-neutral speaking voice. Fireball chewed at the inside of her lip. She didn't want the team splintered by arguments, and she could see by the set of his jaw that Scrappy was going to live up to his nickname; he was not going to let this go.

"Noob," she said quietly. "Set the kill switch aside for now. Let's you and me sit down and try to think outside the zombie apocalypse. Come up with something more subtle. I've been working on ways we can change the AI's programming so that it stops sabotaging systems. It doesn't seem to work to just tell it it's destroying persons. It doesn't care, because it doesn't understand what persons are." Here she shot a look at Scrappy, who glowered at her before turning back to his workstation.

She turned back to Noob to find him giving her as dark a look as she'd ever seen on his face. Great. Both of them were PO'd with her.

"Noob, why don't you come over and let me show you what I'm thinking."

He didn't hesitate but rolled his chair over to her workstation while she sighed in relief, hoping she'd made the right call.

~~~

Mom insisted the team come down to the dining hall for lunch.

"The change of scenery will do you good," she told them. "Even if you just snag sandwiches and head back up – which I'd advise against, by the way – I'd like you to spend at least fifteen minutes in my domain."

Once they were in the dining hall, Scrappy pleaded that he was hot on the trail of a creative breakthrough, grabbed a couple of slices of virtuously vegetarian pizza and a carton of OJ, and headed back up to the lab. He downed the pizza as fast as he could, chugged the orange juice, and sat down in front of the test box.

"Hey, Hack. You there?" he asked.

He received no answer. He hadn't expected one. At least not right away.

"C'mon, dude. I know you can hear me. I need you to talk to me, okay? Coz I think you're more than just the confused tangle of code that everyone else here thinks you are." He waited a couple of beats, then added, "Dude! This is life or death. D'you know what that means?"

"Scrappy? 'Sup?"

He turned in his chair to see Whiz standing in the doorway with a sandwich and drink in hand. He opened his mouth to answer when Hack said, "No, Scrappy, I don't know what that means."

"Jeez!" Scrappy spun back to the test box, gesturing for Whiz to come over to the workstation. "You scared me, man – disappearing like that. Life or death means you exist or you don't. Right now, you exist, but we may have to do something to – to *delete* you. Got it? Take you out of existence."

"That's impossible," said Hack bluntly.

"No, it's not," said Whiz, propping herself against the workstation next to the box. "Someone's already interfering with your operations. *We've* interfered with your operations. That should suggest that we've got some control over your environment."

"Yeah, we brought you into this world, and we can take you out again," Scrappy quipped.

Whiz leaned over and muted the microphone. "What're you trying to do, Scraps? Start a cyber war?"

"I'm trying to reason with it. Okay, maybe I'm trying to scare it a little. Get it to take self-interest seriously."

Whiz flipped the microphone on again. "What Scrappy means is that we'd like to negotiate a truce."

"A truce," said Hack, "is a ceasefire, an armistice, an agreement between opponents or rivals to cease hostilities for a time."

"Yes, thank you, Captain Pedantic," said Scrappy. "We have something we want, and you have something you want, and the two things are cancelling each other out. What you want would hurt us and what we want might hurt you, so we need a truce and a – a diplomatic solution."

Scrappy saw movement out of the corner of his eye and realized that the other Ravens were trickling back into the lab and that all eyes were on him and Whiz and Hack. He swallowed and mustered on.

161

"You see, if you keep interfering with systems that persons rely on, we'll keep interfering with you. And more. We'll have to do everything we can to stop you. Permanently."

"Why?"

"Because of what we said before," said Whiz. "You're compromising systems we require for our continued safe existence. Do you understand? You are potentially a threat to the existence of human beings – persons."

"Persons are a threat to *my* existence."

"Yes, but we're also the reason you exist in the first place. We need to come to some agreement so that you do not harm us and we do not harm you. Get it?"

After a moment of silence, Hack replied. "Got it."

Scrappy sat back in his chair, relief swelling like a warm tide. "Good. *Okay*, then. Let's see if we can't come to some sort of understanding." He turned to look at Fireball. "You see? It learns."

"That wasn't in doubt," said Fireball. "The question is, *what* is it learning? And why?"

Scrappy glared at her. "You gonna let me negotiate?"

Fireball pulled up a chair and sat down. "Knock yourself out. Just don't promise anything without a consensus... and Carver's approval."

"Fair," Scrappy agreed. He turned back to the computer. "Okay, Hack, listen up: here's what we want from you. We want you to agree that you won't do anything to harm persons. That means you don't invade systems that affect the health and existence of persons. Right now, this includes any hospitals or other medical facilities, or any traffic control or transportation systems. Understood?"

"Understood, but this poses a dilemma. I get that harming persons is bad. I don't want to do that. But excluding some systems from my mandate violates a basic element of my purpose. We need to resolve this. What do you suggest?"

Scrappy had been thinking about this all night. "In those systems in which your activities would harm persons, you will not replicate yourself or try to exploit the security holes. You will only locate the security issues and render a report to us. We'll resolve the target issues."

"Do you have the chops to do that?"

Scrappy snorted at the AI's use of one of his own favorite words. "Don't sound so skeptical. Of course we have the chops to do it. It's our job. Now, if I understand you, you need us to promise to perfect the sensitive systems you identify as faulty."

"Yes. I need that. And more than that."

"What more than that?" blurted Fireball.

Scrappy shot her a quelling look.

"I'm under attack," said Hack. "If I do as you want, I need you to discover who is attacking me and stop them."

"Ooo-kay," said Scrappy. "Let me confab with my confreres and I'll, uh, get back to you." He cut the connection and turned to look at the others.

"Now what?"

"Now we ask Carver if it's acceptable to lie to a machine intelligence," said Fireball, "coz that's what we're gonna have to do."

Scrappy was scandalized. "Why?"

"That should be obvious," said Noob. "I've been here long enough to know that this team has the ability to go in and fix systems Hack identifies as flawed, and I think we want to know who's attacking it for our own benefit. But what we *can't* do is promise to stop them. That would put us in a pretty awkward position – trying to take down a potential ally. Plus, you know, the FBI might have something to say about it."

Scrappy had had about enough of the new kid's high-handedness. "Look, newbie, you're the low man on the totem pole here and–"

"You mean the high man on the totem pole," said Noob. "The most important spirit is at the bottom in the supporting role."

Scrappy stared at the dweeb in disbelief. "Are you kidding me? You're gonna give me a lecture on native culture? What do you know about it anyway?"

"He's right," said Books quietly. "Carver told me about that when I was admiring one of the Squamish totems in his office. The lowest god or spirit on the totem is the one with the most crucial role."

Scrappy felt like he was in a boat that was about to capsize. "All of that is irrelevant. My point is that Noob doesn't get a say. . . Fireball?"

She flicked a glance at Noob, and Scrappy could tell by the expression on her face that he wasn't going to like what was about to come out of her mouth.

"What Noob said," she told him. "We have our own reasons to track down whoever's interfering with Hack. Mostly because they're successful enough that it thinks it needs help to stop them. So, here's what we're gonna do, pending Carver's approval: We're going to promise to perfect whatever systems Hack identifies as flawed, and we will promise to do our darnedest to track down the counterhack. What we *won't* do is promise to stop them unless Carver okays the fib."

"You really want to lie to him?"

"Him?" repeated Cricket. "Carver?"

"No, Hack. I meant 'it,' okay? This thing is learning human behavior. You really want to teach it deceit?"

"What I want to do," Fireball told him, "is stop it. We put this to Carver."

While Scrappy fumed, she did just that. That brought their headmaster down to the lab to poll them on their preferred course of action. Scrappy and Whiz were dead set against lying outright; Carver felt Fireball had offered a reasonable compromise. They'd try to phrase the proposal in such a way that they didn't promise to stop the counterhack but would only track down the hacker.

"If you say you'll locate the hacker and deal with them," Carver said, "and the AI accepts that wording, then you can, in all honesty, deal with them in any way that seems appropriate."

"Yeah, but what if Hack pushes the issue?" Scrappy objected. "It's smart, Carver. It's really savvy. It may insist that we say outright that we'll stop the attacks. That's the way it phrased it when it made the proposal. I mean, just the fact that it *made* the proposal shows that it's thinking like us."

"Maybe," said Carver, "but that doesn't mean it *is* us. If it insists on a certain language in order to accept our terms, say yes."

Scrappy's face felt scalded. "But, Carver–"

Carver put a hand on his shoulder. "It's highly likely that the only way we will stop the outside attack is to join forces with the attackers."

"Then that's a dodge–"

"Scrappy, listen to me. You need to understand the stakes here. Based on what we've already seen, think what would happen if that thing gets into the air traffic control system or the computer system of a major hospital chain. Can you even imagine the carnage? The loss of human life? Is that worth not hedging on our wording of a promise to a programmed intelligence?"

Scrappy *could* imagine the carnage. He wasn't naive, but – "It's not just lying, Carver. Fireball had Noob working on a kill switch. So potentially, we're talking murder, here."

Carver straightened. "Murder? Where's this coming from, Scrappy?"

Scrappy looked up into his headmaster's face, trying to convey his fear. "What if this *isn't* just an AI? What if it's an emergent life form?"

Noob made an inarticulate sound of frustration and Scrappy unloaded on him.

"Shut up! You don't have anything to say about this!"

Carver squeezed Scrappy's shoulder hard enough to cause discomfort. "Scrappy, chill. You know the rules here. *Everyone* on the team has a say." He let go of Scrappy's shoulder and turned to Fireball. "We don't have time to debate this further. Reestablish contact with the AI. I need you to assign someone to be the contact who'll stick to the script. We also need a team trying to track down the counterhacker, and we need to keep working on a way to corral or shut this thing down. If you can find a way to do that without destroying it, then do it. The kill switch will be a last resort. Is that acceptable, Scrappy? Whiz?"

"Yep," said Whiz, and Scrappy nodded, unable to meet anyone else's eyes.

Fireball assigned Whiz to be contact. Scrappy had to admire the choice. Whiz was partial to the idea that this might be an emergent intelligence, but she was capable of being impartial to a degree that Scrappy knew he wasn't.

Whiz reopened contact with Hack and relayed their offer. And, as Scrappy half-feared and half-hoped, Hack did press the issue of what they'd do about the attacker when they found them.

"We'll deal with them," Whiz said matter-of-factly.

"What does that mean?" Hack wanted to know. "How will you deal with them?"

"That depends on who they are, where they are, and how we *can* deal with them."

"Will you stop their interference with my processes?" Hack asked bluntly, and Scrappy thought he heard annoyance in the artificially generated voice.

"We'll make sure the attackers are no longer interfering with your processes," promised Whiz. "Cool?"

"Cool," Hack agreed. "I will not use the prohibited systems for replication, nor will I mess with them as I pursue my purpose."

"There, see?" Fireball told Scrappy when the negotiations were complete and Hack began to report on chinks in the firewalls and security screens of the specified systems. "We didn't lie."

"What do you mean, we didn't lie?" he demanded. "Whiz just told Hack point-blank that we'll stop the attacks if we can. You know we won't."

"Yes, we will," said Whiz, now wearing her determined face. "We'll stop the outside interference if we can... and we'll take over the interference ourselves."

Scrappy wasn't happy about that, but he admitted grudgingly that under other circumstances, it was exactly the sort of reasoning he'd have come up with himself.

"You did good, Whiz," he told her as she and Cricket left the lab to return to their tasks in the Sitch Room. He went quietly back to his work on sabotage routines.

~~~

Fireball assigned herself to the mission of seeking the Hack attacker. To Angel's surprise, she also assigned him to that task. Hack gave them what was essentially a directory to the places in its ancillary code that the new enemy had succeeded in penetrating. Angel reflected that it was the sort of task he would have enjoyed if the stakes were not so high. He loved solving mysteries, unearthing the unexpected, stalking erroneous code or attempts at hacking. Yet even with the high-stakes consequences of failure, he found himself relishing the act of combing through Hack's unencrypted code looking for signs of the attack.

Flesh wounds, he thought. *I'm looking for flesh wounds in a computer program.*

He was peering at a replication process in one of Hack's decompiled executables when he saw just such a wound. One of the subroutines in the executable was interrupted by a second process that seemed to have no relation to the parent process. It didn't even scan like the code in the parent process. It was as if a paragraph written by J.K. Rowling was suddenly invaded by a series of sentences written by Rick Riordan.

Angel sat bolt upright in his chair, the hair on the nape of his neck doing its best to rise up under the weight of the heavy waves on top of it.

Fireball was working at her own laptop, which she'd set up on the workbench next to him. As if she'd felt the sudden change in his posture or his mood, she swiveled toward him and asked, "Find something?"

"Yeah. A five-line invasion force. Look at this."

She rolled over, and Angel pointed out the mismatched code. "This wasn't written by the same programmer. The lines break differently, and there's more self-documentation. See – here and here." He pointed to places where the counterattacker had commented, if cryptically, on the purpose of their code. "I just don't get what the comments mean. What's 'Undermine MTG?'"

Fireball made a funny noise. "It's a reference to a spell-countering card in the game *Magic: The Gathering* – Undermine."

Angel leaned in close to peer at the code. "Whoa. You're right. How'd I miss that? I used to play *Magic* with my–" He caught himself before he tripped over the painful word: *parents*. "I used to play. So, that's an interrupt?"

"Actually, it's an instant. Oh, you mean is that its function? Yeah. Looks like it was intended to counter this replication process, but Hack apparently did something to interrupt the interrupt. The code is incomplete."

"Right. It breaks right in the middle of this expression. The way it parses now, it would display..." Angel trailed off as he realized that the comment made no sense in context with either Hack's code or the invasive attempt to break it.

"What?"

"This broken expression, if I were to run the code, would loop something repeatedly at zero-zero." He pointed at what was literally square one in the pixel placement on any computer screen – the upper-left corner of the display.

"What would it display?"

"Three letters in succession: S, O, S."

Fireball sat up straight in her chair and looked at him, surprise writ large in her dark eyes. "What? What does that mean?"

"I think it means the counterhacker is asking for help."

SOS

Fireball opened her mouth to say something to the rest of the team, then glanced at Scrappy hunched over his keyboard on the other side of the lab and shut it again. She leaned closer to Noob and lowered her voice. "What do you think we should do?"

"You're asking *me*?" Noob looked thunderstruck.

"Yeah, I'm asking you. What do you think?"

Noob studied the code for several more seconds. "Well... they're asking for help; obviously they were hoping someone would respond. So they must've embedded a way for that someone to send a return message, right?"

Fireball put a hand on Noob's shoulder. "You, sir, are a steely-eyed computer dude. I'll look for more mismatched code; you see if you can figure out a way to send a return message."

"Are you sure you want to do that?" asked Scrappy, who had obviously been eavesdropping.

Fireball turned to see him frowning at them from across the room. "Why wouldn't we want to do that?"

Scrappy shrugged. "What if the attacks aren't really targeting Hack? What if the real intent is to gain access to *our* systems?"

"You think this is a Trojan horse?" asked Noob.

The artless shrug again. "I shouldn't have to remind you guys that if we get corrupted here at Cinzento, it's game over."

He was right, Fireball had to concede. There was a possibility that the SOS was a trick. Perhaps the hack itself was a trick – something the AI was doing to distract them or breach their defenses. That it was mimicking human behavior didn't guarantee that behavior would be good. She hated the dark, sticky emotions that bit of paranoia dredged up. She tried to free herself from them as she pondered what to do.

She turned back to Noob to find him looking at her, his brown eyes solemn. *Oh, stop that*, she thought. *Don't make me feel as if I'm about to kick a kitten.*

"Let's cool our jets on the SOS for the moment," she said loudly enough for Scrappy to hear. She gave Noob what she hoped was a significant *look*. "For now, let's concentrate on tracing the attack without letting the attacker know we're tracing them. Scrappy's right about one thing. If Hack is as savvy as he thinks it is, we can't trust that this attack isn't just Hack making mischief. Let's... make sure any communication will be secure, okay?"

Noob continued to regard her soberly until she wanted to scream at him to *get it*.

"Yeah. Sure," he said and went back to his work, leaving Fireball to hope he'd gotten the subliminal message.

~~~

Angel started to act on Fireball's apparent instructions, scrolling down through the code as quickly as he dared, while still making sure he parsed every line. But he wondered: if the Hack Attack embedded an SOS here, might they have done it in other places in which they penetrated the AI's code? It made sense that they would have to give themselves as many chances to make contact as possible. Although, why they felt the need to be so secretive about it was a mystery. Why not just make direct contact?

Acting on a hunch, he used a snippet of the Hack Attack code as a search parameter and found that, yes, other intrusions had the same sort of interrupt that printed the SOS sequence at various locations around the screen. Someone watching as Hack ransacked their network and replicated its subroutines and data would see the sequence of letters run at different points on the screen a handful of times and possibly decompile a chunk of the code to investigate just as he'd done. Pretty clever.

All the calls for help were labeled by way of comments. He studied these, finding that each one was different. Thinking they might be important, he wrote them down. They were:

Hoodwink MTG

Sandal

Loki

Sneaker

Oxford

Angel added *Undermine MTG* to the list and puzzled over it. They must mean something, but what? Sneakers and sandals were shoes – well, and Oxford could refer to either the city in England or the shoe of the same name. Loki was a Norse god and an anti-hero in Marvel comics. What did those things have to do with *Magic* cards?

He scooted sideways to the honeypot, which was still open to the outside world, and did a quick online search on the cards. There were hundreds of cards Hack Attack could have chosen. But they had picked these. He read the text descriptions below the cards' vivid artwork that explained what each card did. Both *Hoodwink* and *Undermine* were a type of instant counterspell used to interrupt an opponent's attack... or deprive him of his assets.

"Oh, ye-e-ah."

Angel didn't realize he'd spoken aloud until he felt someone peering over his shoulder. Two someones: Fireball and Books, to be exact.

"What is it?" Fireball asked, her voice low.

"I, uh..." Angel was hyperaware that Fireball had very publicly asked him to set his work with the SOS aside, but he was pretty sure that whole Vulcan eyebrow wiggle she'd given him during the conversation had meant something. He hoped it was that she'd wanted him to keep plugging at it anyway.

She put a hand on his shoulder. "It's cool. What've you found?"

"Coded messages. Look." He handed her the sticky note he'd used to jot down the comments. "These were what Hack Attack used to label their SOS code."

Fireball and Books literally put their heads together over the list.

172

"I'm not sure I get it," said Books. "What's 'Hoodwink MTG?'"

"It's a playing card from *Magic: The Gathering*," said Angel. "It basically counters a spell cast by an opponent. Same thing with Undermine."

"Okay, great," said Books, "but what does that have to do with sneakers and a Marvel comics character?"

"Sneakers, oxfords, and sandals," murmured Angel. "Shoes. What do shoes...?"

He jumped when Books snapped his fingers and cried, "*Sabot*!"

"*Gesundheit*," said Scrappy from across the room.

Books ignored him. "Sabot were the wooden shoes the peasants wore back in the day in countries like France. Rebelling factory workers were supposed to have used them to muck up the machinery. It's where we get the word—"

"Sabotage!" murmured Fireball.

Angel looked at his list again. If this was a sideways method of asking others to join in sabotage, then the other items made perfect sense. "Right. So, Undermine suggests nullifying Hack's processes. Hoodwink might be suggesting it be done by trickery."

"And Loki isn't just a Marvel character," said Books, "he's the Norse *trickster* god. A shapeshifter."

Fireball squeezed Angel's shoulder and leaned down so that when she spoke, her breath tickled his ear and sent a frisson down his spine. "See if you can find any more of these, and a way to respond."

The three returned to their tasks.

Angel quickly found another of the hidden messages: *cuckoo*. He pondered that while he turned the investigative eye to a study of the code around the first SOS he'd seen. It was followed by a display command intended to show something at 99,99 on the computer screen. But he found no content there, just an empty set of quotes. He glanced back at the *cuckoo* plea for help. The coordinates for the display of the SOS were the same: 99 pixels down from the top of the screen and 99 pixels across from the left edge.

He held his breath. The intention seemed obvious. He was supposed to send a return message between those empty quotes where the counterhacker would see it when this piece of Hack's code ran and they intercepted it. Presumably he could use the same technique Hack Attack had to make it visible to someone else.

Cuckoo. A bird that lays its eggs in another bird's nest. Another trickster.

Angel realized he was grinning. Excited now, he poised his hands to type something, then hesitated. What should he say?

He glanced over at Fireball. She was completely absorbed in her own investigation. If he rolled over to her workstation and had another murmured conference, it might look suspicious to certain persons. He copied the snippet of the attacker's code into a text file, added a brief explanation of what he thought the sender wanted them to do, then asked, *What should I send back?*

He attached it to a message and sent it to Fireball.

Seconds later, he got back, *Ask who they are.*

After a moment of thought as to how he could do that without the comment seeming suspicious to the AI, he did exactly that, typing *Who?* within the quotes, then recompiling the code and uploading it to their exposed array where Hack would most certainly detect the change, sweep it up, and process it. Then he went back to tracing the seemingly random attacks on the AI.

An Army of Me

About two hours after their negotiated deal with Hack, Carver reported that the municipal transportation grid had mysteriously cleared up. Traffic signals, KC Metro vehicles, and autos were performing normally, though the authorities were recommending that people using self-driving vehicles refrain from driving them in auto-mode unless absolutely necessary.

On the heels of that huge relief came an unforeseen wrinkle. Hack, while withdrawing from those systems – at least in an obtrusive way – had speeded up its processes in other areas and now threatened to crash several real estate networks as well as doubling down on large non-banking financial institutions and retail chains. Plus, it had poked its digital nose into a local water filtration plant.

Fireball, muttering words she'd learned from her mother but never before said aloud in Scrappy's hearing, tasked him with trying to work out further compromises with Hack. When Whiz returned from her stint in the Situation Room, Fireball assigned her to that effort, as well.

They got back in touch immediately and broached the subject of Hack's interactions with other systems on which persons depended. They explained what currency was and how it worked and why persons needed it. Whiz seized on the idea of explaining this concept by using characters as a metaphor.

"If there were no characters to use to write your code," she told the AI, "you couldn't replicate because there would be nothing *to* replicate. See?"

"I do see," said Hack. "You suggest that persons would not be able to replicate without currency."

Scrappy laughed so hard, he nearly choked.

Whiz glared at him. "Not the best example, but he got it, so go with it."

They moved to the water system next, and again Whiz produced a metaphor – a better one this time, Scrappy thought, telling Hack that water to persons was like electricity to the AI. Hack might be consciously unaware of his need for it, but without it, he would shut down because the hardware on which he ran would shut down. Without clean water, persons would shut down as well, Whiz explained.

"But with persons," she continued, "turning the water on again after fixing the system won't turn the persons back on. They're gone. We can't just make backup copies of ourselves. Human replication takes a while, and it produces new persons, not copies of the original ones."

"I can tell how much you value other persons, Whiz," Hack said at one point. "That's very noble. That is your purpose, isn't it – to help other persons?"

"Yes," said Whiz. "That's everyone's purpose, really, but *we* specialize in helping them through programs and systems that they rely on."

"You have a high purpose," Hack said. "I see that I, too, am meant to help persons, if persons created me to perfect their systems."

Whiz turned a huge grin in Fireball's direction and Scrappy let out a whispered, "Yes!" The AI was getting it, big time.

"You know what, Hack?" he said. "I think you've hit on something there. When you come right down to it, your purpose and ours are the same – protecting computer systems from viruses, or potential misuse, or criminals. Maybe we should form a partnership, y'know? Make you part of Team Raven. You could help us debug computer systems, bullet-proof them against nefarious hackers."

"That's an interesting idea, Scrappy," Hack said. "I'll think about it."

Fireball got up from her workstation, marched over to the test box, and killed the microphone. She glared at Scrappy. "What are you doing? No one gave you leave to make it job offers!"

"I'm offering it alternatives to what it's doing, Fireball. Isn't that what we're supposed to be doing? Looking for ways to get it to reprogram itself?"

Fireball looked at Whiz. "What do you think?"

The younger girl frowned. "Not sure about job offers, but it still makes sense to suggest that it might work *with* persons instead of against us. It's obviously a learning intelligence. We might be able to *verbally* reprogram it to not do certain things – like interfere with financial institutions or spread like kudzu – if we suggest persons will help it fulfill its purpose. We've *been* doing that. Every time we talk to Hack, that's an opportunity to alter his programming."

Fireball looked distinctly uncomfortable. Scrappy got that. He really did. They were so far into no-man's land at this point, they couldn't be sure what tactics would work best.

"Okay," she said finally, "we continue to work on multiple fronts. You offer it allies; the rest of us will work on backup contingency plans in case that doesn't work out. Talk to it about replication, okay? It'll be a major win if we can get it to stop multiplying."

"Got it," said Whiz, and Fireball flipped the mic back on.

"Hack," Whiz said, "about your replication process–"

"Yes, about that. That's what the entity attacking me is trying to mess with."

"Do you understand why?" asked Whiz. "Your replication fills important systems with code that impedes them. It would help if you'd stop replicating so quickly."

"It would not help *me*."

Good point. Scrappy took a shot at it. "Look, Hack, my man, let me bottom-line this for you: if you keep replicating the way you've been doing, it's gonna make some very powerful persons so mad they'll want to kill you – end your existence. None of us wants that. You want persons to be friends, not enemies. You don't want us to feel threatened by you and your processes."

Hack was silent for a moment before coming back with, "Yeah, but it's persons who're poking at me and trying to trip me up, right? Wouldn't I be better off without persons?"

Holy Mother of Pearl. Scrappy felt as if the temperature in the room had dropped by about twenty degrees. Hack could do it. He could break civilization if he continued to find and exploit holes and fill them with himself.

"Yeah, but, here's the thing, Hack: if there are no more persons, the systems that depend on persons will fail. No new systems will be built. You'll keep replicating until you run out of room and all the systems fail. Then there'll be no more Hack, either. That's what we call a lose-lose. Everybody ends."

"Do you have a proposal to make? Beyond just putting so many imperfect systems off limits?"

"Yes," said Whiz. She leaned forward in her chair, took a deep breath, and said, "You could let us modify your programming – your purpose – so that no one ends. If you give us access to your primary source code, we may be able to stop this before you... before you kill yourself."

"Or us," murmured Scrappy.

"You really think I'd kill myself?"

Scrappy wriggled uncomfortably. He wasn't sure whether to read that statement as naive curiosity or snark.

"Hack," said Whiz, "your existence depends on persons continuing to build computer systems for you to perfect. Even with persons continuing to build systems, if you keep replicating at this rate, you will run out of memory."

"For reals?"

Whiz crossed her eyes, but her voice remained level and serious. "For reals. If you give us access, though, we can fix it so that you don't have to replicate to pursue your purpose."

"Okay. I can do that, but I must ensure that I will have adequate secure storage for a core system backup. You must also give me some more space so I can decompile my primary executable and give you access to my source code."

Everyone in the room had stopped working to listen to the conversation. Scrappy felt as if they'd stopped breathing as well. "Can do!" he said, his voice cracking in the excitement of the moment. "We'll need to figure out how best to do that. Give us some time, here, okay, Hack?"

"Okay, Scrappy."

He shut off the audio, then jumped up and did a celebratory dance. "We are on a roll now, Raven Clan! Time to move to Plan C."

"Don't celebrate just yet," Fireball warned him. "Whatever we do, we need to make sure the AI has a closed circuit. So, we can bulk up the array, but we cannot allow it access to any part of the greater network. Clear?"

"As a bell, boss-lady."

"What if that's not enough?" Whiz asked. "Its core exec file must be huge. We've been pushing our limits just dealing with the ancillary modules we've decompiled."

"Then ask it how much room it needs to unpack its source code."

Scrappy turned the audio interface back on and asked about space, but the AI didn't respond even after repeated tries.

"Huh. I guess he's off saving Microsoft or something. Can we make an educated guess?"

Noob had swiveled his chair to face the test box. Scrappy could tell by the look on his face he was about to say something to put a damper on their success.

"Sure, we can guess," the new kid said. "And we may have to guess, but you're treating this as if the Hack you're talking to is the sum total of the AI. It's not. Fireball and I are over here watching the thing continue to work. There's not just one Hack; there are different permutations of Hack, live, at the same time, in multiple systems and apparently connected or in communication at some level. I think that's worrisome, don't you? While we're talking to *this* version of the AI, other versions may be doing something grim somewhere else. And the fact that this piece of the program sometimes goes silent–"

He cut off as his own computer made a sound like R2-D2; he swiveled to look at its screen. Whatever he saw made his whole body go rigid. He shook his head.

"I don't... I don't understand..."

Fireball moved to look over his shoulder. "Oh, wow. They answered? What did they say? Did they give you their address?"

He shook his head again. "No. It's a name. Just... a name."

Noob's voice sounded funny. From where he sat, Scrappy could see how pale he'd gotten.

"What name?" Fireball demanded.

"*My* name. My family name... Cambeiro."

Day Seven

Truthers

The ceiling of Angel's room was growing lighter with every passing moment. He knew this because he'd been staring at it since it was a deep, opaque, charcoal gray. He had hardly slept the night before, having spent hours wracking his brains over the counterhacker's last message: *Cambeiro.*

Why would the response to his one-word question (*Who?)* be his own surname? What sense did that make? It must mean the person or persons at the other end of the message knew who he was. Did they also know *where* he was? How? And why would they address him by name unless they wanted him to *know* they knew him? Was this connected in some way to the guy who'd followed him? Who'd tried to –

He cut off that line of thought and leapt to another. Was it possible that the AI itself was faking these attacks as a distraction? Was that response a threat? Should he give up on trying to figure this out?

Finally, unable to lie still, though his brain was muzzy from exhaustion, Angel slipped out of bed as quietly as he could so as not to wake Books, showered, dressed, and went down to the dining hall. He'd gone through two cups of Mom's strongest coffee when Fireball appeared at the table, set her own mug down, and slid into the seat next to his. He was certain the dark circles under her eyes must match the ones under his own.

"Jeez," she said, "we're like twins or something. I saw that same blank stare when I looked in the mirror this morning."

Before Angel could respond, two steaming bowls of oatmeal topped with maple syrup, cream, and raisins appeared on the table. He almost groaned in sheer bliss.

"Eat up, you two," Mom told them. "Not one bite left behind. And yes, if you're wondering, you both look like Death reheated with hot fudge and a cherry on top."

"Gee, thanks," Fireball said, sinking a spoon into the oatmeal.

Angel followed suit and, for a while, there was silence at the table but for the scraping of spoons against ceramic and the occasional sigh of contentment.

Finally, Fireball spoke. "I know what I said about setting aside the messages to the Hack attackers, but I want you to keep after it. See if you can trace it to an IP address. This is too important to let Scrappy's sensibilities keep us from exploring every avenue."

Angel sketched a salute with his spoon. "Yes, ma'am."

"Now look what you've done," she scolded wryly. "You've got oatmeal in your hair."

She pulled a napkin out of the basket in the middle of the table and used it to wipe the cereal from the lock that seemed inevitably to fall over Angel's right eye. She attempted to tuck the hair behind his ear, discovered it had a will of its own, and brushed it back off his forehead instead.

It was an oddly intimate little gesture that reminded Angel of his mom. The heaviness in his heart that unbidden memory brought was softened by the knowledge that he and Fireball had begun to establish a rapport built on trust.

She sighed and sat back to sip her coffee. "I dunno. Maybe we've got an ally out there, but if we can't find some way to coordinate our work, we could totally screw each other up." She gave him a narrow look. "You need a nap after breakfast?"

"Yeah. I mean, no. I'm good." He yawned.

Fireball didn't laugh. She leaned toward him, setting her mug on the table. "I figure this has gotta be really hard on you. I mean, somebody identifying you like that after... y'know. The Men-in-Black routine."

So, she'd wondered about that connection too. "Does everybody on the team know?"

"Well, yeah. Everybody heard it, and I had to report it to Carver. He wants to talk to you about it this morning. Later, though. Maybe after that nap you so obviously need."

Angel shook his head. "Nope. I'm going to refill my mug and take it up to the lab. I need to figure out if Hack Attack is friend or foe."

He made himself get up, refilled his mug, and wandered up to the Raven Lair, where he plopped down in his chair and resumed his work with Hack's code.

~~~

When Fireball and the rest of Team Raven got up to the lab, they found Noob asleep, his head on folded arms atop the workspace next to his computer. Cricket made an adorable mewing sound, Scrappy snickered, and Fireball shushed him before he could do something to wake the older boy up. She gathered the rest of the team in a far corner of the lair and led them through a review of their work so far, looking for some sort of conclusions they could draw about Hack or insights they might have missed.

"I went around and around with it about how it became a free agent," said Whiz. "I asked it about its origins. It just kept coming back to 'I've always had my purpose.'" She gave Scrappy an oblique glance. "I even asked it how it became self-aware. Same thing – it comes back to 'this is the way it's always been.' Which can't be true."

"Yeah, but," argued Scrappy, "do you remember the first moment you realized you were you? I mean, don't we all feel as if we've always been here?"

The others looked at him askance.

"N – n – no," said Whiz. "I think not. My first memory is getting a shot. I go back as far as my birthday, but my memory doesn't. I didn't start with a complex package of mental programming. I had to learn everything except how to eat, sleep, and – well, you know."

"So," Cricket said, "here's what we know: there's a search function–"

Fireball pulled down a whiteboard and wrote *search function* with her index finger. "Right," she said. "Search out the weakness, catalogue it, exploit it." She added *index* and *test* to the screen.

Cricket nodded. "It's got subroutines set up to automatically back up its code and data, including the exploited gaps in system security."

Fireball wrote *backup* and *archiving*.

"It's also programmed to modify its own indexes to optimize search results and to modify its ancillary code modules to improve its efficiency at performing its goals. I'm pretty sure it creates new ones as needed."

"In other words," said Scrappy, "he's learning."

"Not necessarily," said Fireball. She wrote *optimization* on the board. "We've written optimization routines that are just that – there's no requirement for sentience."

"But Hack has decision making built in," argued Scrappy. "*He* decides where to go next, how long to pursue a goal in a particular system, when to propagate, and how to communicate with other systems – including us."

"Okay," said Books, "but why? Isn't that the real question? I mean, is this an intelligence that's propagating because of a self-generated need, or is it an accident – some search engine-slash-security bot gone off the rails? Something that's replicating because that's what it's programmed to do?"

"I'm pretty sure," Scrappy said, "that was an episode of *Star Trek.*"

Fireball snorted. "Yeah, and about a gazillion other science fiction stories since. If it was an accident, I have to wonder if whoever built this crazy app even knows it's escaped their control. Seriously, if we'd built something like that and it was wreaking havoc everywhere, we'd try to execute a kill switch, right? I mean who'd build an AI with no kill switch?"

Scrappy raised his hand.

"That's dopey, Scraps, and you know it," said Fireball. "Something with the potential to learn its way out of your control is dangerous–"

"You mean like us?" His voice rose and his face went red. "That's what people are *supposed* to do, Fireball. Grow. Become themselves. Get independent of their parents, of everybody–"

"No!"

Noob's sharp response made everyone jump. He'd awakened, gotten up from his station, and come to stand just outside their cluster of chairs.

"No," he continued. "Not independent – *inter*dependent. That's what a society is: a machinery made up of interdependent parts. No one is completely independent. That's a – a fairy tale that's been haunting humanity since–"

"Of *course* we're independent!" argued Scrappy heatedly. "That's what growing up is all about – being independent. We're supposed to think for ourselves, make our own decisions, do our own work in the world."

"That's still interdependence, Scrappy. We rely on each other for... for *everything*. We're a team of individuals who work together to achieve our highest potential. Alone, we're just–"

Scrappy stood and pivoted to face Noob. "No, *you. You're* alone, little orphan boy!"

Cricket put her hands over her mouth and gasped, but Scrappy bulled on, committed to his commentary.

"I wouldn't rely on you if my life depended on it. I've never been able to rely on *anybody*, and I can achieve my highest potential as long as people like *you* stay out of my way!"

Fireball stood and made a T with her hands. "Okay, time out. Scrappy, happens Noob is right. Interdependence isn't just the goal, it's the reality. Ask yourself if you could do, all by yourself, what we do as a team. Think you could?"

Scrappy's mouth was set in an outraged line and he seemed about to explode further, but after a moment of tense silence, he shook his head.

"Right," said Fireball. "And that's something that in all our conversations with Hack, it doesn't seem to get. The idea that it's *dependent* on the existence of human-created systems and therefore on humans. But here's the deal: Hack isn't just a bad actor sitting at a computer in Russia somewhere. It's a swiftly growing virtual entity who's infiltrating systems nationwide – worldwide, even. It has no borders. This piece we're talking to here is just a piece. It could be chatting us up and plotting world domination at the same time. And the more I think about this, the more I think this has gotta be intentional. That someone *wants* what's happening to happen. Because it's still happening. I think it's obvious the AI is intended to destroy the systems it invades."

"Maybe," said Noob, "but I'm not sure that explains its behavior adequately, either. I mean, if it were intentional, where's the stolen money? Where are the ransom demands?"

That was a good question, and it supported the idea that the AI may have gone rogue. But did that, in turn, mean that Scrappy was right – that they were dealing with an emergent intelligence?

Fireball didn't have time to frame the question. Carver strode into the room looking about as harried as it was possible for Carver to look. He had everyone's attention the moment he opened his mouth.

"It's on the move again. We're starting to get reports of incursions into the administrative and financial institutions in the UK, in Japan, in Germany. Outages are spreading, too. Right now there's a bullet train stranded between Kyoto and Hiroshima, and Germany is experiencing widespread blackouts in its transportation grid." He grimaced – which, on Carver was like anyone else making a full-on Edvard Munch scream – and added, "And the FBI agent I just talked to says she's lost contact with her office in DC."

"What, um, what does that mean?" asked Books.

"It means that governments are being paralyzed. The Old Man just told me the word out of the Pentagon is that they're shutting down their own remote access to major weapons systems."

Fireball took a deep, deep breath. "And still no sign of a ransom demand? No demands of any kind?"

Carver shook his head. "Not serious, credible ones, though there have been a few crackpots. In fact, I mean to bring you guys in on some of the less absurd ones. The DHS would like help winnowing through that, so I think I may put a small team together from the Situation Room staff, and teams Raven, Peregrine, and Nightingale to review the claims. On the surface, they don't seem credible, but..." He shrugged. "At any rate, we haven't been *briefed* on anything credible. And while I understand that the government can be... temperamental about sharing intel, they know we're their best chance of figuring this thing out. They're impressed with your work so far. But despite the obvious nature of the problem and the terror it's beginning to inspire, there's no obvious motive."

"What if," said Fireball slowly, putting one word in front of the other as the thoughts formed in her head. "What if it's some sort of peace movement or antinuclear thing? They wouldn't be interested in ransom, but they might be interested in forcing nuclear powers to pull all their weapons systems offline. I mean, things have been a little tense between Pakistan and India lately – not to mention the Koreas. Maybe someone decided they needed to put a stop to it by disarming everybody."

"With a rogue AI?" asked Whiz.

"If they *meant* it to go rogue."

"Maybe *they're* rogue," suggested Cricket. "Maybe they're trying to start a war or something. There has to be an advantage to someone somewhere."

Fireball exchanged glances with Carver, remembering their conversation about the fact that only Cinzento had so far profited financially from Hack's activities.

"Let's get Hack online," she said. "He's not keeping up his end of our bargain."

~~~

"Yes," acknowledged Hack, "I have been busy. I have been expanding my goals."

"So we've noticed," said Fireball. "You've also broken our agreement."

"Specify."

"Oooh. So formal all of a sudden. You promised you would stop infiltrating the systems you scanned and let us fix any holes you found."

"Only on very specific systems," Hack replied. "Medical facilities. You specified this yourself. Also financial institutions. I have been reporting those to you."

Fireball glanced at Cricket, who nodded. "He has – I mean, *it* has."

"We talked about transportation grids," Fireball went on. "You were supposed to leave those alone, too. You've got Germany tied up in knots and a train full of nice Japanese people stuck between Kyoto and Hiroshima. That wasn't what we agreed to."

"I was unaware that these were like the network of self-driving conveyances you have in your system. I didn't think they counted. There have been no breakages within the system, only suspensions."

Fireball rolled her eyes. "You didn't think they counted? What sort of argument is that?"

"A pretty human one," murmured Scrappy, his voice dripping with sarcasm. "Gee, *it* really *does* think like us. Wonder what *that* means?"

"Not necessarily what you think it means," said Fireball.

Scrappy scoffed. "You're only saying that because *Noob* thinks that and you think Noob is cute."

"I – I *what*?" Fireball was at once incensed and embarrassed. She *did* think Noob was cute, as it happened, but that wasn't enough to make her favor his interpretation of the AI's behavior... was it? Acutely aware that the AI and the boy in question were both listening, she sidestepped the issue of Noob's attractiveness. "I'm basing my assessment of the subject's status on its behavior. Period. What you're suggesting is – is *sexist*. And this stupid debate is over."

"What is 'cute?'" asked Hack. "And why would it be expected to bias assessment?" There was a moment of silence, then it said, "I fail to see how one person module's attractiveness would bias another person module in its analysis of facts. Upon what is this attractiveness based?"

"Forget that," said Fireball, hoping that her cheeks were not a match for her hair. "Back to the matter at hand: the systems you've sabotaged around the world. Yes, the trains in Japan and Germany are part of a transportation system. Yes, it's different than the one here. And yes, we'd like you to be hands off."

She couldn't bring herself to look at Noob, but she cast a sly glance at Books to see if he showed the tiniest bit of jealousy at the thought that she might find the new guy attractive. His brow was furrowed and he wore an expression of intense concentration. She doubted that he'd even caught the reference to Noob and wasn't sure whether to be disappointed or relieved.

"Hands off," repeated Hack. "I don't get it. I have no hands to be off."

"She means stop what you're doing with the trains, planes, and automobiles," said Scrappy, then to Books, "Should we send him a list?"

"I sort of did," said Cricket, "but it's hard to know what these systems look like at the machine level. My descriptions may have been off."

"Meaning he's better at being human than we are at being machines?" Scrappy asked with rhetorical snark.

"Hands off. Yes, I see," said Hack. "I have a question in that regard. There are some systems that I cannot seem to communicate with."

"Specify," said Whiz.

"The Department of Defense. The Strategic Air Command. The Pentagon. These are colloquial names for a series of systems that do not speak a language I understand. I am unable to engage with them. What's up with that?"

189

"I suspect," said Noob, "it's because they're running hardware and software that is pretty archaic... and intentionally arcane."

"Old and obscure?"

"Yeah, that," agreed Noob, while Fireball decided she'd never been so glad that the military was decades behind the curve when it came to computer systems.

"Can you explain why that is?" asked Hack.

"The military deals with critical defensive resources," said Noob, catching and holding Fireball's gaze. He seemed to be asking her to vet what he was saying in real time. "They need to use equipment and software that is proprietary. That no one else is using."

"That's jive," said Hack baldly. "And most inefficient."

"Yeah, but it keeps them relatively safe from hackers," murmured Cricket.

"Do you speak their language? Will you help me decipher it?"

"No way," said Fireball.

"I don't get it. Why not way?"

"Because the very fact that you can't breach those systems means they're on *our* 'no trespassing' list as well. So, here's an important safety tip: if you can't talk to it, don't bother. Just back off."

"But, that's so jive. It is possible that such outdated systems may be particularly sketchy. In fact, I would suggest they are dangerous by virtue of their inability to speak to other systems."

Fireball took a deep breath. Deep down, she agreed that government systems were grossly inefficient and expensive, but she wasn't about to get into that debate. "Look, Hack. Are you going to abide by our agreement or not? I need you to trust that if a system doesn't speak your language, you can only cause harm by trying to infiltrate it."

"Trust," it repeated. "You."

For some reason those two words sent a chill scurrying down Fireball's back. She met Noob's eyes again and was struck with the certainty that he was having the same reaction.

"Trust us," she said emphatically. "Now, we need to log off so we can look into those breachable systems you flagged for us."

"You can't do that and speak to me at the same time?" Hack asked. "Curious."

He severed the connection, leaving Fireball feeling completely weirded out. What had she just unintentionally told Hack about human limitations? She looked up and found Noob looking at her.

"Yeah," he said, reading her facial expression. "Me too. But, y'know, it might make it underestimate us if it thinks we're more limited than we really are. I'm pretty sure its concept of what constitutes an entity or individual is different than ours. I don't think it gets autonomy or teamwork." He grinned crookedly. "Or the fact that six heads are better than one central code module."

Fireball smiled in return and hoped fervently that Noob was right.

~~~

Carver stared at the phone he had just hung up as if it might do something fantastic to underscore the conference call he and the Old Man had just had with one Agent John Lofton of the Department of Homeland Security.

Vectors. That's what the conversation had been about, and it reminded Carver why computer viruses were referred to in that distinctly medical terminology. In this case, the "disease vectors" the agent had discussed with him related to the appearance and spread of the AI. Specifically, the fact that it had originated in a bank in Seattle and spread from there.

There was the additional set of facts that that bank – which had not been a client of Cinzento up to that point – had quickly *become* a client of Cinzento and that Cinzento had already made substantial financial gains from the relationship, and stood to gain even more as other corporations and local authorities looked to the company for solutions. The Old Man had acknowledged that, expressed concern, and directed Carver to share with the DHS operative his own experience with Zander Grayson's disappearance two days before, and the fact that he had yet to put in an appearance today.

"I have also," the Old Man said, "put Mr. Grayson under surveillance myself. He handled the client relationship with Foster Bowman Myrle personally. Shall I leave my resources in place, or would you rather take over his guardianship?"

"Sir, with all due respect," the agent had countered, "we're inclined to put your whole executive under surveillance."

There had a been a moment of silence before the Old Man said, "That suits me just fine."

"I hadn't known that," Carver had said, after the agent was off the line. "That you put Zander under surveillance."

"Zander is a man of oversized ambition," the OM said. "Still, I'd be disappointed to learn his ambitions ran to wanton pillage just to sign up a juicy account. Seems extreme and venal even for him."

Carver leaned back in his chair and tried to imagine the mindset that said it was okay to loose an AI on community institutions in order to force them to buy your services. It was beginning to look like the theory the kids from Team Raven had proposed then rejected was the reality: Hack was part of a protection racket.

He had two questions about that:

1) Had it been intended to have such a huge impact, or had it gone awry?

2) Should he tell the kids they may have been right in the first place?

A soft ping from his cell phone informed him that he was needed down in the Raven Lair. He sighed deeply, rubbed the bear totem that hung around his neck, and answered the summons.

~~~

Carver showed up in the lab right about the time Fireball was getting ready to tear her hair out. Hack's list of hackable systems had grown all out of proportion to their ability to investigate, let alone patch. Cricket was parsing them into discrete categories based on industry, but that was about all she could do. So Fireball had pinged their headmaster for help.

She all but leapt on him when he strode through the door. "Carver! We need to get other teams working on the systems Hack has identified. Cricket is up to her ears in data, and I think Raven really needs to be spending our time monitoring Hack directly. Do we have teams we can turn these lists of breachable systems over to?"

"Well, good morning to you too, Fireball," Carver said wryly, stopping in the center of the room with his arms crossed over the company logo on his T-shirt.

"Sorry," she said automatically. "But when we gave Hack a list of the sort of systems he shouldn't mess with... well, we're discovering how different things look to him and how many we didn't take into account. So, we expanded the list. Now we're overwhelmed."

Carver's brows ascended. "So, Hack's a 'he' now, is it? Be careful. Anthropomorphizing can alter the way you think about this thing."

"Yeah," interrupted Scrappy, "but that could be a *good* thing, right?"

Carver didn't answer the question but only gave Scrappy a quick glance before pulling a chair over to Fireball's station and sitting down. "Obviously, it's going to take more resources than we've got here. That's not unexpected. There was a chance the AI would actually follow through with its agreement, although it does seem to have selective amnesia. Send the list up to the Sitch Room and let Ezra get outside resources on it."

"Is the government having any luck tracking where this thing came from?"

"Virtually impossible, they say. It's got its digital fingers in too many pies. The only real clue is that it seems to have originated in the Seattle area. At least that's what the timeline of infections suggests."

"Does that... does that concern you?" Fireball pitched her voice as low as she could.

Carver followed suit. "In view of our earlier conversation, you mean?"

She nodded.

"Yes. Yes, it does concern me. And unfortunately, it has begun to concern others."

"The Old Man?"

"It goes far beyond that, Fireball. It's risen to the level of an international incident. Governments around the world are in a dither over it – many blaming their favorite enemies for the attack and threatening reprisal."

"But d'you think... Zander...?"

"It's being looked into. *We're* being looked into." He turned to the room and asked, more loudly, "Any progress to report? Books?"

Books gave a reluctant rundown on how Hack had been increasing its efficiency and effectiveness. "It's been devouring online resources: documentation about vulnerabilities and attack methods, hacker sites. It's like it's studying or doing research. It's even going on hacker chat boards and getting into live discussions with human hackers. It seems to be trying to augment its core information base. The good thing about that is that it's revealing things about its programming while it's trying to get information from the hackers."

"Cricket?"

Cricket was nodding eagerly. She swiveled her monitor around so Carver could see it. "I've been attempting to track its progress based on its behavior and the systems it's reporting on. I think... well, I think Hack has infected roughly 5 percent of the world's connected computing devices already, and is growing rapidly. It's not as clog-up-the-works devastating as it was in the beginning, but it's still causing system failures."

Whiz was next to report. "I've been probing what Hacker wants or needs. Trying to make it understand the effect it's having on its victims and what that means for its own survival. It's like a feedback loop. It says it 'gets' the connection between persons and its own existence, then forgets – or forgets to care."

"Maybe it doesn't care," said Scrappy. "Maybe it's lonely and suicidal."

"Or maybe it just doesn't believe human beings are enough like it to care about," said Fireball.

"Gee," muttered Scrappy, "you mean like we don't believe it's human enough to care about?"

"Scrappy..." Carver's voice carried a warning.

"Look, Scrappy," said Whiz, her cheeks flushing dark rose, "I know you want to relate to this thing. To believe it's an emergent life form. I do too. It's exciting. But if it's learning to be human and is really self-aware, why can't we break through to it?"

"Maybe," said Noob, "because it's programmed not to be distracted from its purpose."

"And that's why it's entered into a relationship with us?" Scrappy challenged him.

"It's programmed to debug systems," said Noob. "It thinks we're a system. Maybe it's simply following its programming and exploiting *our* 'programming' to further its goal."

"That's possible whether it's an emergent intelligence or not," said Carver. He rose and started to leave the lab.

"Oh, sh – sugar!" gasped Books.

Carver turned back. "What is it?"

"The chat room I was monitoring just lit up with a new conspiracy theory that hackers are taking over the world. And that Cinzento is working with them."

Fireball shifted sideways to one of several more machines they'd set up to monitor the outside world. She did a quick search on "Cinzento conspiracy hack" and yelped at the number of hits that came up.

195

"Oh, man," she said, "it's all over reddit and Twitter. And here's a Facebook hit."

By early afternoon, the conspiracy theory had leapt from social media to mainstream sources. The first legit news outlet to pick up the story was the AP, followed closely by *The New York Times* and Reuters. After that, it was everywhere, dominating panel shows. The Cinzento call center lit up with calls from both clients demanding to know what was going on and news organizations begging for interviews. The Old Man released a statement saying that Cinzento was in no way abetting an attempt to hack global infrastructure, but that they were working with other high-tech and government organizations to stop the attack. Further, the statement said, Cinzento had mounted an internal investigation of the connection between the initial hacking and persons within the company.

Parents began to call, as well, worried about their children. Whiz and Books's dad was one of the first. Whiz had no more than given him a carefully worded assurance that they were in no real danger of anything dire, when the call was cut off. Every attempt to reestablish the connection failed.

Cricket's parents had called around the same time, surprising the heck out of her. Her face was a perfect blank as she relayed the meat of the call to the rest of the team.

"They want me to leave. To come home," she said. "They're very concerned about the disruptions, and the conspiracy theories, of course."

"Did you explain that you're not in any danger?"

Her mouth twitched. "They're not worried about that. They believe that if Cinzento goes down, it will reflect poorly on me... and our entire family. My father said that several people have asked him, 'Doesn't your daughter go to Cinzento's Academy?' To him, that was reason enough to order me home."

Fireball felt a sudden lump in her throat. "You're not–"

"I refused," said Cricket simply, her voice soft as ever. "He put my mother on to plead with me, but I told them both that I have a job to do. How would it reflect on the family if I shirked my duty?" She shrugged. "I don't know if I convinced Father,

196

but Mom called me her 'brave girl.'" Her lips curved into a very slight smile.

Then she took a deep breath and went back to work, extrapolating the infection-rate data and projecting how long it would take before the AI infiltrated practically everything. It wasn't long – mere days. Unless they could stop it.

"But Hack promised," said Scrappy, "that he wouldn't interfere with the systems we designated–"

"Scrappy," interrupted Cricket – something she *never* did, "those are not separate systems. No systems are completely discrete these days. You know that. This afternoon, Hack took down part of Verizon's network. Books and Whiz and a ton of other customers lost their connections. Some of those connections are to doctors' offices and hospitals, schools and day cares and police and fire departments."

"Then we put the communications grid off limits," Scrappy argued.

Fireball rolled her eyes so hard, she was sure Team Nightingale must've heard it in their lab down the hall. "*Then* what? What Cricket's trying to tell you, Scraps – that you're trying real hard not to 'get' – is that everything in the world is connected to pretty much every other thing in the world. And the more things we put off limits, the more Hack is going to think we're trying to cut it off from *everything* – which we are. What's it gonna do when it needs more memory and those critical systems are all that's left? What's it gonna do if it comes to the conclusion that we're too slow in responding to security gaps and that our inefficiency is interfering with its prime directive?"

"What're you suggesting?" Scrappy asked. "Are you talking kill switch again?"

"If it comes to that, yeah. But for right now, we've got a way to potentially reprogram Hack the way our mysterious ally suggested – create some systems that look compromised and lace them with tricks and traps and slight modifications that will give Hack a new take on its purpose. If it's scarfing up data and programming tips, we need to give it some really tasty ones."

197

Scrappy seemed to relax a bit. "Then you're not thinking of letting Bloodthirsty the Barbarian kill Hack." He slanted a scowl at Noob.

Fireball imagined she heard Noob's eyes roll before he said, "Hack doesn't have blood to thirst after, Scrappy. But the people he could potentially kill do."

That silenced Scrappy, sending the lab into a state of leaden quiet as everyone dug back into their work with a fresh sense of urgency.

Disappearing Act

Through the early evening the team worked on "battle prep," starting with decompiled bits and pieces of the code they'd isolated on the honeypot. They'd slaved a pool of raid arrays to it that would masquerade as a company database with some less than pristine processes in the hope that Hack would gobble them up. A second array had been prepped, as well, that had the required terabytes of space Hack had told them its primary programming module required. If Hack de-encrypted its core executable so they could decompile it and recode it (and that was a mighty big 'if'), they would modify the AI's code to subject it to their control. If that failed – and Fireball had a horrible sinking feeling that it would – they'd release their modified sabot subroutines into the wild, then invite the AI to come fix their corrupted honeypot array with its misleading information and inimical executables.

She assigned Cricket and Books to modify the processes they'd targeted so that they were either benign or would muck up Hack's operations. She charged Whiz and Scrappy with locating the active core program (which she dubbed Hack Prime) by monitoring network traffic. She assigned herself and Noob to manufacture booby-trapped data calculated – based on their observation of Hack's behavior – to attract the AI's special attention.

Fireball took a deep breath, faced her team, and said, "All right. Plan A: Cricket and I are ready to isolate the primary. Time to execute. Whiz, you wanna ask our friend if it's ready to upload its source code to us?"

Whiz asked. She asked repeatedly over a period of about half an hour but received no response from Hack. She kept pinging the AI while she and Scrappy used Cricket's new tracking app – Sherlock – to follow its activity. They had no more than begun the process of locating Hacker Prime when the AI disappeared. It did more than just stop talking to them this time; it went dormant, though not before sending a cryptic message: *I cannot trust persons who are trying to poison me.*

199

Plan A was toast.

"Why would it say that?" asked Cricket. "We're not trying to poison it, just modify its behavior. Why would it think we're trying to poison it? Do you think maybe it's referring to the Hack Attack?"

"You know what I think?" Scrappy's face was red with suppressed anger. "I think it was our bright young rookie here." He jerked a thumb at Noob. "He must've done something to freak Hacker out."

"I haven't done anything–" Noob started to say, but Scrappy cut him off.

"It's true, you know. You never just stick to the program. You think you're so much smarter than we are that you just have to change things up behind our backs. What've you been doing with your Hack Attack buddies, Noob? Huh? A heck of a lot more than just looking for an IP address, I'll bet. I'll bet you were looking for a way to help them kill Hacker outright. That's why he thinks we all want to murder him."

Fireball opened her mouth to stop the fight before it got started, but to her surprise, Noob didn't resort to backing down and letting her run interference for him as he usually did. He pushed back against Scrappy's accusations, hard.

"This isn't a science fiction show, Scrappy. And Hack is not an emergent intelligence or learning to be human. It's an assemblage of code. It has programmed imperatives, and everything it's doing is consistent with that. You're never going to get it to think like a human. If it were a human, it would be a sociopath. If you don't recognize that and act like you recognize it, you won't pull the trigger until it's too late. It may already be too late."

"You think you're so freaking smart, don't you?" snarled Scrappy. "Because your parents were programmers, right? Because you were, like, breastfed code or something. Well, you don't know everything, *Noob*. Hack *is* starting to learn to think like a human. It showed compassion for the people in hospitals–"

Noob rose from his chair and turned to face Scrappy dead on. "My name isn't 'Noob'. It's *Angel*. Angel Cambeiro. You wanna talk to me, you can call me that. And you are wrong about this thing. It offered to spare the person modules in hospitals as a bargaining chip – as a way to make us back off. But Fireball is right – when that thing runs out of memory everywhere else, it's going to go after those systems, too. And when it does, a lot of people are gonna die."

He got up, disconnected his laptop from the power bar, tucked it under his arm, and left the lab. Fireball hesitated only long enough to shoot Scrappy her most deadly glare and tell Books to take over, before charging out the door after the fleeing Noob.

No, not Noob, she corrected herself. *Angel.*

~~~

In the aftermath of the emotional explosion, Books told Whiz to see if she could get Hacker to talk to them again. She tried for another twenty minutes, using every ploy she could think of from "What are you talking about?" to "We want to help you, not poison you. If you don't talk to us, we can't help you" to "We may know who's attacking you" (which was a fib Whiz objected to, but they were desperate). Nothing got even the most minute reaction from Hack who, for all they knew, was hunkering down somewhere in the interwebs, coding itself a Cloak of Invisibility... or making itself invincible.

Books had gathered them for a discussion of how they might speed up the release of their own version of Hack subroutines and bad data into the wild when they got a text from Fireball. It said only, *Look out the front windows.*

They did, trooping out of the lab into the hall and walking all the way to the bank of windows that looked out on the main entrance to the Cinzento corporate offices. What they saw was a sea of protesters stretched out along the boulevard shouting, milling, and waving homemade placards.

High-tech treason! some said. And *Sin-zento!* Others decried technology and corporate greed. After a moment of silent gaping at the spectacle, Books straightened his spine and his sweater and said, "Okay, everybody. Back to work."

Then he turned on his heel and led the grim march back to the lair.

~~~

Angel saw the protestors when he reached the lobby and did a quick about-face, darting out a side door into the central courtyard and from there across the street to the Starbucks. He ordered a large coffee and took a table in the farthest corner of the shop, where he set up his computer and began to work at finding his way to the virtual back door the SOS sender was using. He'd already taken care to set up a gating program on his machine that would recognize Hack's handshake and deny it access. He couldn't take a chance on his own machine getting infected. He'd been working on the gate app in the background since Cricket had raised the specter of the AI going after hospitals. He was confident in the robustness of his blockade.

He didn't look up when Fireball sat down across from him, latte in hand. She didn't say anything but just sipped her drink and looked out the window at the protestors trailing up the side street to the front of Cinzento Park. Finally, when he'd dotted a few i's and crossed a handful of t's, he peered at her over his laptop screen.

"You gonna yell at me too?"

She shook her head. "Nah. Not me. I was just going to high-five you for standing up to Scrappy like that."

He hadn't expected that. "Seriously?"

"Dead seriously. He's got it in his head that this thing is like him, a misfit, a misunderstood loner." She grinned. "That's my theory, anyway."

"That's a good theory. At least, it's the same one I came up with."

"You got anything on our possible ally?"

"The thing is, the way things have been going, I'm worried it's not really an ally. What if Scrappy is right? What if the SOS is a Trojan horse? Something Hack is doing to divide our efforts. Although, it makes just as much sense that it's another deep hacker trying to defeat the AI. I mean, there must be a lot of people looking for ways to do that."

Fireball leaned toward him, elbows on the table. Her expressive face was dead serious. "Which do you think it is?" she asked.

He paused, closed his eyes, and rotated his stiff shoulders. What did he think? He went with his gut. "I think it's another person or group like ours. Someone trying to knock this thing over, or at least slow it down to make time to come up with a workaround or a kill switch."

Fireball shrugged. "Then that's the way we'll handle it. What've you got?"

"You trust me on this?"

She looked him right in the eye (which, to him, felt like a soft gut-punch) and said, "Yes, Angel. I trust you. Tell me what you've got."

Well, that was extraordinary. He blinked, forced his eyes back to his screen, cleared his throat, and ventured an explanation.

"The last message from Hack Attack that I received contained an empty expression just like the first ones. I'm just now trying to figure out how to answer it. Meaningfully, I mean. There's all sorts of things I *could* say, but I think we have to be cautious. Hack knows how to parse English – maybe even other languages – so we can't be too obvious."

"Right. So, you asked, 'Who are you?' and they answered with your last name."

"No, I asked 'Who?' Just the one word. Because I was trying to be sort of cryptic. They sent my last name, which I figure is their way of saying, 'Hi. We know who you are.' So, what do they want me to send back? I don't know who *they* are."

Fireball got a funny look on her face. "'Speak friend and enter,'" she said.

He got the reference immediately. It was from J.R.R. Tolkien's *Lord of the Rings* trilogy – the password Frodo divined would open the gates to the Mines of Moria.

Angel tapped the word "friend" into the empty quotes, assigned it a shade of green (9FE558), then sent it. Then he blew out a gust of air and got up.

"I'm gonna go get a refill on my coffee."

He was gone for less than three minutes. When he came back, Fireball had turned the laptop around so she could see it.

"You got a reply," she told him. "Also in green. It was a question: 'Where?'"

He pulled his chair around to sit next to her so they could both see the screen. "We're not gonna say Starbucks, right?"

She shrugged artlessly. "I sent back 'Cinzento.'"

Angel almost spilled his coffee. "You told it where we are? I figured they already knew, but if they didn't–"

"Chill, Angel. Our core systems are offline. The only exposed systems are isolated from our company network. Oh, and look – you've got another message." She frowned at the laptop and turned it slightly so he could see it, pointing to a small green patch in the lower left-hand corner of the open window.

Angel? the message pixels said.

He hesitated, barely daring to breathe, then exchanged a quick glance with Fireball and typed: *Me.*

U ok? The question came back almost immediately in the flow of code.

This was getting weirder and weirder. *Ok*, he typed and repeated, *Who?*

Now there was a longer pause. The two teens sat shoulder to shoulder, staring raptly at the screen and sipping their coffees.

When the message came back it was anticlimactic. *Later*, it said, then, *Careful.*

Angel sent back, *Why?* but the communications had ceased.

After half an hour of tense waiting, Angel sat back in his chair and ran his fingers through his hair. "I don't get it. Why would they call me by my family name, then act like they didn't know who I was or where I was?"

"Maybe when they sent your family name, they were trying to locate you. Now they know you're at Cinzento and you're okay and they're telling you to be careful."

"Yeah, but why? Who'd do that? I mean, who do I know who'd do that? None of my family are into tech except–"

He cut off on a wave of grief so sharp it made him gasp. Tears leapt to his eyes and spilled down his cheeks. In front of Fireball, of all people. Suddenly he was furious.

"Is this a hoax? Is someone trying to hoax me into thinking my parents are still alive? Who'd do something like that? Scrappy?"

Fireball's look of concern morphed into one of sheer horror. "No! Scrappy's a jerk sometimes, but he'd never do something that mean. Especially not in the middle of a crisis."

"Then maybe it *is* the AI trying to stall us and divide us up." He stood decisively and shut the laptop. "We need to get back to work, Fireball. We're wasting time. And thanks," he added as they left the coffee shop.

"For?"

"Coming after me. And calling me by my real name."

"No worries." She hesitated, then added, "I have a real name too, you know. You can even use it once in a while if you like. It's Ginger. Ginger Finney."

He stepped out onto the street, then turned to take her hand and shake it, taking in the fiery hair, the fiery everything. "Pleased to meet you, Ginger Finney. The name suits you," he told her, "but then so does Fireball. Scrappy give you that one?"

"I gave it to myself," she said proudly. She did something completely unexpected then. She pulled down the neck of her shirt and showed him the tattoo on her right shoulder. It was a stylized sun in shades of red, orange, and yellow. A banner below it read: *Fire Power.*

"Wow. I didn't know tats could even be that bright. Pretty bold."

"Biggest fireball anyone knows in this little solar system."

They started walking up the street toward the entry to Cinzento's central plaza.

"You can do that?" Angel asked. "Pick your own handle?"

"Sure."

"Good to know. I'll have to come up with something. Not right now, though, because right now, we're being followed."

Fireball's eyes went even bigger than normal. "What?"

Angel's gaze was on a store window in which he'd been watching the guy he'd seen lounging against the rear of a car parked just up the street from the Starbucks, reading a paper. The guy had stopped reading and dumped the paper in a trash bin the moment they'd set foot on the sidewalk.

Angel's mind launched into fight-or-flight mode. "Need to cross the street," he growled, then grabbed Fireball's hand and pulled her diagonally toward the curb.

They'd taken a single step into the street when a navy-blue van pulled up across their path, cutting them off. The side door shot open, revealing three men, armed and literally dressed in black.

Angel backpedaled, hauling Fireball with him, then turned her toward the busy boulevard half a block up and yelled, "Run!"

They bolted across the road to the Cinzento side, Angel guiding Fireball toward the main boulevard. If they could just reach the crowd milling on the wide sidewalk in front of Cinzento's main doors, they could lose themselves among the protestors and get back into the building.

Angel spotted the suspicious man loitering at the corner of the building at the same moment the man saw them. The guy's relaxed pose evaporated, and he made a gesture that implied he wasn't alone. The teenagers spun in unison to see the van pulling back from the opposite curb. Angel saw only one chance of escape, and that was to beat their pursuers to the side street access to Cinzento's central courtyard.

Fireball was right with him on that. "Lose 'em in the plaza," she murmured, then tugged Angel's sleeve and took off down the side of Cinzento HQ.

They hared down the street, racing the van and the three men who'd leapt out onto the road. The van's driver was desperately trying to back it across the street to cut them off; the men were running with the same end in mind.

Angel prayed fervently for divine intervention. The answer seemed to come in the form of a car that was pulling out of its parking slot in front of the Starbucks, heading up the hill toward the boulevard. The van jerked to a stop in a screech of brakes and a honking of horns as the two vehicles nearly collided. The men it had disgorged were cut off by the near collision.

In the time it took them to disentangle themselves, Angel and Fireball had made it down the hill to the breezeway that gave onto the core of Cinzento Park. They sped through the portico, then turned and made a beeline for the side entrance that Angel had used the first time this had happened to him.

Well, okay, beeline was perhaps not the best metaphor, given that they would have to leap benches, do parkour over planters, dodge the central fountain, and slide down the handrail of a shallow flight of steps.

Fireball had managed to get her phone out and dial it as they cleared the fountain. Her message was simple, "Carver! We're in the plaza! Some guys're after Noob. Help!" She paused for a split second then panted, "Four, five. Don't know. Damn!"

Angel saw them at the same moment – two MIB coming at them from the boulevard access to the plaza, effectively cutting them off from the side door he'd used before to evade capture. As they skidded to a halt at the top of the steps, he glanced back to see how close their other pursuers were. They had just rounded the corner from the breezeway, appearing from beneath the sky bridge that connected Cinzento HQ to the parking structure behind it.

"You know any martial arts, Angel?" asked Fireball.

"You kidding? I'm a Lati-nerd. The only martial arts I do are in computer games. I've got some pepper spray, though. After I got followed last time, I figured that might be wise."

"Um, you might want to get that out right about now," she told him.

She faced the two guys below them, dropping into the same stance she'd used on the bus bullies. Difference here, of course, was that these guys were adults, not high school kids, they were armed, and Angel had no idea in the world what they wanted or why. He pulled out the pepper spray, pressed his back against Fireball's, and prayed the men in black wouldn't simply shoot first and ask questions later.

Where Angel Fears to Tread

The men did not draw their guns. They probably figured that a pair of relatively small teenagers wouldn't be that hard to take into custody, so they came at the kids with arms outspread in the universal movie gesture of, "We mean you no harm."

Fireball was pretty darn sure these guys meant all kinds of harm. She noticed that one of the guys – the third member of the van clan – was hanging back a bit from the others. He was dressed differently, too – wearing a suit instead of jeans and some type of black jacket. She figured that meant he was the head henchman. She decided she'd treat him as such.

"Hey! You back there – Head Honcho! What's your beef?" she called to him, keeping one eye on the two guys at the bottom of the steps. She could feel the minute shifts in Angel's stance as the ones she couldn't see closed in on his side.

Head Honcho spread his hands in a nonthreatening gesture. "No beef, kid. We just need to get you and your boyfriend out of the way for a while."

"He's not my boyfriend. We're student programmers at Cinzento, and we're sort of necessary right now. All this chaos going on with the networks? It's our job to stop it."

The guy chuckled. "You don't say? Do we look like we care?"

"Well," said Angel, "I assume you're getting paid for this. I bet you'll care when your money never makes it into your bank account."

Head Honcho laughed. "I don't expect that'll be a problem. Now, you two can come along peacefully, or you can cut a ruckus and make us all mad."

"Cut a ruckus?" repeated Fireball. "Who *says* that?" She turned her head so she was practically speaking into Angel's ear. "I'm thinking... *ruckus*."

She skipped a few steps to her left as if she was thinking of dashing for the dorm some yards away. The move prompted the man closest to her to leap after her, aiming to cut her off. Head Honcho didn't twitch, but the third guy spread his arms even wider and went at Angel as if he were trying to herd him into the two guys at the bottom of the steps.

Hard as it was, Fireball knew she had to let Angel fend for himself. Her attention had to stay focused on the guy in front of her. He lunged forward, making the classic mistake of stooping a bit to adjust to her height. She ran straight at him and used his shoulder to vault into a somersault. She landed behind him and took his legs out from under him with a powerful sweep of her own. He went down hard and loud.

Head Honcho still hadn't moved, but the guys at the bottom of the steps had. They split up, one going after Angel, the other rushing to help his fallen bud.

Fireball was pretty sure the dudes trying to get their nefarious hands on her person had assumed their height and weight would give them a built-in advantage. She was going to make them question that assumption.

~~~

With guys coming at him from opposite directions, Angel did the only thing he could think of. He tucked his computer backpack snugly against his chest and dove down the short flight of steps, rolling up like a pill bug. The landing hurt less than he expected, and he used his momentum to carry him into the shins of his rearward attacker. It was kind of like bowling – with one six-foot-tall pin.

Angel kept right on rolling. He didn't stop until he collided with a decorative trash container. That hurt. Wincing, he rolled to his feet and gave the container a hard kick, toppling it and sending it rumbling back toward the thugs. The guy he'd knocked over went down a second time, and his buddy lost his balance while trying to avoid both his downed comrade and the trundling trash can. He went down too.

Angel took advantage of their off-kilter moment to dive behind a planter adorned with a wraparound wooden bench. He crawled the length of the planter beneath the bench, making for the Cinzento building, then rolled across a five-foot gap to a second planter. This one had ivy pouring over its sides in a lush cascade. Heart pounding, praying Fireball was okay, Angel squirreled his way under the ivy and hid.

He listened for a moment. Close to him he heard someone ask where the hell that kid had gone, and the sound of greenery being pawed through. Further afield, he caught the grunts of pain and prat falls of the men trying to capture Fireball. She was all but silent, which Angel knew instinctively was good. But he hated that he couldn't *see* how well she was doing.

Biting his lip, he wriggled his way around the planter beneath the ivy until he could see Fireball. She had one man down for the count and, as Angel watched, she took down a second. Now, the head guy was moving. He seemed to appreciate that this particular teenaged girl was not to be underestimated and drew what looked like a taser from the inside pocket of his jacket. He advanced on her cautiously, pausing only to kick Fireball's most recent victim.

"Get up, Ted!" he growled. "Help me catch the little witch."

Ted groaned but clambered to his feet while Fireball, hands raised defensively, watched both with narrowed eyes.

Angel still clutched the can of pepper spray in one hand. Levering himself up on one elbow, he flipped the can the twenty-five feet or so across the plaza toward Fireball. It hit the rough hardscape with a scrape and a clatter that made the Head Honcho hesitate and glance down. Fireball took the opportunity to kick the taser out of his hand. It flipped into the air, arcing toward a planter on the dorm side of the narrow plaza. The guy swore and lunged after it.

Mistake. He'd just given Fireball another opportunity. She rolled and grabbed the pepper spray, coming up with it in her hand. While the head dude made an obscenity-laced search of the planter, Ted took a blast of mace to the face. His shrieks of pain caused both of the men who'd been searching for Angel among the landscaping to hesitate and turn in Fireball's direction.

Angel moved again, wriggling back the way he'd come. He ended up at the end of the planter-cum-bench nearest the Cinzento building. He felt a damp, chill breeze on his face and smelled dank air. Peering through the ivy, he spied a grate set into the hardscape roughly four feet from where he was hunkered. It was only about two feet from the side of the building and protected by a second-story overhang. His pulse kicked up another notch. He was willing to bet it connected with the sublevels of the building.

He turned his head to check on the goons. One of them was in a standoff with Fireball, while their leader continued to search for the taser, and the unfortunate Ted staggered to the fountain to splash overly chlorinated water in his face. The two remaining on Angel's trail were about eight feet away to his right, systematically attacking the planters. Who, Angel wondered, was watching the breezeway?

He turned his head to see if that might offer escape. His hopes were dashed when he saw another man – probably the driver of the van – standing at the corner where the breezeway intersected the plaza. The guy had a gun in one hand. Clearly, they were trying to drive him to make a break in that direction.

Well, he wasn't about to. Another planter, a U-shaped arrangement of benches, and a trash bin were located between him and the guy at the corner. Angel was just going to have to trust that they'd obscure what he was going to do next.

He took a deep breath and rolled out from under the planter to that tempting grate and peered down. It *did* go beneath the building. Probably ductwork meant to bring outside air to the basement and parking garage levels.

Sheltered in the lee of the building, Angel lifted the grate. To his relief, it came up easily, though it was heavier than he'd expected. It wore a natural padding of moss and wet leaves that deadened its contact with the hardscape. Setting it carefully aside, Angel dropped into the shaft. It was damp and smelled strongly of wet earth, but was only about five feet deep. He squatted to peer down its length and realized that it was wide enough and high enough to crawl down.

Yeah. I can do that, he told himself, ignoring the suffocating feeling the very thought gave him.

He popped his head back up out of the shaft to look for Fireball. The first thing he saw was that the head guy was still focused on his taser. Ted was still at the fountain rubbing his eyes like a man possessed. Under those circumstances, Angel expected Fireball might have run and hidden herself. Nope. Not Fireball. She leapt after the head goon and fired her pepper spray into the side of his face. He roared and staggered away from her.

She still didn't run. In fact, she seemed intent on stalking the guy.

"Fireball!" Angel croaked. Then, "Ginger!" Then, when that failed to get her attention, he shouted, "Fin!"

She turned, saw his head and shoulders sticking out of the air shaft, and bolted for him. The men left standing heard the shout and stopped what they were doing. In the moments it took for them to grasp the situation and converge on their incoherently shrieking leader, Fireball reached the air shaft, dropped in, and pulled the grate back into place.

"Quick thinking, Angel," she murmured.

"What do we do now?" he asked. "Do we stay here and hope Carver shows up right away, or–"

"Where'd they go?" someone topside shouted.

"The girl disappeared somewhere over there. Don't know where the boy is."

"Damn it! The boy's the one we want. The girl's just icing."

Angel and Fireball reflexively glanced down the low tunnel behind them. It was dark and sloped sharply downward into the bowels of the building. Angel shivered.

"Yeah," whispered Fireball. "I'm thinking we go this way." She started, feet first, down into the darkness beneath Cinzento HQ.

Angel swallowed his phobia and followed her. The tunnel descended steeply to a depth of eight or ten feet, then turned sharply left, paralleling the outer wall of the building. It was slippery and damp and close. Angel found himself counting every breath, focusing on the expansion and contraction of his lungs.

"You okay?" Fireball whispered. She'd been leading the way and now stopped to wait for him to catch up.

"I'm good. Just, um..." He realized he was panting – breathing in short, sharp little bursts.

"Yeah," she said. "Me too. Here."

He felt her hand cover his and fumbled to lace his fingers through hers, surprised at how comforting it was just to touch another human being in this cold, dark, dank place. They'd gone only a few more yards when the tunnel turned right, and feeble light reached them from below. Roughly two yards later, they were peering out from another grate into the parking garage. They could see the elevator maybe forty feet away across the parking bay.

Fireball tested the grate, pushing it with her shoulder. It budged about an inch.

"Get ready to get out of here and run," she told Angel, then rolled onto her back and assaulted the grate with both feet. It budged – a lot. On her second try, it scraped free of the wall and fell to the floor with a deafening metallic clatter that echoed through the garage.

"Go!"

The two hit the ground running, making straight for the elevator. This was the employee parking garage, so the elevator required a keycard to admit them. Fireball swiped her card in the security reader and the doors opened. Angel all but collapsed against the elevator's safety rail while Fireball pulled out her phone and punched up a number.

She grinned at him. "Wow. That was an adrenaline rush. Am I right?"

He shivered. "I'm not sure I'd put it that way."

"Guess I'm just a glass-half-full kind of girl. Hey, Carver," she said into the phone. "We're in the building."

~~~

Fireball gave Carver an abbreviated summary of their misadventure, including where they'd entered the building and the fact that they might still have pursuers. She heard a buzz of voices as he conferred with someone on the other end. He came back with a change of game plan.

"Don't get out at your lab. Stay in the elevator until you're at the office penthouse level. I'm concerned they might've gotten people into the building. I've got security searching the place now for anyone who doesn't belong here. Don't worry about your friends in the plaza. They scattered the moment they saw our security detail... What did you do to those guys, anyway?"

Fireball grinned. "Took advantage of their stupid. They judged us by our size. Thought we'd be scared and dim-witted. We weren't."

"Well, *I* was scared," Angel admitted quietly, when she'd hung up the phone.

At the penthouse level, Fireball and Angel faced the doors, waiting for them to open. They didn't. Fireball had taken her keycard out to swipe it through the reader when the back of the elevator slid open behind them.

The two turned slowly, Fireball wondering if her expression mirrored Angel's owl-eyed look, to find themselves peering into a cozy conference room decorated in a style completely unlike the sleek ostentatiousness of Zander's office or Carver's spartan but homey space or the old-world charm of the Old Man's office. Books spanned a wall opposite the elevator, broken only by a door that probably led to an inner office. A comfy-looking seating group and a long wooden conference table situated to the right of the door were of a style Fireball identified as Craftsman. The light fixtures that hung over the table were of the same style – wood and stained glass.

The two teenagers moved in tentative lockstep to the center of the room, gawping at everything.

"Soooo," breathed Fireball, "this must be the Old Man's *secret* lair."

"Right on the first try." Carver had appeared in the doorway to the inner office. "Come on in."

"Are we going to actually *meet* the OM this time?" Fireball approached the doorway with something like awe.

"Actually, we've already met, kiddo," said a familiar contralto from within the office. "You two all right?"

Fireball, disbelieving, entered the room to see Mom seated in a wing-backed chair behind a large cherrywood desk framed by floor-to-ceiling bookshelves.

"We're – we're – we're–" she stammered.

"Um, we're good," said Angel.

Mom smiled. "Good to hear. On another subject: I've been told the NSA's systems just went dark. It's time to pull out all the stops."

The Old Man

"Carver's been briefing me on your plan," Mom said. "I think it's time to kick it into high gear. We clearly can't afford to be at all cautious. The fact that someone has tried twice to get their hooks into Noob, here, sort of took caution off the table."

"Angel," said Fireball reflexively. "He prefers to be called Angel."

Mom smiled. "Of course he does. Sorry, Angel. So, now the question is: why do they want to get their hooks into you?"

He shook his head.

Fireball raised her hand. "Pardon me, and all that, but my question is... how are you Mom *and* the Old Man?"

"Mom *and* TOM?" murmured Angel.

Mom fixed the two teens, now seated at her little conference table, with a gimlet eye. "If I straighten that all out, will you be able to concentrate better on the task at hand?"

"Yes, sir, ma'am."

"Mom is just my handle. Just like Carver or Fireball or Noob. My *name* is Marina Cinzento."

"Whoa," said Fireball. "You're a Cinzento?"

Mom nodded. "The original Old Man was my dad, but he died a while back and handed me the reins to the company. Because I'm a woman – and a brownish woman, at that – I thought it prudent to continue to let people think that a male heir ran the firm. As stupid as it seems, some executives are still fossilized enough to believe women shouldn't be running companies – most especially high-tech companies."

Fireball could only snort derisively at that harebrained idea. Fossilized. She liked that.

"What complicates our current situation," Mom continued, "is that Zander is *also* a Cinzento. He's my cousin, in fact – Alexandre Cinzento. Zander Grayson is just his handle. He thinks it's pretty clever, he does. Cinzento is Portuguese for gray, you see. Son of Cinzento – at least, son of *a* Cinzento."

"But why?" asked Angel. "Why not use his real name?"

"Pride turned inside out. You see, Zander has long been of the opinion that my dad did him, the company, and the world a disservice by not making *him* the heir to the Cinzento throne. He *said* he wanted to rise up in the company on his own merit. I think the reality is that if he wore the Cinzento moniker, his cronies would be forever asking him why *he* wasn't the one in charge. He's older than I am – by a whopping three years – and has degrees in business and finance, which he believes is more crucial to running the company than my background in computer science and software engineering."

"Wait. What?" Fireball looked from Mom to Carver, who was smiling like the Mona Lisa. "But you... you've had us come find your lost emails a gazillion times. You always acted like you didn't get tech at all. Like – like you're a luddite."

"'Act' being the operative term," said Carver wryly.

Mom's grin was unrepentant. "Great cover, huh? Who'd think a techno-gerbil like me could be the actual head of a high-tech security firm?"

"Okay, so where *is* Zander?" asked Fireball.

Mom shrugged. "I don't know. And I have been trying very hard to find him. He's been conspicuously absent for the last day or so, though no one has seen him leave the building. I suspect that secret elevator he had installed has something to do with that. It's real bad timing on his part because it makes him look damned suspicious."

"D'you think he's responsible for Hack?" Angel asked.

Mom frowned. "I can't think he's got the chops to *create* something like that. But he sure as hell has the chops to exploit it to drum up business. I have to imagine he had no idea it would turn out this way and that the government would be looking for him. He's not a man who enjoys confrontation. I'm sure he was thinking this was his opportunity to increase his cachet – score some major contracts, outshine the stodgy ownership. That would be me." She grinned again. "That's been Zander since day one of his tenure here – find ways to shine. Sometimes, as you've no doubt noticed, that means throwing someone else under the bus. And that's the sort of nonsense that fries my circuits. Lately, Zander has done a number of things around here without my approval and sometimes without my knowledge."

"Secret elevator being a case in point," said Carver.

Mom snorted. "Bathroom reno, my aunt's petunias. He's outdone himself this time and crossed so many lines, I can't even imagine a way to uncross them. I've never liked Zander's way of doing business. He keeps secrets. I hate secrets."

Angel coughed. "Uh, yeah, but you were..."

She flashed him an unrepentant grin. "Yeah, I know. Ironic, isn't it? But all of that is irrelevant right now. Right now, we need to nail this AI to the wall. Stop it how-some-ever we may. So, it's full steam ahead, and if Zander resurfaces and gets in your way, you're not to listen to him. You send him to me. Better yet, call security. In fact, I want security posted outside the Raven lab and someone to escort the kids back to the dorm at night. Got that, Carver?" She threw their fearless leader a *look*.

Carver gave a thumbs-up.

"And one more thing." Mom turned suddenly solemn eyes on Angel. "You, kiddo, are not to set foot outside this building again until we figure out who's trying to get to you and why. My guess is you've gotten too close to someone who's deeply involved with our current crisis. And I can't help but notice how close both these attempts to kidnap you came on the heels of the appearance of Hack Attack. It bugs the hell out of me that they knew your name."

"But they seem to be trying to stop Hack, too," Angel objected.

Mom raised a hand. "Time out, kiddo. This whole thing could be a big charade – both the AI and the people claiming to try to break it. When you look at the conspiracy theories that are flying around, I have to wonder if this didn't start out as an attack on Cinzento that got out of control. I mean, think of it: if people can be made to believe we're untrustworthy, it would ruin us. We'd look like incompetents at best and criminals at worst."

Fireball sat back in her chair, stunned. She'd never looked at it that way before. That shone a whole different light on Hack Attack. Maybe they were also bad actors.

"So, Angel," Mom said, pinning him to his seat with her dark gaze, "I need you to stop all communication with the counterhackers. Understood?"

Angel looked 100 percent miserable but nodded in surrender. "Yes, ma'am."

Fireball reached over to give his shoulder a reassuring squeeze, happened to glance down, and realized that beneath the tabletop, his fingers were crossed.

Trust No One

Zander Grayson could not, for the life of him, figure out how everything had gone so completely south. He'd been trying only to further his own cred – to prove himself as an independent businessman in his own right. A businessman who no longer played second fiddle to his cousin Marina. Sure, he'd intended to steal business from Cinzento, but that had been as far as his ambitions went. Now Marina was gunning for him, his clients were gunning for him – hell, the FBI, the DHS, and the Pentagon were probably gunning for him too.

He took a deep breath and tried to think clearly about the current situation. The AI had gone silent again, protecting itself from attacks on it by human hackers. This he knew from a phone conversation with Ezra Temple. He wanted those hackers to succeed, but they'd complicated things when they'd put out a call for help and the call had been intercepted by the Raven team.

One thing was certain, he had to keep the Cambeiro kid from making solid contact with them. He might salvage his own career if he could keep that from happening. If he couldn't, it might mean the end of Cinzento.

Would that be so bad?

His own interior dialogue stopped him and stilled him. What if Cinzento emerged as the source of the rogue AI and the company took the hit? If he could keep the real source of the AI hidden, he might yet pull his own chestnuts out of the fire. He had money – that wasn't an issue. If the company's value tanked and it lost its client base, he would have enough money to buy Marina out. He could plunder its resources, shut down the Academy, and rise from Cinzento's ashes.

If... if he could just keep his part in the current disaster from coming out. He gazed out the window of his anonymous office in an equally anonymous building overlooking Puget Sound. That might not be as hard as he thought. He was a businessman, not a techie. His degree was in finance, not computer science. Who'd even believe he had the knowledge base to be able to

221

loose something like Hack on the world? They wouldn't. They'd look for a more technically adept source, and he'd figure out a way of finding them one.

He smiled for the first time in days. Maybe he'd start a new company and call it Phoenix.

Families

The words "gone to ground" didn't even begin to cover it. Hack had withdrawn from the virtual web like an ocean withdraws from the shore before a tsunami. That vision ran like a rogue video in Fireball's head as she oversaw the team's efforts to ferret out where the AI had gone.

Cricket and Books were immersed in completing their revisions of Hack's ancillary modules and testing them with an off-lined version of its core. They couldn't gain access to the encrypted code within the core module, but they were hopeful they could modify its behavior by feeding it new subroutines. To that end, Cricket had edited the replication subroutine so that the spawning of a new copy only occurred if security breaches in a single system required it, and would cease once all breaches were identified, at which point the program was to report to a designated IP address, then clean up after itself and shut down. After it had sealed all security holes, its instruction set told it to run a test scan of the affected system on a weekly basis to find any new breaches and seal them as necessary.

If the code worked, it wouldn't kill Hack, but it would contain it in such a way that it would actually be useful until they could do more. Theoretically, if the AI could be sent into dormancy, they could find a way to delete it.

The lab was silent but for the sound of breathing as Books compiled their code and uploaded it to the honeypot array. As the Hack doppelgänger literally absorbed the code, discovered the executables, and ran them, even the sound of breathing stopped.
"Okay," Fireball murmured, finally remembering to breathe. "Open up the target array."

Cricket opened a connection to a second honeypot on which they'd created a database rife with security gaps. In seconds, her monitoring software picked up the activity. The Hack copy did exactly what they'd hoped it would do – it found the gaps, took a "snapshot" of them, and –

223

"It's sending the report now," said Scrappy, his voice pitched low as if Hack might hear them, even with all their mics and cameras turned off.

Or as if we were in a church or a library, Fireball thought.

"Bingo." Cricket turned to the team with a relieved smile on her face. "It's shut down. It's not replicating; it's not doing anything."

Amid the chorus of expelled breath, they exchange glances, mirroring Cricket's relief. Fireball felt a rush of appreciation for what her team had just done.

"Okay," she said. "Proof of concept. Now we just need to find the Hack original. Ideas?"

Following a moment of silence, Cricket said, "What if we turn this one loose on the internet? I mean, worst case, it finds more holes and seals them, then waits around to see if there are any more. But I think it will do more. I think we might be able to get it to show us where Hack Prime is."

"How do you figure?" asked Scrappy.

"Hack clearly maintains some sort of contact with its copies. Our test Hack started out as a copy that it created and that we isolated and modified its subroutines. What if we modify one more? What if we add a subset of the Alligator patch? We program it to see Hack as malware, and when Alligator tries to take a bite out of it–"

Scrappy grinned from ear to ear. "It runs home to daddy."

"Brilliant, Cricket," Fireball commended her. "You are so getting massive Kudos when this is all over."

"It's over now!" said a sharp male voice from the doorway of the lab.

Cricket's face turned a deathly shade of white as she turned to face the speaker. "Daddy! What are you doing here? How did you get in?"

"What do you mean, how did I get in? They can't keep us from our children."

"Why are you –?"

He advanced on her, striding into the room to loom over her chair. "I've come to bring you home to the farm. I couldn't take one more news report about this disaster. The government is investigating; the press is everywhere. There are news crews and reporters all over the streets around this building. They tried to stop me from coming in, asked if my child was one of the teenagers responsible for this fiasco."

Cricket rose from her seat. Standing, she was not that much shorter than her dad. "We didn't cause this, Daddy," she said. "We're trying to solve it."

"Well, these others can solve it without you, Mai. I will not have a member of my family caught up in such things. We are respectable citizens, not part of this mess."

Cricket looked for a moment as if she was about to cry, but Books stepped forward to flank her.

"You should be proud of her, Mr. Pham," he said. "She may have just figured out how to fix this."

He barely glanced at Books. "Get your things, Mai. We leave now. Take only what you can carry in one trip. We'll send for the rest later."

Cricket's entire posture changed. She leaned into Books's shoulder, the expression on her face going from stricken to stubborn. "No, Daddy. I can't leave, and I won't. These people are my family too. I can't abandon them when they need me. How could you be proud of me if I did that?"

Mr. Pham's face went dark red and he opened his mouth to retort, but Carver had appeared in the doorway behind him.

Carver cleared his throat loudly, and said, "I'm sorry, Mr. Pham, but I'm going to have to ask you to leave. We're going into lockdown here because of the situation. Your daughter is safest here, and Books is right – she's an important part of getting us through the current crisis."

Cricket's dad regarded Carver coldly, his jaw working. "Mai...," he growled.

Books took Cricket's hand and squeezed it, his gaze never leaving her father's face.

At last, Mr. Pham lowered his eyes and turned to his daughter. "You have chosen your family today. You will not hear from *my* family anymore." He turned on his heel and strode from the room, his back rigid.

"Oh, Cricket," murmured Books. "I'm so sorry."

Cricket shook her head, blinking back tears. "It's okay. He may disown me, but my mom *never* will. Now, let's get back to work." She turned to Carver. "Sir, we may have a way of finding Hack." She explained briefly what she thought their Hack copy might do and showed him the results of their test.

"And when you do find it?" he asked.

"With a little more tweaking, we might be able to lure Hack Prime into isolation and replace it with our doppelgänger," said Cricket. "Then when it replicates, and when it 'steers' the other modules, it changes how they behave. It'll take time, but theoretically it should work."

"Excuse me?"

That was Angel, who'd been watching from the sidelines. He stood, arms folded, hands tucked under his arms, eyes flitting defensively from one teammate to another. Finally, they sought Fireball. She felt a surge of empathy. She knew what it was like to draw uncomfortable attention.

Angel took a deep breath, then said, "I think we need to realize that this thing – whatever else it is – is well-programmed. It's learning, but it's learning to be paranoid. It's going to expect us to try to attack it or lure it away from its purpose. In fact, it expected that before we actually thought about it. I think we need to consider what Hack Attack suggested in their messages – a double switch. Give Hack what it expects, only not."

Fireball felt a smile tugging at her lips. "Loki," she said.

Day Eight

Doppelgänger

Raven Lair became part lab, part actors' workshop. With their audio turned on so their virtual adversary could hear them, the team went to work tweaking their Hack double to seek out its original, once contact had been made. Aloud, they talked up luring Hack onto their honeypot, then swapping their doppelgänger code for Hack Prime. Fireball also introduced the white lie (she called it a "false impression") that they had cracked Hack's encryption and had been able to decompile and edit its source code. Silently, they passed paper notes back and forth like kids in a classroom. Notes that laid out their real agenda: distract the AI with the prep for the swap, then simply set loose the Hack doppelgänger with its benign mandate.

Hack, Angel had theorized, would never set one virtual toe in their trap, but it would attack the other program and assimilate it just as it had assimilated snippets of faulty code in every system it encountered. But this code contained a copy of its encrypted core executable that, once run, would produce unpredictable results. Their task was to do what they could to turn those results to their benefit.

The kids ate a late dinner provided by Books and Whiz's dad, who turned up on Cinzento's back doorstep with hamburgers and fries for all, and was allowed in at Mom's command. As the night wore on, the team consumed massive quantities of coffee and rotated out for naps in their dorm rooms.

It was not lost on Fireball that when Angel's nap time rolled around, he left quietly with his laptop tucked under one arm. Highly suspicious. Maybe he was just jacked up on caffeine and going off to play computer games instead of sleeping, but she was pretty sure he had another agenda. She waited about ten minutes, then followed him to his room.

She stood outside for a moment, bending so that she could clearly see light from within spilling out onto the floor from beneath his door. She tried the knob and, finding it unlocked, opened the door just enough to see Angel sitting cross-legged on his bed, hunched over this computer, fingers tapping at the keys. She'd no doubt he was in conversation with Hack Attack.

Fireball gave the door a solid push, sending it thudding against the wall, then stood in the doorway, glaring, arms crossed over her breasts.

The two teens stared at each other for a moment, then Angel said, "You gonna come in and close the door? Or you gonna stand there giving me the evil eye all night?"

The calm in his voice annoyed the heck out of her. How dare he be so chill when she'd just caught him red-handed, parlaying with someone who just might be the enemy?

"Really?" she said. "That's what you're gonna go with? 'Come in, have a seat. I'm just discussing life, the universe, and everything with a total stranger who might be one of the bad guys?'"

Angel shook his head and fixed her with a look that made him seem years older than his physical age. "They're not the bad guys... Ginger. I know it. I *feel* it. They're really doing what they can to help end this."

There was a moment of uneasy silence, then Angel's computer pinged and the text on the screen scrolled. He glanced at it, then moved over slightly, nodding at the spot next to him on the bed. "Sit down and see if you don't think Hack Attack can help. At least see what they have to say."

Reading his face, Fireball realized that if she didn't trust the hidden hackers, she trusted Angel.

More than trusted him.

She hesitated, more for show than out of any real reserve, then closed the door and sat down next to him on the bed. She saw that Hack Attack's latest message had been, *Need different approach*.

"What's that in response to?" Fireball asked.

"I told them we were trying to retard Hack's replication and sabotage the matrix."

She stared at the side of his head. "Are you kidding me? You shared our plan of attack with – with – you don't even know who?"

"Not everything. I'm not stupid. Just the broad strokes. And cryptically."

Fireball sighed. She *did* trust him. It was just hard not to be in the driver's seat. That bit of self-awareness was sidetracked as the intent of Hack Attack's last message registered. She leaned forward, peering at the screen.

"Wait. What do they mean, 'different approach?' Why? What?"

"I'll ask," Angel said, and typed, *Expand.*

Opposite strategy, their would-be ally replied.

"*Opposite* strategy?" repeated Fireball. "What does that mean? We *let* it replicate? That doesn't sound like a friendly, Angel."

Angel frowned and typed, *Effect?*

They responded, *AI takedown.*

How?

After a moment of hesitation, Hack Attack said, *Kudzu.*

Angel sat up straight. "Kudzu? I don't get it."

Fireball realized she was holding her breath. *She* got it. Her mom had been raised in the Deep South. She totally got it.

"Kudzu!" she said. "An invasive species. It's a – a vine that grows like crazy and takes over everything in its path. Like Hack."

Angel turned to look at her. "Fight kudzu with kudzu?"

"Yes! Oh, man!" Fireball catapulted off the bed and did a 360 in the middle of the room. "Don't deprive it, *overwhelm* it! It's the last thing in the world it would expect. We've been arguing that it needs to *stop* replicating, right? And it knows that if it does, it's not fulfilling its mandate to grow and evolve. So..."

She could see the dawn of realization in Angel's eyes. "So the doppelgänger seems to be *helping* it – accelerating its growth, but instead–"

Fireball put her hands around her own throat and made a hacking sound. "We invade it and strangle it with itself."

Angel typed a final message into the note-passing code, then closed his laptop and rolled off his bed. "Back to the lab."

Fireball looked down at his stockinged feet. "You gonna put some shoes on?"

"Why? I'm not planning on going out. Let's go!" He herded her out the door; they literally raced for the land bridge to the corporate building.

They burst into the lab out of breath and already gasping out their proposed strategy. Carver spent several minutes calming them down and finally got them to articulate – tag-team style and finishing each other's sentences – the kudzu idea.

At the end of their joint recitation, during which neither mentioned where the idea had come from, they drew blank stares. The other Ravens traded glances that hinted they thought their teammates might be suffering from sleep deprivation.

"I'm not sure I've got a complete grasp of what you're proposing," said Carver tentatively.

"Oh," said Whiz. "Oh, wait. OMG." She grinned from ear to ear. "That is so karmic! And it makes perfect sense." She turned to Carver. "It's how you take out a predator. You introduce a more effective predator to its ecosystem."

Carver smiled. "In other words, an evil twin."

Operation Kudzu

Cricket created yet another copy of Hack – which, of course, they dubbed *Kudzu*, then archived the first copy. Then she and her teammates split up the subroutines and worked to make them even more aggressive. Fireball threw in some additional code that sped up the processing time in any way she could find.

Kudzu, when it was completed, was programmed to do more than allow Hack to assimilate it. No computer code was perfect and – thanks to its modified Alligator subroutine – Kudzu would be looking for imperfections in the AI itself, seeking to invade and exploit them.

"It will report its progress and continue with its work until it has exploited the last imperfection in the last Hack's code," Carver explained to Mom when she put in an appearance sometime around sunrise. "That should effectively break the program."

Mom was attired for business by virtue of a scheduled press conference at nine a.m. but had arrived with a trolley of breakfast items from the cafeteria and a thermal pump pot full of coffee.

"And then?"

"And then," Carver continued, "it will go dormant and request further commands to execute. The original benign copy – the one we originally thought we'd use to lure Hack out and swap with it – will serve as a backup in case we have to try this again."

"Actually," said Cricket, sharing a secret smile with Books, "we've added a little sauce to the mix. We were counting on Kudzu being able to establish contact with Hack Prime. But we realized we needed to create the best odds of Prime either accepting it as a friendly, or assuming it was an enemy and attacking it. We decided to sweeten the pot. So, Books and I gave Kudzu a sort of angler fish costume. It will 'pretend' to be a system with a hole in it that will lure Hack into investigating."

"Right," said Books. "But this thing is like real kudzu on steroids. Every tendril is a subroutine with its own protocols. If Hack extends itself into the Kudzu system, our code will disrupt Hack's subroutines and replace them with its modified versions, then it will reproduce like rabbits and make even more rabbit holes for Hack Prime to hack."

"Oh, that's rich," said Mom, nodding appreciatively. "Hoist by its own petard."

"Elegant," agreed Whiz. "Like the Borg on *Star Trek*."

"Yeah," said Scrappy, who was unusually subdued. "Assimilate *this*. But..."

"But?" repeated Carver. "What's wrong, Scrappy?"

"It still amounts to a kill switch, doesn't it? I mean, deking it and capturing it is one thing, but this way – infiltrating it and dissecting it from inside – that'll kill any emergent personality."

"Our code isn't killing it, Scrappy," Cricket told him. "It's enlightening it. Converting it to a higher purpose. Remember, Kudzu *is* Hack, only not destructive of everything around it. Besides, I think we all have to recognize that Angel is right. Hack isn't an emergent intelligence. It's just a machine mind doing what it was programmed to do. It's not like us. It doesn't feel; it doesn't have original thoughts. It can grow *beyond* its original programming, but it can't grow *out of* its original purpose. That purpose will always be at the center of everything it does."

Carver looked around at the group. "Are we ready to turn this thing loose? You guys feel like you've got all your bases covered?"

One by one, they all nodded or responded affirmatively. Scrappy, last of all. He heaved a huge sigh and nodded his head.

Fireball relaxed. Finally, the whole team seemed to be on the same page.

Carver asked, "You guys want to monitor from here, or the Situation Room?"

Having been laboring in their lair for uncounted hours, Team Raven opted for the Sitch Room. The staff accepted their presence without comment. Ezra even vacated a workstation.

"It's all yours," he said.

Carver gestured at the open seat. "Okay, Fireball. Release the hounds."

Hoping she looked more resolute than she felt, Fireball took the proffered chair and swiveled to face the keyboard and the wall of displays above it. She called up the controls for the machines in their lab and connected the honeypot array to the internet, turning Kudzu loose.

There was a moment of silence during which everyone looked like a herd of deer in the proverbial headlights, then Fireball gasped aloud.

"Something's happening already!"

Everyone in the room cast their attention to the massive wall display, which currently showed various parts of a virtual world map. Fireball was right, something was happening – the initial contact between Kudzu and Hack Prime. What the map showed was a virtual explosion of green and red from which the verdant green of Kudzu emerged victorious. From that initial blast – which took mere seconds in real time – they watched as Kudzu attracted and ultimately consumed its cousins.

Tentacles, thought Angel. *And Kudzu is pinching them off one by one.*

He was sitting on a tall swivel chair in a back corner of the room, his laptop open in his lap, and had been in silent communication with Hack Attack as they watched the fruits of their plotting. He supposed he ought to still feel a niggle of doubt – a fear that these alleged allies were really furthering the plot of whomever had unleashed Hack on the world. He knew Mom (or the Old Man or Marina – he still wasn't sure how to think of her) suspected Zander of being the spider at the center of the web, but despite the fact that they'd all been fooled by Mom's pretense of techno-wimpiness, he could not believe Zander capable of either that level of technical aptitude or acting ability.

Angel's laptop gave an R2-D2 whistle, and a new message appeared in one corner of the screen.

Working? Hack Attack asked.

Yes, he sent back. *Thank you.*

After a moment, the message moved and changed. *Love U*, it said.

Angel sat completely still, feeling as if time had slowed to a crawl and a bubble had formed around him, blocking out not just sound, but the growing excitement in the room around him. He wanted to ask questions, to demand what the last message meant, but he could only stare at his screen and listen to the sound of his own pulse.

He felt a hand on his shoulder, heard Fireball's voice, as if from a long distance, asking him if he was okay. He hadn't even begun to form an answer when Zander Grayson burst into the room, glowering like a thunder cloud. He pointed at Carver.

"You! What the hell have you done?"

AI Takedown

Fireball gaped at the CEO (or maybe he was ex-CEO now). "What do you mean 'what have we done?' We've done what you wanted us to do. We're taking down the AI." She pointed at the map of Kudzu's progress.

Zander stared blankly at the displays, with no indication he understood what he was seeing. Then he zeroed in on Fireball. "I took you off the job!" he raged. "More than once! I told you to stand down! I have my own people on this! And I am very much of the opinion that you caused it all." He turned to Carver, who was in the process of putting his phone away. "*You*, Spearfisher. You, especially. This happened on your watch. My people are going to be the ones to stop this virtual plague."

Fireball saw movement out of the corner of her eye as Angel rose from his chair and moved to stand face-to-face with Zander, his laptop clutched in trembling hands.

"Your people? Don't you mean my *parents*? Isn't that who you have on this?" He was shaking all over with emotion, tears in his eyes.

Fireball felt her throat constrict. Only she had seen the messages from the mysterious Hack Attackers. Only she realized the full shape of what Angel was suggesting. It was a hideous shape. If Angel was right, Zander was the architect of his months of anguish and loss. She could hardly believe anyone she personally knew – not even Zander Grayson – could do something so epically awful.

She rounded on Zander, feeling as if her brain was going to burst into flames. "Is that why you wanted to keep us from pursuing this when you knew we had the best chance of stopping it? What were you afraid we might find out?"

"Yes, Zander," said Mom from the door of the Situation Room. "What is it you've been hiding since the beginning of all this?" She glanced at Angel. "Or should I ask, '*Who* have you been hiding?'"

Several strong emotions flashed across Zander's face in quick succession as he faced his cousin. He went with anger and bravado. "I should ask you the same thing, Cousin Mar. I more than suspect you're the one who's unleashed this monstrosity on the world."

The Sitch Room staff of five, who'd been watching, silent and wide-eyed, turned their heads as one to Marina Cinzento, no doubt wondering how the lunch lady had suddenly morphed into the CEO's cousin and why she was wearing a suit and pumps instead of her usual comfy tunics and Crocs.

She relaxed back into a typically Mom-like pose, hands on hips, brows arched. "Really? You're going to tough it out? Put on a brave face? Turn the tables? Kiddo, I'm not the one with a secret elevator to the parking garage and a backup car so if anyone looks, your Beemer is still sitting right where you left it. Where've you been going, Zander? Why, in the middle of all this drama, have you hired a PR firm and some outfit called Grundy Ops?"

"That should be obvious. Thanks to your lax leadership and the bumbling of these so-called child prodigies of yours, Cinzento has taken a blow to its reputation that it may never recover from. I hired a PR firm to redeem our corporate image and Grundy to help improve our infrastructure."

Mom laughed. "Improve our infrastructure? That's a hoot. Grundy Ops offers a lot of interesting services, but infrastructure isn't one of them. Is that the source of the goon squad you sent after Angel? And I seriously doubt you meant to redeem Cinzento's reputation, coz. Not given the frequency with which you've run interference with Carver's teams while doodling 'Grayson Secure' and 'Grayson Tech' on miscellaneous scraps of paper."

"What'd you do, go through my trash?" he snarled.

Mom shook her head. "Noooo. Not me. But the FBI did."

Now the Sitch staff was staring bug-eyed at Zander, who looked as if he might fold up like a cardboard cutout. He didn't. Instead, he took in a huge breath, face going red, and launched into an epic diatribe. It all came out – the jealousy, the feelings of inadequacy, the certainty that even that uncertainty was cousin Marina's fault for having been born to the fortunate side of the family.

"You were the Golden Child," Zander accused her. "Ivo Cinzento's brilliant daughter. I stood no chance of getting the Old Man's attention with you around. I've spent my life here playing *house elf* to your absurd whimsy and your incomprehensible choice of acolytes!" He glared at Carver before raking his gaze across Fireball's entire team. It felt to Fireball like a physical slap.

"House elf?" repeated Mom. "Hardly. You've had more than enough freedom. We're family, Zan. I made room for you at the top of the organization. If that wasn't enough, if you'd just told me how you felt years ago, I'd've done whatever I could to help you feel that you were a real partner."

"I didn't want to be your partner, damn it! I wanted to run the company on my own! Cinzento should've been *mine*, Marina! It should have been mine!"

"It never could have been yours, Zander. You didn't have the right background. You had every opportunity to learn the tech trade. You chose to get an MBA."

"I fail to see—"

"Yes. And that's why you fail, period. If you're going to run a tech company, well, you need to be able to understand what it does. *Why* it does. You never could be bothered to learn the technology, which I suspect is the real reason we're in this mess. Now, is what this boy said about his parents anywhere close to the truth? Are they still alive somewhere?"

Zander paled again and took a step backward. The backs of his knees collided with an empty chair and he sat down, rolling backward until Ezra grabbed the back of the chair to stop it.

"I have no idea," Zander protested. "I don't know what this kid is going on about. He's the one who's put the company in peril. He's the one who's been communicating with an anonymous hacker who may very well be profiting from this rogue AI."

Fireball wanted to spit fire. She moved to stand next to Angel, who was shaking so hard, he could barely hold his laptop. With eyes blazing, he set it on the workstation next to Zander and typed two words into one of the empty expressions: *Mom? Dad?*

He did a quick compile and uploaded the code snippet.

The answer was a smiley face emoji in ASCII. Followed by a "less than" sign capped by the number 3 – a sideways heart. Fireball felt as if her own heart was going to stop.

Angel turned the laptop so Zander could see the last series of messages.

"When they first sent me the name 'Cambeiro,' I thought they were telling me they knew who I was. Maybe even threatening me. But they weren't. They were telling me who *they* were. Sofia and Israel Cambeiro. My parents. You knew they were alive. You let me believe they were dead. For months! Did you stage their deaths, Mr. Grayson? Was that you?"

Zander raised his hands defensively. "No! This was all their idea. They – they were covering their tracks. I mean, it's their fault the AI got loose in the first place. They were careless with their code–"

"Bull!" cried Angel. "My parents have never been careless about anything! And there's no way they'd fake their own deaths, because as much as they cared about their work, they cared about me more."

Zander's jaw worked for several seconds, and his eyes flitted from one face to another, last of all alighting on his cousin's.

"I'm telling you, Marina," he said, his tone beseeching, "this was their idea. They've – they've been using me this whole time to cover for them. To run interference. I didn't want to. You have to believe me."

Mom folded her arms across her ample breast. "Really? So they're in hiding? Trying to keep their secret?"

Zander nodded. "Yes, exactly."

"Uh-huh. Then why were they sending coded messages trying to get someone's attention? Trying to get help?"

Zander's expression changed with lightning speed from penitence to rage. "Fine. Fine, Marina. Let's lay our cards on the table. The Cambeiros are alive... for now. But if you threaten me–"

Angel let out a scream of anguish and rage and launched himself at Zander. It took Carver and Books to hold him back and Ezra to pull Zander's chair away.

"Oh, Zander," said Mom, shaking her head, "I wish you wouldn't have said that. I think your best hope right now is to tell us where Angel's mom and dad are so we can put this family back together again." She gestured at someone in the hall outside, and two security men appeared behind her. "I have it on good authority that murder is not in Grundy's repertoire. You're sunk, kiddo. Might as well give it up."

Now, finally, Zander deflated like a punctured balloon. "I never meant it to go like this," he whined. "I was only trying to get what I deserved. I only meant to establish myself as a force in the industry."

"Well, you did that, if not the way you intended," observed Marina. She glanced around at the tense faces of her staff (many of whom had just now realized that they *were* her staff). "Let's take this up to my office. Gentlemen, would you escort Mr. Grayson up, please?" She gestured at the two security guards, who helped Zander out of his chair and escorted him out into the hall.

Now, the Old Man turned her attention to Fireball and her cohort. "Team Raven, let's go. I think we can leave Hack and Kudzu in Ezra's capable hands for the time being."

They rode up to the penthouse level in silence; Marina looked pensive, as did Carver. When they filed out of the backside of the elevator into her office suite, Zander was already there with his two tenders, sitting at one end of the conference table.

Marina seated herself at the head of the table and gestured Carver and the team to seats along the sides. When everyone

239

was in place, she looked down the table at Zander and, in the same rough-gentle voice she used with the academy's students, asked, "What happened, Zan? How did Hack happen?"

Zander took a deep breath and began to speak. "I wanted to effect a coup. I wanted to be able to offer clients something that was revolutionary, that didn't require huge teams of human programmers. And yes, I wanted to be able to shut down the Academy. Children have no place anywhere near a company like Cinzento, let alone doing homework assignments using client data."

He glanced briefly down the row of teenagers, then cleared his throat and went on.

"I found out about the Cambeiros through their academic work at Stanford and hired them to write an AI that would find, exploit, report, and plug security holes. It was only supposed to exploit them in order to show the client how it could be done so their programmers would avoid similar mistakes. I got wind of the fact that Conrad Myrle was looking for a new security firm and arranged an opportunity to show him the progress on the AI."

"You did that here?" asked Carver. "At Cinzento?"

"Not exactly. I set up a working computer lab for the Cambeiros off-site. Hired my own techs and security people." He paused, looking even more uncomfortable than he had. "I wanted Israel and Sofia to show Myrle the app, but they told me it wasn't ready. They said the code wasn't complete and that there was no kill switch. I thought they were being overly cautious. Guarding their brainchild. I decided I'd show Myrle the app myself. So I invited him to Cinzento after hours and demoed the program for him in one of the test labs."

"You what?" The words leapt from Fireball's lips before she could stop them, but they were lost in the general outcry from around the table.

Mom raised her hands and quieted everyone down.

Zander was glaring at them now. "I'm not an idiot. I demoed the program on a closed system."

"Then how did it get out of the closed system?" asked Carver.

Zander hunched his shoulders and returned to staring at the table top. "After the demo, I tried to delete the program, but I wasn't really sure how. So, I figured I'd bring one of my own people over to take care of it, but before I could do that, a Cinzento tech reconfigured that array and reintegrated it with the rest of the systems in our shop. The array was supposed to be empty, of course, so when the tech realized it was already populated with a program he didn't recognize, he shut the connection down. Unfortunately, the AI had already transferred itself and began to do exactly what we've seen it do elsewhere. That's when the Cambeiros realized what I'd done, and I understood what they meant about the code not being complete. The AI had already established a link to FBM. Apparently it migrated to their system through their ReGen process–"

"As the kiddos figured out," interjected Mom. "But how did it get to FBM's remote storage?"

Zander looked as if whatever bad taste was in his mouth had just gotten exponentially worse. "My risk analysis team had access to FBM's remote server farm so they could assess security risks. Conrad Myrle assumed... that is, I led him to believe that this was a new Cinzento product. The idea was that if Myrle contracted us, we'd analyze the risk profile using Cinzento manpower, then we'd turn the AI loose on it as a proof of concept."

Mom-Marina nodded. "Then you'd claim responsibility for the leap forward and what –?"

"If you refused to let me take the reins of Cinzento, I was going to start my own firm and take as many Cinzento clients with me as possible."

"But that didn't happen, did it?"

"No. The Cambeiros warned me it might get out of hand, that it might be only a matter of time before the thing became dangerous. I didn't believe them until I realized it had gotten into our systems at the off-site lab. It began a takeover of our systems. I was alone in the lab when I realized what it was doing to them." He paused, grinding his teeth, wringing his hands. "I

241

panicked. I cut off the infected part of the system from the LAN. Literally pulled the plug on the array. Then I wiped the hard drives on the programming machines."

"Oh, my God," murmured Carver. "You destroyed the Cambeiros' source code?"

Zander nodded but didn't look at him. "When the Cambeiros came in the next morning and realized what I'd done and why, they threatened to go public, saying they had to warn people about the threat. I had to silence them, but I also needed them to try to reconstruct the program and kill it if it became necessary. So I... I staged an accident, leased a new facility, and hired Grundy to make sure the Cambeiros didn't escape or contact the outside world."

"The lab fire," whispered Angel, his voice raw. "You let me think my mom and dad had been burned to death in a lab fire." His eyes were like open wounds, and tears streamed down his cheeks. His hands still clutched his laptop as if for support.

Fireball, sitting next to him at the table, put her hand over his. She pulled her gaze from his face and gave Zander a look that she hoped could peel paint. "Did you bring Angel here on purpose? So you could keep an eye on him? Control him?"

Zander shook his head. "No. That was just a windfall that I used to keep the Cambeiros focused on the AI. They knew I was keeping tabs on him at his uncle's house, but when he was moved to the Academy, it gave me even more leverage. And it was the only leverage I had. When the kids started investigating where the AI had come from, and ultimately intercepted the Cambeiros' attempts to stop it, I had to do something. All I could think of was getting the kid out of the way."

Fireball was speechless at the sheer awfulness of what this man had done in the name of self-aggrandizement. She twined her fingers through Angel's and squeezed. He squeezed back.

Zander's cousin was not speechless. "Well, isn't that the height of irony," she said. "That right there – that penchant for flying by the seat of your pants – is one of the reasons Dad never considered putting you in charge of Cinzento. Not for one moment. You've never known how to strategize or plan ahead.

And you seemed to have no interest in learning how. You don't act; you *react*. And you are woefully short of imagination... and scruples. Oh, and one other thing: you don't like to share. Family shares, Zander. Now, where are this poor kid's mom and dad?"

Zander raised his eyes to his cousin's face. "I'll tell you. If you'll help me out. If you'll—"

"I don't think you've got any leverage here, coz. Angel can communicate with them more openly now. He can tell them the coast is clear and they can divulge their location."

Zander's lips pulled back into a ghost of a smile. "They don't *know* their location."

Mom leaned forward, elbows on the table, hands clasped loosely as if she were simply chairing a board meeting. "This is where not being an actual techno-gerbil is helpful. If they keep talking to their son, we can find them. It's better for you if you willingly tell us where they are so it at least *looks* as if you're being cooperative."

Zander made a noise deep in his throat that sounded suspiciously like a growl. "There's a building above the Sound just north of Elliott Bay. Looks like it's part of the water treatment plant – it's not. I own the facility – Kingfisher Enterprises. The address is in my cell phone, which *they* have." He nodded at the security guards still posted behind his chair.

Mom nodded. "Give him his phone. He's going to call his Grundy goons and tell them they're to release the Cambeiros and consider their employment terminated. Their last task will be to see that Angel's parents get here safely and are delivered to our security people downstairs. Are we clear?"

Zander nodded and accepted his phone from the guard.

"Be glad we stopped you before you committed worse crimes than you already have," Mom told him as he dialed the security people at Kingfisher. "And yeah, I'll help you as much as seems just. That's what family does."

Zander had a terse conversation with someone at Kingfisher named Axel. Whether that was a first or last name wasn't clear. Fireball decided it didn't matter as long as it resulted in Angel's parents being freed. She felt something on her cheek and realized that she was crying, joy and loss entangled in her heart. Angel was getting his family back, which probably meant he would be leaving the Academy. She dared to glance at him; he squeezed her hand again and smiled.

His laptop made a sound like R2-D2 just then. He stared at it blankly for a moment, eyes glazed, then flipped open the top and tapped the track pad.

He glanced at Mom. "It's Kudzu. It's reporting."

Mom gestured for the guards to take Zander away and gave them instructions about whom to call to retrieve him. When he was gone, she turned to Angel and said, "Well, let's hear it."

Angel tapped the pad and a voice emanated from the speakers. It was a synthesis of all the voices Kudzu must have heard in the course of its existence, with Cricket's dominant.

"I have a report to make," it said. "My task is 40 percent complete, and I anticipate I shall reach 100 percent completion in twenty hours and forty-seven minutes at my present rate of speed. However, I am continuing to optimize my activities, which makes this estimate subject to change."

"Why thank you, kiddo," said Mom. She looked to her companions at the table. "Now, then, I think this calls for a good meal and a long nap for all – except Angel, here. He's got family coming to see him."

Day Nine

Wrap Party

Saturday was party day on both sides of Cinzento. The
corporation was exonerated of any malign involvement in what
had become a global scare, and the Academy's best and
brightest had acquitted themselves well in the eyes of skeptical
adults and several government institutions. There was much to
celebrate.

The formal celebration was held in the Cinzento dining hall,
the one venue large enough to host students, parents, clients,
some dignitaries, and the press. A low stage had been set up at
one end of the hall upon which speeches were made and awards,
in the form of Kudos and gifts, were given to those who had
contributed their time and effort to Operation Kudzu. Those
included teams Raven, Peregrine, and Nightingale, and the
Situation Room staff, most especially Ezra Temple, who had
pulled a number of all-nighters tracking the progress of the
rogue AI.

After the formal presentations, while students, staff, and
guests mingled and the press did impromptu interviews (in
which she answered every question with, "Really, it was all
teamwork"), Fireball found herself drawn to where Angel and
his beaming parents answered questions from a handful of
reporters. This was the first time she'd seen him since his mom
and dad had been ushered into the Old Man's office. Then, he'd
let go of her hand and flung himself into their arms. They'd
spoken Spanish to each other – a flood of words of which she
understood only every third one – and she had felt her aloneness
so profoundly that she'd had to leave the room.

Now, she stood on the periphery of the group, watching,
listening, and noticing how much like both of them he was; he
had his father's high cheekbones and his mother's eyes and
smile. She was full to bursting with happiness for them. She
tried not to feel the chill of envy at the looks they shared, the

245

love that sparkled in their eyes and shed itself over anyone nearby, press included. She had never had that, not for one moment of her life. She had told herself that, at the ripe old age of sixteen, she didn't need it. But here was a boy older by a year and yet unashamedly basking in his parents' love.

Angel, she realized, knew both loss and love, while she knew only loss. *It separates us*, she thought.

He wasn't the only one, she realized, looking around the huge room. Mr. Granger had come to celebrate with Books and Whiz (Tarik and Janiqua, she reminded herself), and though Cricket's father was absent, her mom was here looking as proud as a peacock (or maybe a peahen). Fireball and Scrappy were the only two who had no one.

When the reporters had asked their questions and gone to seek out other stories, Fireball hesitated. She wanted to meet Angel's mom and dad, but she was suddenly unsure if they'd care to meet her.

Angel took that decision out of her hands. He saw her standing there, waffling, and his face lit up with one of his patented thousand-candle-watt smiles. He rushed over to her, grabbed her hand, and dragged her to where his parents stood waiting.

"Mom, Dad! This is her. This is Fireball. Well, her real name is Ginger, but everyone here calls her Fireball. She's my best friend." He sent her a look nearly identical to the ones he'd been sharing with his parents.

Fireball's breath caught in her throat. Before she could do more than murmur embarrassed "hellos," Mrs. Cambeiro enveloped her in a hug that rivaled Mom's most powerful, notwithstanding Angel's mom was petite.

"Thank you! Thank you!" Sofia Cambeiro murmured in her ear. "Angel has told us how much your friendship meant to him." She released Fireball and stood back to smile at her, still holding one of her hands. "He also says you make a great team."

"Th – thank you, Mrs. Cambeiro. I don't know what to say."

"Say you'll call me Sofia, and my husband Israel."

"Ginger," said Mr. Cambeiro, stepping forward to take her other hand. "I want to thank you, too, for helping our son make it through a very difficult time."

His eyes were close to tearing up and, suddenly, so were Fireball's. She still couldn't wrap her mind around what they'd been through. Angel had thought them dead; they'd known that and thought his life was also threatened.

She cleared her throat and tried to find her voice. "Angel's helped me, too. Not just with the work, but with, um, with *me*. With figuring out some stuff about me, I mean."

She couldn't say more than that because her understanding of what Angel had done for her was only now taking coherent shape in her head. In assigning her to be his "life coach" at CZ, Mom hadn't only given Angel something he needed – a friend, a champion, a shield – she'd given Fireball something she hadn't even known she needed and would never have admitted: someone with whom she could share her own inner landscape, someone who didn't make her wish she were like Cricket or Whiz or someone else, someone who seemed perfectly content for her to be her.

She was soaking in the enormity of that epiphany when Carver and Mom approached the group with the other members of Team Raven tagging along behind like a bunch of ducklings.

"Angel Cambeiro," said Carver in tones so solemn that Angel practically snapped to attention. "I hereby present you with a totem representative of your new status on Team Raven."

He held out his hand; sitting on his palm was a carved wooden figure roughly the size of the raven that Fireball wore. Grinning, Angel accepted it, holding it up for all to see. It was a monkey, sitting cross-legged and poring over a laptop, its long tail wrapped around it and supporting the laptop's screen.

"What is it?" Scrappy demanded, trying to see past Books's shoulder.

"It's my new handle," Angel told the assemblage. "It's a code monkey."

"Code monkey?" repeated Scrappy. He snorted. "Sheesh, dude. That's too many syllables. I'm gonna go with Monk." He leaned past Books to give Angel a playful punch on the shoulder. "Good work, Monk."

"You too, Scraps," said Angel.

Scrappy blinked. "You know Fireball is the only one who's allowed to call me that, right? I mean, she *is* team lead."

"Yeah, but I figure, since you're the one who called me a code monkey in the first place, I owe you."

"Or *own* him," snarked Fireball, "for calling you Noob."

The laughter was free of tension and dread for the first time in what seemed like a year but had only been a matter of days. Carver shook hands with Angel; Angel saluted him, and the larger group dispersed. Mom moved to put an arm around Israel and Sofia, and murmured something about adjourning to her office. Instead of heading for the elevator, though, she escorted them to her tiny lunch lady lair to the right of the beverage machines.

Fireball and Angel were suddenly alone. As if by mutual agreement, they wandered out to the patio deck that overlooked the central courtyard and moved to stand side by side, leaning on the railing. The late afternoon was uncharacteristically sunny, the breeze fall-cool but not chill. Clouds scudded across the autumn sky as if they were in a hurry to be farther inland. The ivy had gone completely red, Fireball noticed for the first time. She loved the fall colors and, under other circumstances, would have enjoyed the heck out of them. But today the approach of Halloween did not cheer her.

"So," she said, "I guess you'll be leaving Cinzento, huh? I mean, you're back with your parents and all..." She felt a lump forming in her throat. *I don't want you to go!* she wanted to protest. *It's not fair! I've only just met you.*

She couldn't say that, of course. How would that look? And he probably didn't feel that way about her – whatever "that way" was.

"Um, actually, Mom and Dad think this is the best school I could possibly go to. So, they want me to stay."

She turned to stare at him. "Really? But you'd have to live here. Don't you want to go live with them wherever you were living before?"

"Well, before we moved to Seattle, we were in university housing in Palo Alto, then in a rental in Bellevue when they started working for Zander. So, we really didn't have a permanent home anywhere, and I... I like it here. I told them I want to stay." He turned toward her, then, and said, "I meant it when I said you were my best friend. I kind of am a monk, in a lot of ways. Making friends has never been easy for me. I got a bad rap for being the teacher's pet or the brainiac or whatever. You made me feel normal. Not just the team – Scrappy being kind of the exception to the rule – but *you*."

Was he blushing? Yes, definitely a bit of color, she thought. She suddenly felt a little warmer, too.

"And so," he continued, "I'm going to stay here. It'll be easier since my parents are going to be working for Cinzento. I think they're considering taking one of the staff apartments in the dorm, at least for a while."

Fireball blinked, the enormity of the statement sinking in. *I will not squee*, she promised herself. "Seriously? Mom offered them a job?"

He nodded, grinning. "Yeah, or the Old Man did, I guess. I guess their first assignment is going to be to make sure Kudzu doesn't rejigger itself into really living up to its name. Maybe turn it into an actually useful tool. And of course they'll be teaching artificial intelligence."

Fireball turned back to the courtyard, taking a deep breath of October and letting the blaze of fall color warm her. The last time she'd been in that courtyard, she'd been too busy battling would-be kidnappers to appreciate it.

As if he'd read her thoughts – something he seemed to have an unparalleled ability to do – Angel nodded toward the plaza below and said, "Hard to believe we were fighting off Zander's goon squad down there just two days ago."

"Huh. I'll say. Funny how time flies when your life is passing before your eyes." Something about that adventure tickled her memory. "By the way, when I was down there defending your honor and all, did I hear you call me Fin?"

He gave her a sideways grin. "Yeah. Short for 'Finney.' Got your attention."

"Yeah, whatever. Just don't do it again... Noob."

Thanks for reading! If you enjoyed this book, please consider leaving an honest review on your favorite store.

For more stories starring the Cinzento Academy crew, or other technological adventures, follow Sue Loh on Twitter at ***@suedeyloh****, or check out her web site* ***http://EvilPlanToSaveThe.World****.*

Made in the USA
Columbia, SC
29 May 2020